The Nose Rules

A Spunky Murder Mystery 🐾

The
Nose
Rules

Holly L. Lewitas

The Nose Rules: A Spunky Murder Mystery

© 2019 Holly L. Lewitas.

This novel is a work of fiction. Any resemblance to actual events or persons, living or dead, is entirely coincidental. The humans in this book are fictional characters whose personalities and actions I invented for the purpose of entertaining my readers.

ISBN Paperback: 978-1-7344067-0-2
ISBN eBook: 978-1-7344067-1-9

Cover artwork and interior design: Creative Publishing Book Design

Dedicated to

Abba
Who made it all possible.

CHAPTER  1

"What if we had a big, tough guy cuddling a little puppy?"

"That's a good one, Spunky, but what if we had that same tough guy sweet-talking a tiny, fuzzy-wuzzy kitten? Now *that* would be totally cute!"

"You're right!"

"Spunky, what are you (*breath*) and Sweetie jabbering about?" Fearless asked as he meandered into the room.

Sweetie answered, "Spunk and I are trying to imagine the cutest video possible. Of course, if we were only using critters it would be as easy as fish pie. But we made it more challenging and said that it has to include a human. We've narrowed it down to a big, tough guy snuggling a baby kitten. That's our winner."

I quickly added, "Yeah, but only if the dude is the real deal. Those phony-baloney toughies can't show honest mush. They're too worried about protecting their image. A real, honest-to-goodness tough guy is a totally different story. He would be sweet-talking a kitten while giving you the look that says, 'Go on, smirk, I dare you.' I just love those guys. They're a hoot!"

Sweetie began prancing and babbling at the same time. "Yeah, like Mr. Ellis down the street. He's super huge, bald, covered in tats, and his biceps are the size of hams. Most all the humans are scared stiff of him, but when Ms. Whiskers plunked her kittens down on his front porch, he was like a sweet little old lady."

"Ms. Whiskers told me he sounded just like this," Sweetie's voice went up an octave as he mimicked Mr. Ellis. "'Oh, you little darlings! You're so sweet! You come to Poppa, and I'll protect you.' Ms. Whiskers said he gently snatched those babies up and whisked them inside. Of course, he invited Ms. Whiskers to join them, but being the committed outdoor gal that she is, she respectfully declined. But her babies, Fluffy and Tuffy, are living a life of luxury now, with matching furry beds, good food, a ton of toys, and a whole mess of primo catnip!"

Fearless licked his paw and began preening his face as he said, "It appears Ms. Whiskers knew *(breath)* Ellis had a good heart, or else she wouldn't have *(breath)* brought her babies to him. Obviously, she made a wise choice."

"She sure did," I said. "And then she made another smart move. She finally let Mom catch her and take her to Dr. Steve to get fixed. Now Ms. Whiskers doesn't have to worry about any more babies, and those nasty old toms aren't bothering her anymore. She's one happy lady!"

"Spunk, you'd better watch what you say about us toms," Fancy-Pants grumbled as he tromped into the room. "Or one night when you're asleep the four toms in this house could become your worst nightmare."

Sweetie quickly intervened. "Now, Fancy, you know Spunky isn't a tomcat bigot. She didn't mean us, did you Spunk?"

"Certainly not! You four are always perfect gentlemen." I quickly turned and started biting my butt to cover my smirk. You did hear Fancy say that his attack would occur while I was asleep, right? He knows all too well that would be the only way he'd ever overtake the Spunk.

Luckily, this conversation was cut short when a car pulled into our driveway.

Bobby was first to reach the window and reported, "Hey, guys, it's Frank and Detective Tony. I wonder why they're here?"

"We'll know soon enough," I said. "I'll let Mom know they're here." I dashed to the back of the house and gave Mom the alert for an impending doorbell—one soft woof combined with a rapidly wagging tail. Without this advance warning the bell startles her, and she has been known to drop or spill whatever she's holding. So if I do my job properly, there are fewer coffee spills and fewer curse words uttered.

"What is it, Spunk?" said Mom. "Is someone here? Who is it?'

Why does she ask, "Who is it?" She never understands my answer. Still, out of respect I barked twice to tell her who it was, but once again she failed to comprehend. But when she saw Fearless and Fancy-Pants standing by the front door, she correctly deduced it must be someone we knew. Those two rescued cats had a terrible history with men, so they never stick around when strangers arrive.

3

But these two men we knew well. Detective Frank Taylor was Mom's new honey bun, and Detective Tony Martinez was his partner on the Clearwater, Wisconsin, police force. Frank is about six feet tall, with a slim but strong build, blue eyes, fair skin, and light brown hair. Mom describes him as ruggedly handsome. Tony is about four inches shorter than Frank, rounder in the hips and middle but not fat, with dark brown hair, a tanner complexion, and warm dark brown eyes. After ten plus years of being partners, they have a strong bond of friendship and trust.

"Get back, you nosey felines!" Mom said as she gently pushed them with her foot. Mom is petite, fit, and slender. She is five feet, four inches tall with light brown hair, and hazel eyes. Many have said she is pretty and Frank frequently calls her beautiful but Mom laughs and says that proves beauty really is in the eye of the beholder.

As she opened the door she smiled. "Frank! Tony! What a nice surprise." She ran her hands through her hair and said, "Come on in. I'm sorry I look such a mess. I was busy cleaning out closets."

Her sideways glance at Frank suggested she was not pleased that he had showed up with Tony without first giving her a heads-up. Apparently, Frank knew the look. "Sorry for the surprise visit, Hannah, but this is official business. We need to borrow Spunky."

"Borrow Spunky? What for?"

"There's been a possible kidnapping, and we're hoping her nose can help."

Mom's hand flew to her mouth. "A kidnapping? Here in Clearwater? Oh, my gracious! What happened?"

4

Tony answered. "I apologize for arriving unannounced, but when we got to the murder scene…"

Mom's brow furrowed. "Murder scene? But Frank just said it was a kidnapping."

"Well, actually it's both," said Tony. "We got a call to the Pederson house over on the west side of town on Miller Street. We found Mr. Pederson stabbed to death and it appears that his sixteen-year-old daughter, Amanda, may have been kidnapped. It's also possible that she ran away on her own. Right now all we know is that she's missing."

"Oh, my, that's terrible!" Mom wanted to hear more, and she wasn't about to let these two get away quickly. "Come in, come in. Can I get you guys some coffee? I just made a fresh pot, and I have some cinnamon buns."

Frank looked at Tony and said, "Sounds great to me. It's been a long morning. But we can't stay long. We need to get back."

The felines and I joined the procession heading to the kitchen. Like Mom, we too wanted details.

CHAPTER 2

After pouring the coffee, Mom brought out the freshly baked buns. Now that she had the deck stacked in her favor, she sat down and asked, "What can you tell me?"

A few months earlier, in recognition of Mom's professional skills as a psychologist and the unique services that her "family" of pets had rendered in solving difficult cases, the Clearwater Police Department had officially contracted with her to be a psychological consultant. That made it legal for her to hear about their cases and provide input. This arrangement protected both the police and Mom, and now we got updates straight from the horse's mouth.

Tony began, "What we know so far is that at approximately seven thirty a.m. yesterday the next door neighbor, Mrs. Wagner, was outside getting her morning paper, and like every school morning, a kid in a blue Volkswagen pulled up in front of the Pederson house to pick Amanda up for school. This kid always waits a minute or two before beeping his horn to get Amanda to hustle, but yesterday there was no need to honk because Amanda came running out the door right away. Mrs. Wagner called out her usual

'Good morning, Mandy,' but this time her greeting was ignored. Mrs. Wagner said she thought it odd, because Amanda always answers, 'Good morning, Mrs. Wagner.' But yesterday Amanda said nothing. She ran out with her head down, carrying what looked like a wad of tissues in her hand. Mrs. Wagner said she remembered thinking Amanda's allergies must be acting up. That was yesterday. She didn't see Amanda leave this morning, but she thought maybe she had simply missed her."

"Did Amanda arrive at school yesterday?" Mom asked.

"Yes, she did." said Tony. "I talked to the kid who picked her up. He picks her up every morning, and just like every other day they arrived at school about seven forty-five. They went inside, and Amanda veered off toward the restroom while he went on to his homeroom. The hall monitor confirmed that he saw Amanda go into the restroom. But no one has seen Amanda again since then. She didn't get to her homeroom or any of her classes yesterday or today. The kid honked for her this morning, but when she didn't come out he figured her father might have taken her to school early, which he sometimes does.

"Meanwhile, her father, Mr. Henry Pederson…"

Mom interrupted. "Wait a minute, is that the same Henry Pederson who's president of Clearwater Savings and Loan?"

Tony nodded. "Yup, same one. His wife…"

Mom's looked confused and interrupted again. "His wife? I thought he was divorced."

"So did a lot of people, but they're still married. Apparently, years ago his wife, Ruth, left him and moved to New

7

York City, but we've been told Mr. Pederson was a devout Catholic and would never consider a divorce. The wife arrived in town this morning and says Mr. Pederson didn't know she was coming to town. She says she called his cell phone when she arrived but got no answer, so she called the bank. They told her Mr. Pederson hadn't come to work yesterday or today. So she went to the house, and when she got no answer to the doorbell she realized she didn't have her old keys with her, so she went next door to see if Mrs. Wagner still had a key, which she did. She and Mrs. Wagner then went into the house together, and they found Mr. Pederson dead on the kitchen floor with a large carving knife sticking out of his belly."

Mom's hand flew to mouth. "Oh my, that's terrible! Was there a break-in?"

Tony shrugged. "We saw no sign of forced entry, and no sign of a struggle. Unfortunately, we also found no obvious clues. That's why we want to give Spunky a shot at it. The crime scene is fresh, and the team knows not to move anything. I'm hoping she'll find something we've missed."

"Well, of course, you can use Spunk. But I have two counseling sessions coming up, so I can't go with you. Are you sure you can handle her?" My head jerked around and I loudly snorted my objection. "Mom, who do you think I am, Patches, that ornery Chihuahua who lives down the street?"

Tony quickly defended me, "I'm sure Spunky will cooperate." He reached down and scratched my head. "We had no problem the last time we worked together, did we, girl?"

I jumped against his leg and gave a quick, soft bark. Correct, oh wise one!

8

Mom smiled. "You're right, she'll be fine, but to make sure, let me put on her harness. That way you'll have better control of her."

I whined. Aw, Mom!

She looked down and silently gave me "the look" to remind me of all the episodes that justified her concern. Okay, already, if wearing the harness meant we could get this adventure started, then bring it on!

Just then Bobby, the bobtail wonder cat, butted his head into my rump. "Wow, Spunky, a murder *and* a kidnapping. That's exciting!"

"Yeah, but if there was a kidnapping, I'm not sure I'm the best one for the job. I'm no bloodhound." I turned to Fearless and said, "While I'm gone, would you hightail it over to Nosey's house and alert him that we might need his assistance?"

Bobby butted me again. "Hey, Spunk, why don't you ask *me* to hightail it over to Nosey's?"

I glanced at Bobby's stubby bobtail and said, "Sorry, bro, no offense intended."

The truth had nothing to do with the brevity of Bobby's tail, but with the fact that Fearless never dawdled. Bobby, on the other hand, was known to get sidetracked even when he went out to pee. If I had sent Bobby, there was a risk Nosey might not get my message until tomorrow!

Fearless interrupted. "Asking Nosey to help is a great idea. *(Breath.)* That boy can track down anything." He turned and said, "Bobby, do you want to (*breath*) go with me?" Fearless's crooked head and breathing issues may slow down his rate of speech, but he never misses a beat when it

9

comes to diplomacy. Off they went, and five minutes later I was in the car, sitting on Tony's lap and listening to the detectives discuss the case.

"It just doesn't feel like a kidnapping to me," Frank said. "Why would someone kidnap Amanda after killing her father? If they want to collect a ransom, why kill the parent?"

"Maybe they took her because she was a witness," said Tony.

"But if she saw the killer, why did they let her leave the house and go to school?"

"Good point. Besides, no one at the school saw anything to suggest she was taken against her will. It seems she went into the restroom and just vanished. Hey, maybe she decided to play hooky and just took off."

"For two days? Even with the air conditioning slowing down the decomp, the medical examiner said Pederson was killed yesterday. So where was Amanda last night? In the house with her dead father?"

"Okay," said Tony, "I agree that part makes no sense. Maybe she took off with her boyfriend or something. Does she even have a boyfriend? The kid in the car says he's just a friend, and I saw no reason not to believe him."

"I guess it is possible she split with an unknown friend or boyfriend before her father was killed," said Frank. "Mrs. Wagner said she saw an unfamiliar black sedan parked in the Pedersons's driveway earlier that morning."

"Yeah, too bad she didn't know the model of the car or get a plate number. All she said was a mid-size black car."

"But she did say she thought the plate started with the number twenty-two. If that's true, then the car must be registered to someone right here in Franklin county and that narrows the field."

"Great, now we only have several hundred mid-size black cars to check out."

"Yeah, a pain in the butt, but given that there was no sign of forced entry, I'll bet Mr. Pederson knew the man, which increase the odds that he's a local."

"Could be," Tony agreed, "but the perp might not be a 'man' at all. It could have been a woman. And the driver of the black sedan may not be relevant to any of this. Remember, Mrs. Wagner also said she didn't find anything odd about a car being in the Pederson's driveway, because people from the bank were always stopping by to pick up or drop off documents and stuff."

"Yeah, but the bank said it had been several days since they sent someone over there," Frank objected.

"True, but the uniform we sent to the bank only talked to Pederson's secretary."

"We'll have to interview everyone at the bank," said Frank. "And we need to spend a lot more time talking to that wife of his, Ruth. Something about her and her story just seems odd."

"I agree, why did she come to town anyway?"

"She said she wanted to see Amanda."

"Then why arrive when Amanda would be in school?"

"Like I said, odd. But right now we have no reason to suspect her of anything. It sure would help if Spunky could find something for us to work with. What do you really expect her to find?"

"I don't know," said Tony. "I just don't want to risk missing something. Remember my last murder scene?

Spunky found clues that both the forensics team and I completely missed."

I raised my chin, stuck out my chest, and sat a little taller. It was nice to be appreciated.

"Hey, this traffic is getting heavy," said Tony. "We need to get to a move on. I'm turning on the siren!"

Frank chuckled. "One of the reasons you love being a small town cop, my friend. Less rules, more noise!"

I wagged my tail vigorously. Yippee! Siren and flashing lights!

CHAPTER  3

Unfortunately, the siren had an irksome flaw. As a dog I have a much wider auditory range than humans, so I wasn't surprised that my companions were oblivious to the grating high-pitched squeal that emanated from the siren's motor. Thank goodness Frank has had a few dogs in his life. He correctly interpreted my repetitive ear-pawing and switched the siren to intermittent blasts, and the problem was solved. Shortly thereafter, the heavy traffic cleared and Frank shut off the siren.

Despite the siren, it still took a while to reach the far west side of Clearwater. The usual route went through the college campus, but the student-filled streets were no place for a speeding police car, so Frank took a longer way. When we reached the other side of town, Frank made several turns before turning onto a side street. There was a mass of people crowded in front of a two story white house with black shutters. There were smaller windows at the ground level indicating a possible basement area below ground. After we approached, Frank flashed his badge and a pathway opened. I felt like the famous Mr. Benji arriving at one of his movie premieres. I admit, I did puff up a little!

But my swagger ended abruptly when I entered the house and my nostrils filled with the smells of blood and death. I waited while Tony decontaminated my paws with alcohol and snipped a sample of my fur. Having worked with him before, I knew the paw-cleaning decreased the amount of contaminates I brought into the crime scene, while the snippet of fur would allow the lab to distinguish mine from other hair samples.

When he finished, Tony knelt down and gave me the speech. "Okay, Spunky, you know the rules. Don't move anything. If you find something, bark and I'll come running. Okay?"

After receiving my affirming woof he undid my leash, and my nose went to work.

I quickly concluded that the entryway wasn't the best place to start: too many scents. I needed to establish which scents belonged to the girl, and which belonged to her father. I looked around, saw a stairway, and ran up it with Tony trailing behind me. The first door was shut, so I pawed the corner. Tony obeyed and turned the knob. Inside I found a desk, a chair, a computer, and file cabinets. It looked like a home office. There were several male and female scents in the room.

The next door stood wide open, so in I went and found items that suggested it was a girl's room. There were stuffed animals, flowery scents, and a closet packed with feminine-scented clothes. I pawed the laundry hamper, looked up at Tony, and he again responded correctly by dumping the clothes out on the floor. My previous tutelage of Tony was paying off! I shoved my nose into the pile of clothes and quickly identified the freshest scent. Until additional data told me otherwise, this was Amanda. I moved on and explored the rest of the room. My nose lingered on a teddy bear lying on the floor. Amanda had held him tight; his head and chest were caked with the salt from her tears.

Upon entering the last of the upstairs rooms, I concluded this was where the father slept. There was a strong presence of a male's pheromones, as well as his dirty socks and underwear littering the closet floor.

Now that I was armed with scent images of Amanda and her father, I headed back down the stairs. At the entranceway I paused and glanced around at all the people working the crime scene. It was a good thing that everyone was wearing blue paper booties. Although I was glad that Tony had never found booties small enough to fit my paws, I was relieved that he had made the humans follow the rules. Booties diminished the strength of the scent trails left by the cops, making them less likely to overpower earlier scents.

I continued my research. After several minutes of intense nose work, I knew that several non-bootie feet had recently entered and exited through the front door. Other than Amanda, two other females had recently entered the house. One wore high heels, and the other sneakers. There was a gap in the middle of the print made by the high heel and I smelled leather. The other imprint had peaks and valleys in the scent, suggesting the sole had ridges, but there was no break from the toe to the heel and the chemical smell was similar to the soles of Mom's sneakers. In numerous places the sneakers had stepped on top of the high-heeled prints, which meant the high heels had walked there first. The high heels had also gone places the sneakers had not. These two females then left the house together, escorted by a bootie-covered man.

I began tracking the next trail. A third non-bootie person had entered the house. This one was a man, and he had entered and left the house alone. Both of the women had stepped on top of his prints, so he had been in the house before them. I followed his trail outside. He had walked over to the driveway. Then his scent trail abruptly vanished.

I turned around and retraced his trail back inside the house. Tony probably wanted me to stop and have my paws re-wiped, but I ignored him and kept on moving. I needed to maintain my focus. Tony must have noticed my intensity, and he too ignored the rules.

Since smells lose potency over time, the weaker ones mark the beginning of the trail. I followed this man's trail to the living room and then to the sofa, where he had sat down. Further exploration revealed that Mr. Pederson's scent was on the recliner opposite the sofa, and several areas of his scent had the same degree of freshness as the scent of the unidentified male. They had been in the living room at the same time. Amanda had been in the room with them, but she hadn't sat down. When the mystery man walked away from the sofa, his steps were farther apart, meaning he had left the room at a faster pace than when he entered. He had followed Mr. Pederson out of the living room, and Amanda had brought up the rear.

Their trail led to the kitchen.

It ended at Mr. Pederson's dead body.

CHAPTER  4

Mr. Pederson was lying on his back. His eyes were open, devoid of moisture and no longer reflecting light. Decay begins the instant life stops, so identifiable odors were present. An animal detects internal decay long before a human can see it or smell it, and although the odor of decay isn't disagreeable to us, it is distinctive. The same smell is present in every fresh carcass I find in the woods, and it was also present the moment my human Dad left this earth. Mom couldn't smell it, but we critters could. It is the smell of a body void of life.

Mr. Pederson had that smell.

I saw a slender male body. He had fair skin and light brown hair. His face was also slender and lacked deep wrinkles but had enough creases to attest that he was no longer a youngster. He was dressed in a white shirt and dark blue jeans. But a large portion of his shirt was no longer white. Dark brown blood covered the front and left side of his chest. The wooden handle of a large knife protruded from the center of his body, beneath the rib cage. A puddle of congealed blood was on the floor to his left.

I carefully backed away from the body and examined the kitchen floor. I found four different sets of non-bootie male feet. Three of these men had entered through the back door. I tracked the first one and learned that he and a second man had entered the kitchen at the same time. They had stood near the body, and one of them had touched Mr. Pederson's neck before they both walked out of the kitchen. I followed their trail. One had gone upstairs, while the other had gone down to the basement. They met again in the kitchen, and proceeded together out the front door.

That was where I found them—two patrol officers now in charge of crowd control. The shorter one looked down, smiled, and patted my head. "Hey there, cutie, where did you come from?"

Tony was right behind me and supplied the answer. "That's Spunky. She's with me. Apparently she tracked you two from the kitchen. If I'd known what she was up to, I would have explained to her that you were the first to arrive on the scene. Come on, girl, dead end. Back to work!"

It made sense. First responders don't stop to put on booties. Oh, well, no stone left unturned! I headed back into the house. This time I did wait for Tony and his alcohol wipe.

I returned to the kitchen and continued my inspection there. The third new non-bootie man had walked around the kitchen more than the first two and had left many footprints near the body. I followed his trail. He had walked toward the living room, stopped, turned, and then gone up the stairs. He had gone into the office room, sat in the chair, touched the drawers of the desk and file cabinets, and then headed back to the kitchen, where he went out the back door. Perhaps he was a cop and realized he had forgotten his booties and wisely left before incurring Tony's wrath. Mistakes happen. But I was the only one who knew he had screwed up, and I'm no snitch.

I next turned my attention to a more thorough investigation of the body. The scent of this third man was only on Mr. Pederson's neck. The other male scent on his neck I now knew belonged to the police officer standing outside. When I ran a nose scan of the whole body, I found that Mr. Pederson's chest, arms, shoulders, and both of his hands contained scents from several sources—Amanda, a watermelon, cookies, the high-heeled woman, and the first unknown male I had tracked from the living room. The scents of the last three non-bootie men who had entered through the back door were only on his neck. The first responder and the third man had probably touched Pederson's neck to check for a pulse. But it was clear that, in addition to Amanda, two unknown people had put their hands on various parts of Mr. Pederson's body. Those scents belonged to the first non-bootie man from the living room and the high-heeled woman.

One of them had to be the killer.

I moved closer to the body and leaned in to sniff the handle of the knife. I pulled back. Something wasn't right. Once again I carefully stretched across Pederson's chest and funneled all of my concentration into my snout. I hovered above the handle's surface and scrutinized the imprinted scents. There were only two.

The first one belonged to the victim himself, Mr. Pederson. I drew in another sniff and focused solely on the second scent. Abruptly I sat back on my rump, looked up at Tony, and cocked my head.

"What's the matter girl?" Tony said. "You look confused."

The second scent left no room for doubt.

The killer was Amanda.

CHAPTER  5

I turned away from the body and quickly ran up the stairs and into Amanda's room. As I hoped, Tony followed obediently, and when he caught up with me I barked three times.

"What is it, girl? What are you trying to tell me?"

I raced back downstairs and into the kitchen. Steering clear of the blood, I put a paw onto Mr. Pederson's chest and waited. When Tony entered the kitchen he said, "Okay, now what?"

I pointed my nose at the knife and whined softly.

"I know, girl. It's terrible."

I whined again and bobbed my nose up and down close to the knife.

"I know, I know. It's terrible," he said again.

I turned and glared at him. This wasn't the time to be thick-headed. I jerked my nose back to the knife and growled. Tony's denseness was getting annoying.

"Okay, already! What?" Tony began scratching his head. "Frank! Can you come in here?"

Frank hurried into the room. "What?"

"You see how Spunky's pointing her nose at the knife?"

"Yeah. So?"

"Well, first she sniffed the body and the knife, then she ran up the stairs, went into Amanda's room, barked three times, ran back down, and put her nose right there. What do you think she's trying to tell us?"

"That the knife came from Amanda's room?"

"Maybe, but that doesn't sound right. Why would such a big kitchen knife be in Amanda's room? Besides, my guess is that the knife was being used to cut that watermelon sitting right there on the counter. I think Spunky wants us to see something else—but what?"

Tony began vigorously scratching his head. Maybe the scratching increased the blood flow to his brain, because all of a sudden he stopped, smacked his hands together, and said, "Or...maybe she's telling us Amanda's prints are on the knife."

"What! Amanda stabbed her own father?"

"Could be."

"No way!"

Tony bent down and said, "Spunky is that it? Is that what you are trying to tell us?"

I barked twice.

Frank's eyebrows shot upward. "Well, maybe way after all."

Tony leaned over the body. "Frank, I didn't notice this before, but look at this knife; it's tilted slightly upward. A shorter person would thrust upward like that, right?" He stood up, bent his knees, and demonstrated his theory on Frank.

"Yeah, in all likelihood it was a shorter person."

"I don't think Amanda is very tall." Tony shook his head. "I don't like this, not one little bit. I sure hope I'm wrong, but..."

Frank sighed heavily. "Bag the knife. We'll find out soon enough."

Yes, they certainly would.

CHAPTER  6

I headed outside. It was time to broaden the search. I retraced the footprints of that first unknown man and confirmed that his footprints disappeared by the side of driveway closest to the house. If that black sedan had been parked here, perhaps the unknown man had gotten into it.

I moved forward and located the spot where one of the tires had stopped. From there I sniffed out where the other three tires had stood, and determined the outline of the car. It appeared as though the unknown male had entered the car close to the front tire, so he must have been the driver. But wait a minute—something else was peculiar.

"What the heck is she doing, Frank?"

"Darn if I know. Something between the house and the driveway sure caught her attention. She's covered that same route three times."

That's because it took three trips to be certain. The footprints of the female in high heels also vanished on the same side of the driveway, closest to the house, but her steps ended closer to the car's rear tire. Either this woman had gotten into a different car that had parked in almost the same place, or she had gotten into the same car and sat behind the driver—the unknown male.

I resumed my search, and at the location of the rear tire I found my next clue. I pawed the pavement to the right of my discovery.

"Look, Frank, Spunky found something smeared on the payment. Looks like mud."

Frank knelt down to examine the smear. He leaned in. His brow furrowed when his nose got close to the smear. He said. "Scat."

Tony jerked backwards and said. "What? Are you crazy? Why should I scat?"

Frank grinned. "No, I don't mean *you* should scat. The *smear* is scat."

"Scat? What the heck is 'scat'?"

Frank chuckled. "I keep forgetting, you're a city boy. This here is coon scat, or as you'd say, raccoon poop."

"Poop! Well, poop can't help us."

My head jerked around and I stared at Tony. It never ceases to amaze me how much important stuff humans miss. The fact was that this particular scat provided me with three major pieces of information. One, by tracking the scent down the driveway, I knew the car had come and gone from the left. To understand the next tidbit, one needs to know that raccoons are territorial critters. They like to stay close to their dens, and if food is plentiful, they don't travel far. Hence, their territory can be small. Now, this particular scat was loaded with fresh parsnips and turnips. That meant that, in all likelihood, the car had driven over this particular scat somewhere near one of two places: either the dumpster at the supermarket, or Mr. Gifford's produce farm. At this time of year, those were the two places where one would find an abundance of these early fall vegetables.

If I were a raccoon, Mr. Gifford's farm would be my first choice.

Third, the freshness of the scat meant the car had driven through it recently. Tony had said the black sedan might have a local license plate, and if that was true, then maybe this unknown male was similar to a raccoon. He, too, might be a homebody, and perhaps he had headed back to his den, which I now thought was probably somewhere near Mr. Gifford's farm.

Although Frank made no mention of noticing the vegetables in the scat, he was smart enough to scrape it up and put it in a bag. If the lab tech was a clever country boy, he'd see what I had smelled and confirm my findings.

Right now, however, all I had to work with were these two, so I kept it simple and revealed their next clue in stages. I put my nose to the ground, walked away from the scat, down the driveway, turned left, stopped, and ran back to the starting point. They didn't get it, so I did it again. It only took two tries before Frank exclaimed, "Well, at least we know the car turned left."

Good boy! Now it was time to mosey down the road. Tony quickly caught up with me, attached my leash, and said, "Spunky, no way I'm letting you walk down this road on your own. Hannah would skin me alive."

Although I didn't need protecting, I knew Mom would appreciate his vigilance. I began leading Tony down the road. When my nose could no longer discern the smell of scat from the multitude of other smells, I plunked my rump down.

Tony called out. "Frank, it looks like we're on our own from here on."

Not true, my friend, not true. Had he forgotten I am a terrier mutt? My dominant traits are tenacity and cleverness. The fact that my nose had given out didn't mean my brain had. It was time to bring in Nosey. He is one hundred percent bloodhound, and comes equipped with a top-of-the-line platinum-class nose. He was definitely more qualified for this nose job.

Spunky's rule number fifteen: Never let vanity interfere with the mission.

CHAPTER

W hen we got back home this time, the detectives didn't stick around.

"We can't stay, Hannah," said Frank. "I'll fill you in later. We have to get the evidence to the lab ASAP. Spunky was a big help, and she behaved perfectly."

What? Had he expected anything else? Mom's smile conveyed pride, but not surprise. She knows I'm a professional.

After they left, Mom went to her office. I headed outside, with the felines right behind me. These guys were not about to wait for the details, they wanted to know now.

"What? The girl stabbed her own father! Why would she do that?" Sweetie began pacing. The scenario I presented made him very uncomfortable.

"Sweetie, I can only tell you what I smelled. There were two scents on the knife—and only two—Amanda's, and her father's. I'm sorry to say it, but she *must* have stabbed him."

"Maybe Mr. Pederson stabbed himself, and Amanda tried to pull out the knife!" In silent unison, all heads swiveled toward Bobby. He got the message, "Okay, dumb idea. But it *could* have happened! Remember when Miss Tabatha stabbed herself with that fishhook?"

Sweetie sighed. "Bobby, Tabatha was just a baby when she fell off the shelf in the barn and accidently landed on that fishhook. That doesn't count as stabbing herself!"

Bobby began grooming his hindquarters as he muttered, "So what? It's possible."

Fearless answered. "Possible perhaps, Bobby-boy, but highly unlikely. *(Breath.)* Spunk, I spoke to Nosey. *(Breath.)* He said he'd be glad to help *(breath)*, but he's not sure how he can get away. *(Breath.)* His human put up a new fence last month after he caught Nosey *(breath)* returning from one of his adventures."

"Is the new gate going to be a problem for you?" I asked.

"Naw, I checked it out. *(Breath.)* The latch is simple *(breath)*. I could undo it with one paw tied to my *(breath)* tail."

"Great!" I smiled. Although I've never actually seen Fearless with one paw tied to his tail, I do know cats can be remarkably clever at undoing latches. I asked, "Does Nosey still stay outside all night?"

"Yup. He wouldn't have it any other way."

"Okay. Can you arrange a rendezvous for tonight after his human goes to bed?"

"Sure, I'll head over there right now. *(Breath.)* Fancy-Pants, want to tag along?"

"Sure thing!"

Now that I had updated the boys, I headed inside to my soft bed. All this brainwork had plumb worn me out. But if the truth be told, a dog never needs any justification for a nap.

CHAPTER  8

When I awoke I went looking for Mom. I found her in her office at the rear of the house. Several years ago when Mom started seeing her patients online she converted one of the bedrooms into her home office. Mom was currently online with a client. I entered the room quietly and climbed into my bed beside her chair. She looked down and smiled. Mom conducts most of her therapy sessions via computer, and she knows I'll be quiet. Well, I should say I'll be quiet as long as I have nothing to say. Some clients do require a critter intervention, but for now, I would just listen.

"So, Samantha, let's summarize: You're twenty-five years old, you have two children, by two different fathers. Your mother has legal custody of your oldest child, your son, Christopher. He's six years old, but she doesn't allow you any contact with him, and you have no contact with his father. Currently you're living with the father of your second child, a girl named Caroline. Her father is Robert, and he's unemployed. You graduated from high school, but never held a job longer than a year, and at present you're cleaning people's homes. Last week, a friend of yours agreed to pay for your therapy. She told you she was willing to do this because you were 'all screwed up and needed to straighten out your life.' She also said you were 'clueless as to how to manage your life.' Does that seem like a fair assessment of what you've told me so far?"

Samantha laughed. "Yeah, that's about it."

"Do you think you're screwed up?"

She laughed again. "Not really. But I'm not married, I haven't seen my son in three years, and I've never had a steady job, so maybe I am."

"What would you like to accomplish in your life?"

"To make enough money to pay the rent every month."

"That's it?"

"That's hard enough."

"When you were younger, did you have a dream for your life?"

"Sure. I wanted to get married, have kids, and be a good mother."

"What about a career?"

"I wanted to be a nurse, but school was too expensive."

"Did you look into a college loan?"

Samantha laughed. "No. I never had a good job. No bank was going to loan me money."

"Did you try?"

"No."

"Okay, so now you're twenty-five, and you still don't have a clue what to do with your life?"

"That's right, but I'm not afraid of hard work. I've worked hard all my life and managed to do fine."

"Are all your bills paid?"

Again she laughed. "Of course not! No one pays *all* their bills. But I keep a roof over our heads and food on the table."

Mom paused and silence filled the room. Her brow furrowed as her mouth twisted slightly to the left. I've studied this woman's face for more than thirteen years, so I know that this particular expression means she's reached a crossroads, and she isn't sure which route to follow. While she was thinking I studied Samantha more closely. Since it was her first session with Mom, it was the first time I'd seen her. She was a pleasant-looking woman with dark, straight hair that reached her shoulders, sparkling eyes. She had a quick smile, but her laugh was loud, quickly triggered, and sounded forced. She reminded me of an anxious little yappy dog.

"Okay, Samantha, let's talk about how and why your mother got custody of your son."

Samantha laughed again. "Because she's a rich, crazy bitch who hates me. She gets to do whatever she wants."

"Hold on a minute. You must have done something wrong, or the judge wouldn't have granted her custody."

"Well, yeah. I was arrested for stealing from my employer—but I had no choice. He wouldn't pay us, and I needed the money to feed my kid." Her voice grew louder and she laughed, "Besides, I didn't really 'steal' anything. He owed me that money. See, part of my job was to pay the company's bills, so I simply paid the bill that he owed me. I wrote myself a check for the exact amount he owed me, not one penny more, so actually I didn't steal a single dime." She threw back her shoulders, raised her chin, and presented a proud posture.

Mom asked, "Who signed the check?"

Samantha's shoulders slumped and her voice fell off. "Okay, so I forged his name."

Then her voice rose again. "But he hadn't paid me in over a month. So what was I supposed to do?"

"How about notifying the police?"

She laughed. "Yeah, and who would buy the groceries while I waited for the law to do something?"

"I grant it wasn't a good situation. Why did you stay so long if you weren't being paid?"

"He kept saying he'd pay us next week, but he never did."

"After you forged the check, how long were you in jail?"

"Only twenty-four hours, then a friend bailed me out."

"And what happened at your trial?"

Again, the laugh. "I didn't have a trial."

"Why not?"

Samantha mumbled. "I didn't show up for my hearing."

A cringe flickered across Mom's face. She asked softly. "You mean you jumped bail?"

"Yeah, I ran."

"With your son?"

"No. When I was arrested, my mother took him to her house, and then when I got out on bail she wouldn't let me see him."

"So you ran and left your son behind?"

"Yeah, I left the state."

"Was a warrant issued for your arrest?"

She laughed. "Probably, but that was in Florida, so as long as I don't get pulled over for a ticket or something like that, I figure I'm safe."

"Is your Florida license still current?"

"No, it expired a long time ago."

"So how did you manage to get a Wisconsin driver's license?"

"I didn't."

Mom's eyebrows rose. "So you're driving without a license?"

"Yeah, but what choice do I have? If they run my name, they'll see the warrant. There are no buses in this town, so unless I drive, I can't get to work."

The girl did have a point. Mom sighed and opted to change topics. "Samantha, when was your daughter born?"

"Two years ago. I got pregnant when Robert and I were living together in Florida. My daughter is the reason I had to run. No way was my kid going to be born in jail! I could never let that happen. I had no choice but to run, right?"

Mom took a deep breath and exhaled slowly. "Samantha, the only thing I know for sure at this moment is that your friend is correct—your life is indeed screwed up."

That certainly was an understatement! I've seen dogs taken to the pound for fewer violations. Obviously, Mom and I had our work cut out for us.

CHAPTER  9

When Mom finished her session with Samantha she said she needed to get out of the house, so we headed to Puppy Park earlier than usual. It was a warm and beautiful fall day, and the walk to the park took less than fifteen minutes. Our park-pals, Jacob and Quincy, were nowhere to be seen, but today maybe it was a good thing no one was around.

Mom was in her monologue talking-walking mode. This is when she walks briskly and talks softly to herself. To an observer it looks like she's talking to me, but the truth is that it has nothing to do with me; the woman is just talking. She's most likely to do this when she's upset and verbalizing her emotions. She says it helps her process her thoughts, but she admits she might be doing it too often now that she's lived alone for so many years. Fortunately she hushes up when someone gets close.

Today her monologue was all about Samantha. "I swear, as the years go by I have less and less patience with women like Samantha. I know I shouldn't be so judgmental, but at this moment all I see is a flakey, selfish woman who produced two children before she even knew how to take care of herself. Why do people do that? If you want to screw up your own life, fine, be my guest, but don't bring kids into your crazy, unstable world.

"Okay, maybe the first pregnancy was an accident, although we know an 'accident' is too often an excuse for not thinking or caring about the consequences. But the second time? With two different men? That goes beyond selfish; that's self-filled to the max. I wouldn't be a bit surprised if she also blames her mother, 'the bitch,' for that too.

"The question is, what am I supposed to do with this girl? Wave a magic wand and make her life all hunky-dory? I doubt her friend has enough money to pay for all the fixing-up this one needs. In fact I'm not even sure Samantha believes she has a problem, or that she really wants to be fixed!"

After a while Mom's fast pace and rapid talking began to pay off. She began slowing down. Finally she took a deep breath and said, "Okay, Spunk, it's time to examine my choices."

Now she was talking to me.

"Samantha's next session is tomorrow, and I need to make some decisions. You know I don't usually schedule a second session so soon, but I couldn't get a handle on her in one day. I wonder what I can do to help her change. Given the strength of my negative reaction to her, I'm also wondering whether or not I should even continue to see her. But after only one session it wouldn't be professional to refuse therapy simply because she annoys the snot out of me."

Mom took another deep breath, let it out slowly, and continued, "Okay, enough venting. It's time to kick myself in the butt and regain a professional perspective, right?"

I barked twice. Correct! Besides, look around, woman, we're already well inside the park, and it's time to play! I pulled on my leash and Mom laughed. "Okay, you're right! Enough about Samantha. It's time for a good romp." She undid my leash, and I sprinted across the field toward the big oak tree. The warmth of the sun felt good on my back, and the air was full of sweet smells. When I reached the tree I stopped, turned around, and waited. True, I didn't want to go too far and make Mom fret; but between you and me, with my thirteenth birthday around the corner, I needed to catch my breath.

I waited while Mom covered the distance. "Look at you! Bet those people over there think you're still a puppy!" She sat down, leaned against the tree, patted her lap, and whispered, "But I know your secret, my sweet old gal. Come up here and take a rest?"

I climbed up and enjoyed the softness of her lap beneath my rump. Her hands gently massaged my spine. The warmth of her love as it flowed through me felt even better than the sun. A true friend never scolds an elder for acting like a youngster. They know there are times we need to prove we still can, and although I know I still can, I also know that I can't as often.

"Hey, Hannah! Are you okay?"

Our heads jerked up at the sound of Jacob's voice. He and Quincy were still a way off. Quincy was pulling hard on his leash, but Jacob restrained him.

"Hi Jacob! We're fine. I just needed to rest a minute."

I turned and gave Mom a sweet lick on her cheek. A friend also never reveals your secrets.

"Is it okay if I release Quincy? I didn't want to disturb your rest."

Mom laughed. "Sure, turn him loose." She leaned forward and spoke softly, "Spunky, go see your friend."

She didn't have to say that twice! I pushed off from her lap and bounded toward my buddy. I only had to run a short way, since Quincy's long Labrador legs quickly covered most of the distance. I love greeting my friend Quincy; he's all wiggles and wags. You just have to stay clear of that tail! That flailing appendage could knock you for a loop.

"Slow down, Quincy! You'll turn yourself into a pretzel!"

"Hiya Spunk! How are you? I missed you. C'mon let's play!"

Quincy took off running. He ran full-out for about a hundred yards, while I stayed exactly where I was. I knew he would turn around and run back. He always does. Quincy is eight years younger than I am, and very considerate of the differences in our stamina levels.

When he returned he said, "Okay, Spunk, now I can turn it down a notch." We set off together at a brisk but tolerable speed. I glanced back and saw Mom walking with Jacob. Since he would watch out for her, I didn't need to, so it was time for some fun.

Of course, the best doggie fun means getting dirty. The trick is to find dry dirt without any stinky stuff in it. At my house, getting dusty will not land you in the bathtub, but getting stinky is a one-way ticket to lavender bubbles. Yuck!

We found the perfect dirt at the baseball field. There were no people on the field, and plenty of good, stink-free dirt between the bases. We ran, rolled, and chased each other until our tongues were hanging long. Then we headed to the outfield and stretched out on the cool grass.

"That was fun, Spunk! I think it's so neat that you don't mind getting dirty. Why is that? All the other ladies avoid dirt at any cost. They don't want to mess up their pretty pink bows."

I snorted. "Quincy, have you ever seen me do *anything* that's typical female?"

"Point taken. You don't even squat like the other gals. You lift your leg."

"Darn tootin'! Why should the boys be the only ones who get to aim high! My body might be compact, but the next dog that sniffs that tree will think I'm twice my size. Besides, why should a little dirt get in the way of fun? I'll bet you a new rawhide, those fluff-balls don't have one tenth the fun I do."

"Spunk, those fluff-balls might be half your age, but they can't even *do* one-tenth of the stuff you do!"

"Mindset, my friend. It's all about your mindset."

By the time Mom and Jacob had finished catching up on each other's lives, we too were ready to quit. We had managed to get in three good romps and several long rests. It's great when your friend cares enough to slow down so you can keep up, yet never makes you feel self-conscious about your limits. Quincy does this with ease and grace. When we said goodbye, I gave him a special lick on his nose and said, "Thanks."

As Mom and I were walking home she said, "A good walk with good friends makes for a good day."

My sentiments exactly.

CHAPTER  10

Frank behaved himself this time and called first. About an hour later, he and Tony arrived with Chinese food.

Tony said, "Hannah, I hope I'm not making a pest of myself."

Mom chuckled, "Absolutely not! Besides, Frank knows that if he brings Chinese ribs, I'll agree to just about anything." I couldn't agree more. Both Mom and I love those tasty, tangy ribs. She knows the bones are too soft for me to gnaw on, but I get my share of meaty tidbits.

The humans took their places at the table, and the cats quickly chose their targets. Since Mom's ribs belonged to me, they divided the two men between themselves. Fortunately, the younger cats had finally mastered the art of begging without becoming nuisances. About a month ago I had to have a very stern talk with Bobby after his unrelenting head-butting of Mom's leg resulted in us being locked outside until the meal was over. Tonight I was quite confident that the boy wouldn't dare risk costing me my ribs.

Begging styles and techniques vary greatly, but one thing is certain: humans have a hard time ignoring a skillful beggar. I've found that men are often suckers for a cute face with pleading eyes. Apparently female humans agree with me, as I've seen that exact same face on many a woman when she wants something from her man.

My cats swear by the rise-and-pat method. They start by sitting next to the target's leg. Then, at the right time, they slowly raise up on their hind legs, placing one paw on the human's thigh while gently patting the human's belly with the other paw. This causes the human to look down and see their sweet face and pleading eyes, and soon a tidbit follows. The drawback to this method is that only one cat can pat at a time; too much patting only aggravates the human. Tonight, with only the two men to work on, the four felines had to take turns. I had already made it clear that any squabbling would result in significant fur loss from someone's butt.

Bobby, Sweetie, and Fancy-Pants all love shrimp. However, Fancy-Pants learned the hard way that he should smell Chinese shrimp before gobbling. One night he greedily pounced on and devoured a hot-and-spicy Szechuan shrimp. Afterwards he had to lap up a whole bowl of water, and he swore never again. To makes matter worse, it was only later that we learned he should have begged for milk! Sweetie, the cautious one, smelled first and quickly backed away. But Bobby was not as smart, and he, too, ate a spicy shrimp; but, amazingly, it didn't seem to bother him one iota. Given that it was Bobby, it's very possible he suffered in silence rather than admit that his tongue was on fire.

Fearless, however, is the odd cat out. He hates shrimp, but the boy does love egg rolls.

As we settled into our places under the table, our mouths were watering.

"So, detectives, what have you learned so far?" Mom asked.

Tony began, "So far, we don't have a lot to go on. The preliminary lab results aren't due back until tomorrow morning, and the team is still canvassing the neighborhood, so we hope to find someone who saw something we can use. One thing is certain, though: this is not shaping up to be a typical kidnapping. If Amanda really was kidnapped, it happened in broad daylight, at the school, and no one saw anything. But if Ms. Spunky is correct, then the whole case is really twisted."

Mom raised her eyebrows. "Twisted? How?"

"It's possible Amanda murdered her own father."

Mom dropped her rib. "What? Why in heaven's name do you think that?"

"Because we watched Ms. Spunky smell the knife handle, then run up the stairs, go directly into Amanda's room, bark three times, run back downstairs, go back to the body, and point her nose directly at the knife handle."

Mom looked down at me. "Whoa! That is a strong message, girl." A large tidbit dropped from on high. Mom always shows her appreciation.

Mom continued, "Listen guys, for a sixteen-year-old girl to kill her own father, especially by stabbing him, something had to be terribly wrong. Maybe she was defending herself, or under the influence of something that could have pushed her to the point of insanity. I don't know the facts, but she must have been terrified of something. A kid might accidently *shoot* her father, but to shove a knife into him is a whole different story."

Tony replied, "Yeah, we agree. Maybe she stabbed him, maybe she didn't. Maybe she had a good reason to stab him. But our immediate problem is that she's a minor, and we still don't know where she is. For all we know, she could be in great danger. We listed her as a probable kidnapping, and every patrolman out there has her picture, plus we've issued an Amber Alert."

"What have you learned about the girl?"

Frank swallowed his shrimp fried rice before answering. "We know that she's an only child, and the neighbors describe her as smart, quiet but friendly, somewhat shy, and quite pretty. There are no reports of any recent problems at school. She regularly attends St. Patrick's church, where she's in the youth group and sings in the choir. Her mother, Ruth, left home permanently twelve years ago. I say 'permanently' because she'd already left numerous times before that. The last time she left, she moved to New York to become some kind of designer or something, and she hasn't returned to this day. There are some unanswered questions about all that, but the neighbors were unanimous in their opinion that Ruth Pederson was not a nice woman. Mrs. Wagner, the next-door neighbor, has lived there more than twenty-five years. She was there when Henry and Ruth first moved in as newlyweds. She said they were all lovey-dovey the first year or so, but then they started to argue more and more. Mrs. Wagner heard some of those arguments when the windows were open or when they were out in the yard. She says most of their fights were about Mrs. Pederson's drinking too much. After a big fight, Ruth would usually storm out of the house, suitcase in hand, and drive away. Sometimes it was just for a day or two, but on several occasions she was gone so long that the neighbors didn't think she was coming back. But she always did. After her last return, years ago, Mrs. Wagner said Ruth seemed to settle down. She thought that maybe she'd been in rehab, because she didn't smell like booze anymore, and the arguments stopped.

"About a year after that, Amanda was born. The arguments started up again when Amanda was about three, and the neighborhood scuttlebutt was that Ruth had started drinking again. That was about the same time Ruth told people her father had died and that she was going to inherit a lot of money. Mrs. Wagner said Ruth showed no grief over her father's passing, only immense joy about the upcoming inheritance.

"Then, right after Amanda's fourth birthday, Ruth left again; and this time she didn't come back. Mr. Pederson had no idea where she was until about a year ago. We talked to several neighbors, and they all agreed Ruth drank too much and yelled a lot at both the toddler and Mr. Pederson. In fact, we couldn't find a single person in the neighborhood who was sorry to see the woman go, though many were sad that Amanda didn't have a mother around.

"Amanda was only four when she lost her mother, and initially she had some problems, but everyone I talked to said Mr. Pederson was a great dad, and after several months Amanda seemed like a happy kid again. Then last year, when Amanda was fifteen, her mother made contact and invited Amanda to spend part of the summer with her in

New York. According to the neighbors, when Amanda got back she told everyone how wonderful it was to be in New York with her mother, and that she was going to go again next year. This summer she *did* go to New York again, but she came home after only a short time. No one knew what had happened. When I questioned Ruth Pederson about it, she said Amanda simply got bored and wanted to spend the rest of the summer back home with her friends.

"If something did happen in New York, it may have affected her schoolwork. The principal told us that at the start of school this year her grades were far below her usual work, but she recovered quickly and was soon back to her usual straight A's. The principal also told us she was an excellent student, and he expected her to qualify for scholarships to several big-name colleges."

Fearless rose up and patted Tony's belly. Tony must have just picked up his eggroll. He looked down and asked, "Hannah, cats don't eat eggrolls, do they?"

Mom chuckled. "If that's Fearless patting you, then the answer is yes. I don't have a clue why, but that boy loves egg rolls—unless they contain shrimp, but these don't, so he'll like them."

Tony pinched off a piece, showed the size to Mom, who nodded her approval, and he gave it to Fearless. "Well, I'll be. He wolfed that down in nothing flat. Who would have thought?"

Frank snickered. He knew all about Fearless's odd tastes. In fact, about a month ago I noticed that Frank had started bringing an extra eggroll. I think he was tired of Fearless eating half of his.

"So what happens with the case now?" Mom asked.

"Well, as soon as we're done eating, we'll head to the precinct," Tony said. "We need to get the casebook started and see if any new evidence has turned up."

"I guess there won't be much sleep for the two of you tonight."

"If it gets too late, we'll catch a few winks at the precinct. We have cots in the record room."

When everyone finished eating Tony offered to help with the dishes, but Mom declined. "Naw, you two need to get back to finding that girl." As they headed toward the door, Mom pulled Frank back and kissed him. She whispered, "Will you try to get some rest if you can?"

"I will." He kissed her gently and said, "How about we meet for breakfast tomorrow around eight?"

She smiled. "It's a date. I'll meet you at the diner. If you can't make it, give me a call."

After shutting the door, Mom shuddered and hugged herself. "Spunky, this case gives me the creeps. According to what your nose found, that poor girl is going to need a whole lot of help. I sure wonder what happened."

My nose knew the facts, not the story behind them.

CHAPTER  11

Turns out Nosey's human is a night owl. We couldn't risk Nosey getting caught leaving his yard again, so our rendezvous had to be delayed until two a.m. I used the wait time to get some shut-eye. As usual, Fearless was an effective alarm clock.

"Fearless, how come you always know what time it is?"

"I make sure one of my nine lives (*breath*) is always awake."

I wasn't sure if he was serious or not, but I was too sleepy to conduct a proper debate, so I let it slide. "Come on, we don't want to be late."

"Why? Nosey can't go anywhere (*breath*) until we get there?"

"True, but I said we'd be there at two a.m., and you know my rule number two.

After all our years together, Fearless certainly had heard it more than a few times. He repeated it perfectly: "Your word is your bond and it must be honored."

I made a quick rest stop before we headed to our own gate. When we got there, we were surprised to find Lion

King waiting for us. "Evening, Spunky, Fearless. How are you two this fine night?"

To show my respect, I acknowledge his presence by nodding my head, but I didn't look him directly in the eye. "Good to see you, Lion King. What a pleasant surprise. This time of the night, I thought you be out there overseeing your catdom?"

Lion King is the alpha feline, not just on our property, but also for miles in every direction. Even the campus ferals acknowledge his authority, and in fact I have yet to discover any boundaries to his tom's territory. This cat is the king!

Lion King stretched and answered, "I've already made a quick inspection tour. I'll make a more thorough one before dawn, but tonight I have a special rendezvous planned with Miss Gidget, that Persian beauty over at Mr. Tidwell's farm. When I heard that you and Fearless were heading in that direction to see Nosey, I thought it best I provide some extra protection."

I snorted. "Why? Is Ollie up to mischief again?"

Lion King began grooming his whiskers. "Spunky, when is that crazy owl *not* up to mischief? However, since he now considers you two friends, I doubt he'll be buzz-bombing you again. No, tonight Ollie isn't the problem, but I've received reports of a young coyote who's gotten too big for his britches. I thought you'd be safer with an escort."

Fearless stepped forward. "A coyote? No offense intended (*breath*), Lion King, but I'm not sure that the three of us (*breath*) are an adequate militia against a full-grown coyote (*breath*), especially if he's a young, hungry one. Spunky and I (*breath*) can't run as fast as you."

49

I smiled. Fearless was downplaying his own abilities in an effort to protect my ego. Even with his breathing issues, Fearless and his long, lanky legs could still out-sprint any cat, including Lion King.

"No offense taken, Fearless. I agree, we all must choose our fights wisely. That is why tonight I've taken measures to improve our odds against this nasty coyote boy. First, I had my trackers locate his den. Then, before dusk I asked Ollie to drop some fresh roadkill on his doorstep. A full belly should knock his aggression down a notch or two, but just to be sure, I made arrangements for Ms. Massey to accompany you the entire way this evening."

"Ms. Massey, the donkey?" I said.

"Yup, she's the best coyote-kicker on the planet! Even though her pasture gate can be a bit tricky, I've successfully busted her out many times."

I replied, "I do remember hearing that farmer Grant hasn't lost a single sheep since he made Ms. Massey his guard donkey, but I didn't know she did outside work."

Lion King stood and stretched. "Well, she and I have a special arrangement, and when the situation warrants, she rides shotgun for me. Come on now, we should get a move on. I already freed Ms. Massey and she's waiting for us."

As Lion King turned away, I looked at Fearless and whispered, "A special agreement between a cat and a donkey?"

Fearless shrugged. "Don't ask me."

Cats can easily climb most gates; I cannot. Using his expertise, Lion King quickly unlatched ours. Once we were through, I then used one of my own assets to shut it—my butt. We headed out, and we soon reached the stream and found Ms. Massey waiting for us there.

"Good evening, Ms Massey," I said. "Lion King told us of your kind offer to be our security guard this evening. But who's watching the sheep?"

"Good evening to you all. To answer your question, Spunk, when I accompany Lion King, he arranges plenty of backup security for the sheep. Even though I know they're well protected, I did promise I wouldn't be gone too long, so we'd best get a move on."

Again, I looked at Fearless and whispered. "Backup security?"

This time Fearless's only answer was to stretch his long body and follow Lion King and Ms. Massey down the path.

Now that we had our donkey protector along, Lion King was free to leave us when we reached Tidwell's farm. As we proceeded on our way, I glanced back and saw that he stopped outside the barn and begin grooming himself. I snorted, "Apparently Lion King spruces up before he calls on Miss Gidget."

Fearless replied, "Well, she *is* mighty *(breath)* finicky about fishy whiskers."

I turned and stared at him. "And you know that how?"

Fearless smirked and bumped me with his head. "Spunk *(breath)*, you know a gentleman never tells."

Just then, off in the distance, I heard Nosey. The wind must have carried Ms. Massey's scent ahead of us, and his warning growls told me he was not pleased with what he smelled. Donkeys are also known to be dog-kickers.

Nosey's growl had abated by the time we reached his backyard. He approached the fence and said, "You three do make an unusual nighttime procession. I got a snootful of Ms. Massey, and I was just about to release a full-blown warning howl—no offense intended, Ms. Massey—but then I smelled you and Fearless mingled in with her. I figured you must know what you're doing, bringing her here."

"Fear not, Nosey," I said, "Ms. Massey is a friend and, in fact, tonight she's also our personal security guard. So come on and let's put that nose of yours to work!"

Nosey hesitated. "Ms. Massey, Spunky would never lie to me, but I'd feel a smidgen better if I heard directly from you that part about being my friend."

Ms. Massey said softly. "Fear not, you're safe with me, Nosey."

Nosey said, "I thank you kindly, ma'am."

Fearless unlatched Nosey's gate, and we headed through the woods toward town. While it's simple for a cat and two dogs to sneak through town without being seen, it's a tad difficult to conceal a donkey. We opted to leave Ms. Massey at the edge of the woods, where she could safely wait while enjoying the tasty campus grass. Since, unlike humans, we were not required to stay on the roadways, we made good time reaching the crime scene.

When we reached the Pedersons' driveway, Nosey easily picked up the scat trail and began following it down the road. Fearless and I trotted alongside him, acting as his lookouts. I learned long ago that when Nosey's nose is fully engaged, his eyes and ears shut down. It helps to have friends watching for oncoming cars and other hazards.

When we got to the spot where my nose had given out, Nosey didn't miss a beat. He just kept on going. Wow! What a schnozzola! Several hundred feet later he made a left turn, and at the next street he turned to the right. Ten minutes later, he started going in circles. Apparently even his powerful proboscis had finally lost the trail.

"It's okay, Nosey, you can stop now," I said.

But Nosey didn't stop, so I barked louder. "Nosey, stop already!"

No response.

I backed up, lowered my head, and gently butted his side. He stumbled. "Hey, Spunk, what did you do that for?"

"Because your ears were shut tighter than a refrigerator door. Didn't you hear me barking for you to stop?"

Nosey snorted. "Nope, didn't hear a thing. Tracking is all about the nose. Sorry, Spunk, but it looks like I've lost the trail. I tracked the scat up to those big puddles back there, but then the trail faded. Maybe the water washed off the last of it. Sorry I can't be more help."

"More help? Are you kidding? Nosey, lift your nose off the ground and look around! You just proved my theory."

Nosey raised his head, looked down the road, and saw what I had seen.

At the top of the hill stood Mr. Gifford's farm.

CHAPTER  12

We had accomplished all we could for the night, so we headed back. Ms. Massey was right where we left her, and together we started back through the woods. Midway on our journey home, she and Nosey simultaneously came to an abrupt halt.

Ms. Massey snorted. "Hold up, Spunk. Something stinks."

Nosey concurred. "I wouldn't say 'stinks,' but I too smell coyote."

Ms Massey moved forward to stand directly over me. She said, "Spunky, stay under my belly, you'll be safe there. Fearless, see that big rock up ahead? When we get there, use it to jump onto my back, but please be kind and sheath your claws."

Fearless jumped on and quickly hunkered down at Ms. Massey's withers.

"Nosey, the path is too narrow to walk side by side. If you're behind me you could get kicked, so it's better if you stay in the front. That nose of yours should provide you with plenty of warning if that coyote attacks us. Trust me, I have a plan."

Once Ms. Massey established her gait, I had no trouble trotting along beneath her. It was like when Mom put me on a slow treadmill. I started at her front legs, and when I slipped back and my tail aligned with hers, I just scampered up to the front again.

With Fearless riding on Ms. Massey's back and me trotting beneath her, I'm sure we made an odd nighttime silhouette. A few minutes later, our parade came to a sudden stop.

Nosey whispered, "He's a few hundred yards ahead and moving fast in our direction."

Ms. Massey snorted. "Spunky, stay right where you are. Fearless, grab a big mouthful of my mane and hang on tight. Nosey, get behind me. Now!"

Nosey hesitated, "But, I thought you said…"

"Now, Nosey, now!"

As Nosey moved toward the rear, Ms. Massey quickly turned her massive body.

The bushes rustled for only an instant before the coyote flew out. Apparently his plan was to attack Ms. Massey head on, but where her front end had been was now her lethal back end. Her powerful hind legs rose as she let loose with a bray so loud I thought my eardrums would burst. As instructed, I stood my ground; but let me tell you, a coyote coming straight at you at the same instant a huge donkey belly is launching right over your head is enough to age you fast!

I readied for the assault, baring my fangs and issuing a ferocious growl. The coyote's feet left the ground and he lunged right at me. At that exact moment, Ms. Massey's hind legs hit his chest. His yelp was loud and sharp. The force of her kick sent that coyote high into the air end over end. He landed a good thirty feet down the path. He rose, shook himself, paused for a second, and then ran off in the opposite direction. He might be a young coyote, but apparently, he was not a stupid one.

"Ms. Massey, that was amazing!" I barked.

"Shucks," she said, "I could've kicked that stinker twice as far, but I was afraid if I bucked too hard, I might dislodge Fearless. You okay up there, Mr. Fearless?"

"Yee-haw! (*Breath.*) That was some ride! If that's what you call a half a buck (*breath*), you're right (*breath*), I couldn't have held on for your best."

"Someday I'll show you my all-out buck," Ms. Massey said. "It's pretty awesome, as long as you're not the recipient."

We all took a few moments to catch our breath and let the adrenaline rush wear off, then we accompanied Ms. Massey back to her pasture. Fortunately, she and Lion King had thought ahead and secured the gate with a big rock instead of refastening the tricky latch. Ms. Massey rolled the rock back with her powerful hoof, and once she was safely inside Fearless fiddled with the latch until it snapped shut again. Now all was as it should be.

"Thanks again, Ms. Massey, for taking such good care of us," I said. "If there's ever anything we can do for you, give us a holler and we'll come running."

"Thanks, Spunk. Now I'd better get back to work and relieve the hired help. You two have a good sleep."

As we headed down the road, I paused to look back. I watched as at least thirty cats left Ms. Massey's pasture.

I snorted. Thirty cats! Wow! Then I cocked my head and thought, given the way Ms. Massey handled that coyote, maybe thirty to one was a tad understaffed.

CHAPTER  13

Later that morning, Mom returned from her breakfast with Frank and told us there were no new leads. Obviously, the humans didn't know what we had learned hours before. But for now that would have to wait. We had an appointment for another online counseling session with Samantha.

The session had gone on uneventfully for about ten minutes when Mom asked, "Samantha, do you want your son back?"

"Of course, I do. What kind of mother would I be if I didn't want my kid?"

"Well, Samantha, as they say: talk is cheap. The question is, what are you willing to do to get him back?"

Samantha's cheeks flushed and her voice rose. "What can I do? That bitch has all the money."

"So you're powerless and can do nothing?"

"Without any money all I can do is kidnap him, and then I'd be in even more trouble than I am now."

"Well, let's say you did have enough money to hire a lawyer. Why should a judge give you your son back?"

"Because I'm a good mother, and a child should be with his mother!"

"Okay, but let's look at it from the judge's point of view. You violated your bond, there's an outstanding warrant for your arrest, and you live with a man who's not your husband and with whom you've had another child; but that man is unemployed, and you yourself have changed jobs several times in the past year."

Samantha's shoulders slumped as she mumbled, "See, I told you, there's nothing I can do."

"You could turn yourself in and serve your time."

Samantha reared back and exclaimed, "Go to jail?"

"Yes, go to jail. How long was your sentence?"

"A year. But what about my daughter?"

"Can't her father take care of her?"

"Hell, no! He only wants to party all the time."

"Then why are you still with him?"

She laughed. "Because I love him, of course, and because he's really good to Caroline."

"You say he's really good to Caroline, but he doesn't even help keep a roof over her head or food in her stomach."

"Well, no, but he's kind to her, he plays with her, and he loves her a lot. He just has trouble holding down a job."

"What if you reconciled with your mother, would she take care of Caroline?"

Samantha's face turned a very deep crimson. It looked like she might explode. She leaned in toward the screen and yelled, "I'll never let that witch near my daughter! Never!"

"Okay. Okay. Let's try approaching this from another direction. Maybe it's time you tell me why you hate your mother so much."

"I told you, she's a crazy rich bitch."

"But what did she actually *do* that made you hate her so much?"

Samantha was silent. The color drained from her cheeks, and her eyes became moist.

"Samantha, please, this is important. Please tell me what she did."

Then the floodgates opened. Samantha spent the rest of the session telling story after story of how when she was young her mother would go out partying and leave her alone. She said she lost track of all the "step-fathers and uncles" her mother brought home. Some would live with them for a while. Two had abused her sexually, and when she told her mother about it, she was called a liar and other choice names. Inevitably her mother got tired of each man, or vice versa, and they'd leave.

Samantha didn't know her biological father, but according to her mother his name was William and he died when she was a baby. Samantha assumed that was a lie, and that her mother just didn't know which man had actually fathered her. When Samantha was fifteen, her mother married a wealthy man; then, on Samantha's eighteenth birthday, her mother gave her a thousand dollars and told her to take her stuff and leave.

That was when Samantha began working at whatever jobs she could to keep a roof over her head, often working two or three jobs. She had worked as a secretary, a receptionist, a waitress, a sales girl, and even a crossing guard. Eventually she'd get in a fight with her boss, and so she had never kept a job longer than eight months. Then she met Terry, fell in love, and got pregnant with her son. The only time she stopped working was for two weeks right after he was born. Now she earned her living cleaning people's houses.

If the session had not run out, Samantha might still be talking. When she had signed off, Mom sat quietly in front of the blank screen. Sweetie climbed onto her lap, and his purr filled the room. Mom stroked Sweetie, closed her eyes, and her breathing slowed. She said, "Perhaps I judged Samantha too quickly. True, she shouldn't have had those two kids; but even with such a tragic and lousy start in life, she's managed to find respectable work, keep a roof over her head, feed her daughter, and stay off welfare. And despite the fact that she hates her mother, can't see her son, and could be arrested at any moment, she doesn't whine about how hard her life is. Maybe that's the part that makes me uneasy. She complains bitterly about her mother, but not about her own life, yet her body language and that obnoxious laugh clearly show a high anxiety level. Granted, she has plenty of reasons to be anxious. She won't be able to escape her past forever. If she gets pulled over for running a red light, she'll be arrested and probably also lose custody of Caroline. From what I can see, she has very little support and few options, yet she never complains about *her* life. Either this woman lives in an enormous bubble of denial, or she has a huge reservoir of grit. I guess my job is to find out which one it really is."

Sometimes, my mom can be very wise.

CHAPTER  14

Samantha might be Mom's current quandary, but at the moment mine was how to let the detectives know that the unknown man had driven toward Gifford's farm.

This required feline input. I found Fancy and Fearless lounging on the couch, and explained my predicament.

Fancy-Pants came up with the winning suggestion. "Go find something that belongs to Frank and take it to Mom. Maybe she'll get the message that you need to see him."

"Good idea, Fancy!" The boys helped me search from room to room looking for something that might work. The problem was that Mom had already tidied up. We couldn't find one thing that belonged to Frank. Now what?

Fearless came to the rescue. "Hang on, Spunk *(breath)*. Let me check under the bed." He flattened himself and under he went. A few seconds later, he emerged with one dark gray dirty sock. "I remembered that I saw this last week when I went under the bed *(breath)* seeking some peace and quiet."

"Thanks, buddy." I picked up the sock and trotted off. I found Mom outside working in her garden. "Whatcha got, girl?"

I dropped the sock.

"A sock? Now, where did you get that? Hey, that's one of Frank's! Isn't that just like a man? I'll bet one morning when he couldn't find it he hightailed it out of here sockless. Thanks, girl, I'll try to find its mate." She stuffed the sock into her pocket and returned to her weeding.

Luckily, the toe of the sock remained sticking out. I leaned in, plucked the sock out of her pocket, and began shaking it vigorously.

"Spunky, stop that! You'll put holes in it. Here, give it to me." She reached for it, but I ran off a way, dropped it, and barked.

Mom got off her knees and started toward me. "Okay, Spunk, enough messing around with the sock. Let me have it." Her tone was firm.

Before she got too close, I picked it up and ran. Then I dropped it again and barked twice.

"Spunky, quit it! Give it to me!" She started to advance. Now she was definitely annoyed.

Once again, I snatched it up and ran. This time I ran big circles around her, then I turned and raced toward the house.

"Spunky Richards, you come back here!" As I hoped, she followed, but her annoyance had now progressed to anger. She didn't like it one iota that I was ignoring her commands.

I waited until she entered the kitchen, then I jumped onto a chair and draped the sock over the phone. When Mom reached for it, I whined. Unfortunately, even this failed to get the desired response. She picked up the sock, glared at me, and stomped off to bedroom, muttering some drivel about the questionable state of my sanity and how no snippy little dog was going to dictate the rules in her house. I didn't take her ramblings seriously. I knew I had crossed a line, but for some reason, today she was being unusually dense. I had no choice. I had to push the limit further.

"Fancy-Pants, I need your help. Mom's being really difficult. I assume she went and put that sock on the dresser. Will you sneak into the bedroom and get it for me? Please don't get caught!"

"Sure, Spunky. Be right back." Another handy bonus is that cats are great at getting the stuff a short-legged dog can't reach.

Fortunately, before Mom headed back outside, she stopped at the sink to get a drink. When she turned around, there I stood with the sock in my mouth.

"Spunky, how in heaven's name did you get that sock again?" She glared, set her jaw, lowered her voice and commanded, "Give it to me, now."

Once again I jumped up onto a chair and draped the sock over the phone. This time, after whining loudly I added three quick barks.

"Goodness gracious! What *is* this all about?" Finally, she paused and took the time to look at my face. I stared her in the eye, cocked my cute head, and focused on Frank's name.

Her brow furrowed. "What could you possibly want?" She studied my face intently and then, to my relief, she said, "Do you want me to call Frank?"

I barked twice to let her know she had hit the bullseye.

"What the heck for?"

Since Mom doesn't speak canine, I settled for two more barks.

"Okay, already, I'll call him." She dialed Frank's number. After all our years together, I trusted her to present my request reasonably. "Frank, I don't have a clue what's going on, but I'm pretty sure Spunky wants to see you.... How should I know what she wants? All I can tell you is that she found one of your socks and has repeatedly draped it over the phone. No, she is not playing. This dog is serious."

Mom studied my face and then added, "Maybe she found something you and Tony need to know about.... Okay, see you soon."

Good job, Mom! Now, how the heck was I going to get the detectives to understand me?

Unfortunately, they arrived before I had come up with a plan. As they walked through the door, they asked in unison, "What is it girl? What did you find?"

Heck, it wasn't like I had an actual object to drop at their feet! I needed time, so I headed outside with the humans following close behind. Maybe they thought I had buried the clue. A few moments later, Bobby returned from an outing. He leaped over the fence, got an update from Fearless, and then intervened. "Spunky, let the humans follow you around for a while before you lead them back to their car. I've got a plan."

At this point, I was willing to try even one of Bobby's harebrained ideas. I did as he requested and meandered around the yard with Tony, Frank, and Mom right on my tail. I heard Bobby's yowl declaring I needed help. After about five minutes, I led the humans slowly back around the corner of the house and turned into the driveway. Wow, every cat within earshot must have responded to Bobby's call! I snorted with glee. Bobby's plan was not only obvious, it was brilliant.

Frank's car had a bumper-to-bumper fur coat.

Frank chuckled. "Hannah, what the heck is going on? My car looks like a zoo-mobile."

I ran to the gate and barked twice.

Tony laughed. "It has to be about the car. I think Ms. Spunky wants us to take her somewhere, and I'm betting she wants to return to the crime scene. Am I right, girl?"

I barked twice, jumped against his leg and vigorously shook my booty.

Mom laughed. "Well, Tony, I'd say you guessed correctly. You're getting pretty good at translating critter talk."

Tony puffed out his chest and beamed. "Come on, Frank, Ms. Spunky needs a ride."

CHAPTER  15

When we arrived at the Pederson place, Tony and Frank immediately jumped out of the car and headed toward the house. When they finally noticed that I hadn't followed them, they quickly reversed course

"Spunky, come on. You wanted us to bring you to the crime scene, right?"

I barked once, but still didn't budge.

Tony put his hands on his hips and cocked his head. "So?"

Frank rubbed his face and muttered, "Think like a dog, Tony, think like a dog."

They both stared at me. Okay, now that I had their full attention, I made my next move. With my leash trailing behind me, I ran down the driveway and into the street. Fear not, I looked both ways first.

"Whoa! This isn't good. Frank, where's she going?"

"Heck if I know. Run and catch her before she gets too far. I'll get the car."

Tony started running and yelled, "Spunky, stop! Wait for me. Wait, girl, wait!"

I kept moving. Most humans are no match for a dog on the run, but sometimes they might get close enough to step on your leash that's trailing behind you. Hey, whiplash hurts, so my advice is if they get too close, it is far less painful to halt and let them think you're being obedient.

This time I decided to be kind. I stopped, turned around, and let Tony catch up. Good thing I did, he was huffing and puffing like an old man. When he reached me, I plunked my rump down. Enough running! It was time to wait for the car.

A few moments later, Frank pulled up alongside and asked, "Now what?"

I jumped against the car door, and Tony got the message, "I think her highness wants a lift."

We climbed into the car, and I perched on Tony's lap with my front paws on the dashboard. I snorted softly and pointed my nose forward. Frank laughed, "Aye, aye, Captain, off we go."

When Frank drove past the first street too quickly, I protested loudly. He behaved himself after that and stopped at each cross street to look at me for directions. He quickly figured out what I wanted when I either turned my head or stared straight forward. Life is so much simpler when everyone follows the rules!

When we reached the road leading to Mr. Gifford's farm, I whined softly and dropped down onto Tony's lap. Frank pulled over, we got out of the car, and I put my nose to work. I had no trouble finding Nosey's trail, and the men quickly realized I was tracking something. When I reached the puddle and crossed to the other side, I stopped and sat down.

Frank examined the road. "Tony, I don't see a thing."

"Obviously Spunky knows something we don't.", said Tony. "She brought us here from the crime scene, so there has to be a connection. I say we call the station and get a bunch of men out here to start searching and canvassing the area."

"And what are you going to tell the captain when he asks why we want to search here?"

"Are you referring to our Captain Swenson, the diehard dog-lover? Have you forgotten how he bragged about Spunky after she helped us solve our last murder case? The man was ready to give Spunky the keys to the city!"

Frank laughed. "You're right. Spunky probably has more credibility with him than we do."

"Yup. So all we have to do is tell him Spunky led us here, and I'm betting he'll call out the troops."

As Tony pulled out his cell phone to make the call, I licked my paw and began swiping my face. Hey, cats aren't the only ones to use this technique. If Captain Swenson was sending the troops, I wanted to look my best.

CHAPTER  16

Three patrol cars arrived, and the police began going from house to house. Two hours later, Frank and Tony drove me home.

"Nothing, Hannah, absolutely nothing," said Frank. "No Amanda, no sign of a black sedan, and no one in the area saw anything out of the ordinary. We couldn't find a single clue. I don't know what Spunky smelled, but we found zilch. Of course we'll keep looking, but there's a lot of countryside out there. We don't even know which direction to go. Right now we're stumped."

Mom furrowed her brow and looked down at me. "I wonder why Spunky couldn't show you anything more."

"Because the kidnapper was in a car. Spunky couldn't possibly track a car."

Mom put her hands on her hips, let out a puff of air, and said, "Well, she tracked *something* to that point, didn't she?"

Frank held up his hands in surrender and chuckled. "I stand corrected. You're right. It's possible she took us to where the trail ended. She obviously knew where she wanted to go, but once we got there, she wandered around, never going far in any one direction. I think she was stumped too."

The humans could continue this useless babbling, but I had work to do. Being stumped and staying stumped are two very different things. Every terrier knows a rat's tunnel has more than one entrance, and I needed to find a way into this rat's maze. I called to the felines to follow me outside.

"Spunky, tell us what happened!" said Fancy-Pants.

"I had no trouble getting them to the farm," I told the assembled cats. "I was hoping they would see something after that, but they didn't. I know the kidnapper drove that way, but I don't know whether he kept on going or he's hiding out somewhere. I need help."

"You want to use Nosey again?" Bobby asked.

"No, there's too much terrain to cover. First we have to narrow down the search area."

Fearless knew exactly where I was heading. "The Campus *(breath)* Cats!"

"Yup, the Campus Cats and every feline they can recruit. Do you think you can arrange a meeting with Einstein and Goliath for tonight?

"Can't hurt to try. *(Breath.)* I'll head over to the college and ask."

Sweetie interjected. "But, Fearless, it's not dark yet. Won't it be hard to find the ferals while it's still light?"

Fearless called back, "Not for me."

I snorted. We tend to forget that before Fearless got hurt and came to live at Mom's he, too, was a free spirit. He knew most of the feral cats' hiding places.

It was only recently that I had had the honor of meeting those two magnificent cats, Goliath and Einstein. They had proven themselves resourceful allies in helping us solve our last mystery. Making their acquaintance had also resulted in an unexpected family reunion, of sorts. We learned that when Fearless was a feral kitten, he and Einstein had been like brothers. Their mothers had been best friends and had raised their babies together. In the feral world, this meant they were family. However, after Fearless's injuries forced him to give up his feral ways, he had lost track of all of them, even his momma. When he and Einstein were reunited, Fearless learned that his mom had lived a good life but had gone over the Rainbow Bridge a few years ago. Einstein's mom, Lady Gray, was still around, living behind Casey's Laundromat. Although Ms. Lady Gray was now long in the tooth, she was still a force to be reckoned with. Of course, given that Einstein was her son, I doubt any feline would be foolish enough to confront her. No sane cat would knowingly insult Einstein's momma. Even Lion King was wise enough to never directly challenge her or her son.

Like many before me, I soon learned that Goliath's and Einstein's names didn't represent their true personalities. Goliath was a huge long-haired, crossed-eyed, scary, dumb-looking bloke, but in fact he was a wise, judicious, gentle creature. On the other hand, Einstein was the one you never wanted to meet in a dark alley. He was a scrawny, mouse-gray dude whose toughness far exceeded his brains. Between Goliath's intellect and Einstein's warrior skills, they were the chosen leaders of the feral colony on and around the campus.

My new relationship with these two had also revealed a delightful tidbit about my friend Fearless. Much to my amusement, I learned that Fearless's momma had called him Baby Cakes, while Einstein's childhood nickname had been Shrimp. Isn't that a hoot! Of course, I could never divulge this information to any other critter. Payback can be painful. But when no one is around, I do love to get up close to Fearless and whisper, "Ah, you're such a cutie, Baby Cakes." Man, you should see that boy's fur ruffle!

While Fearless, a.k.a. Baby Cakes, was away arranging a rendezvous with the Campus Cats, I asked Sweetie and Bobby to go in search of Lion King and respectfully request that he come see me at his convenience. Given the size of his territory, finding him could take a while, so I settled in for a nap.

The sun was setting when Bobby batted me on my rump. "Hey, Spunk, Lion King is outside waiting on you. Sorry it took so long, but he's one hard dude to track down. We finally found him over at that Persian chick's house."

"Thanks, Bobby. Sorry, my mistake: I should have thought to tell you to look there first. Come on, let's not keep the King waiting." We headed outside.

"Evening, Spunk. I heard you wanted to see me," said Lion King.

"Thanks for coming, Lion King. I'm sorry if we interrupted your wooing of Miss Gidget."

"No problem, the whole night lies before me. Whaddaya need?"

As I explained our dilemma, and Lion King caught on quickly. "I'll go find Ollie. It sounds like some owl

73

surveillance might be needed. I'll check in with the campus boys and find out when your meeting is scheduled so that I can be there. I don't think you'll need Ms. Massey tonight—no one has seen hide or hair of that coyote's sorry ass. I heard she really drop-kicked that bad boy. I'll bet he didn't stop running until he crossed the river.

"But here's another thought. I could also spread the word among the raccoons. I'm sure one of them has kinfolk near Gifford's farm. They could be related to the one whose scat Nosey was tracking."

"Thanks, Lion King. I'll take all the help you can muster."

Too bad the humans didn't know—help was on the way.

CHAPTER  17

Free-spirit felines love the night. If the moon is up, so are they. This can make it difficult to arrange meetings during "normal business hours." I felt honored that the Campus Cats had agreed to meet me at midnight. That's prime feral time, normally reserved for prowling, hunting, and all manner of secret cat antics.

When Fearless and I arrived on campus, we headed to our usual meeting spot by the big oak tree. Goliath and Einstein's home is nearby, underneath the college library, but many of the ferals come from all over town and the outlying farms. Tonight, besides Lion King, Goliath, Einstein, and Einstein's mother, Lady Gray, I estimated there were at least fifty cats of all shapes, ages, colors, and breeds. It's difficult to spot a motionless free spirit in the dark, so I concede that there were probably many more.

"Good evening, Ms. Spunky, Fearless," said Goliath.

"Evening, Goliath," I replied. Then I turned and acknowledged Einstein and his mother with a nod of my head, "Good evening, you two."

Lion King murmured. "Spunk, don't forget Ollie, he's up in the tree."

I swung my head upward. "Evening, Ollie. You were so quiet, I didn't know you were up there."

Ollie hooted. "Just waiting to hear what you need, Ms. Spunky."

Cats and owls are natural-born enemies. In fact, an owl as big as Ollie could easily carry off a kitten or a small cat, so it's quite unusual to find them working together. However, during our last adventure, I learned that when given the proper respect and a worthy cause, even adversaries can become allies. The fact that owls pride themselves on being honorable creatures made my job much easier. But feral cats? Honorable? Well, if they call you friend, then absolutely, yes; otherwise I think the feral code is more akin to honor among thieves.

As if to prove my point, just then Einstein backed up, sprayed the tree, and hissed in Ollie's direction, "Make sure you keep those talons to yourself, you big flapping bag of wind."

Ollie opened his wings and transformed himself into a large, menacing beast. Einstein was not deterred; he arched his back and hissed again.

Well, I didn't say *everyone* had accepted my principle of mutual respect, but thankfully Einstein's momma had. She immediately stepped forward, boxed Einstein's ears, and said, "I apologize for my son's rudeness, Ollie."

"Apology accepted, Lady Gray. Some kids are all mouth." Ollie pulled his wings back in and settled down on the limb.

I slowly let out the breath I had been holding. Ollie and Einstein would make for one ugly fight, and one I hope never to see.

76

All eyes then shifted to Lion King as he stepped forward. "Spunky," he said, "tell us what you need us to do."

I told them about the murder, the suspected kidnapping, the raccoon scat, and the trail that ended by Gifford's farm.

Lion King then added some new information. "Today, before the sun went down, I found Bandito the raccoon and filled him in. Tonight he'll spread the word among the other raccoons, and ask them to report anything unusual. He also said he would personally talk to the raccoons living on or near Gifford's farm. I expect more info before morning."

"That's great, Lion King, thanks." I turned to the ferals. "Goliath, I need you and the free spirits to spread out and keep your eyes and ears open. That's feral territory out there. If anything is amiss, they'll be the first to see it. If the kidnapper lives around here and has taken Amanda back to his home, I'm sure you'll notice something. That something might be our next big clue."

Goliath stepped forward and spoke for the rest of the ferals. "We'll get right on it, Spunk. I'll send word to you if anyone reports anything unusual." Then he leaned in and lowered his voice. "But be forewarned, we might be inundated with a bunch of false alarms. Some of these felines are a little *too* observant. They could file a report simply because a human moved his trash can to a new location."

"That's okay, Goliath. I'd rather track down false leads than miss something that could help us find Amanda."

"Tell you what, if I get a report of something suspicious, I'll go and check it out first to weed out the red herrings. It might cost us a little time, but believe me, it will definitely save time in the end. You have no idea how persnickety some of these felines can be."

I snorted. I knew all too well about persnickety cats, but I kept that thought to myself and simply said, "Thanks, Goliath. That'll help a lot."

Next I looked upward. "Ollie, would you be willing to make some flyovers and see if you spot anything unusual? I hate to ask, but the reconnaissance should be done during daylight hours. I know that cuts into your sleep, but humans don't do as much moving around after dark as you do."

"I'm more than willing, Spunk, but if it's okay with you, I'll go talk to the captains of the crow union, Russell and Kaw. Crows are a nosey bunch, and I'll bet they know everything that goes on at that farm. They could easily carry out your daytime reconnaissance. Besides, if they're busy helping you, maybe they'll have less time to dive-bomb me."

"Great idea, Ollie! Go sign them up."

Goliath and Einstein then assigned the cats to various quadrants on and around Gifford's place. Some would be team leaders, others would be scouts, and some would be runners carrying messages back and forth. In my experience, a cat hotline can be mighty handy.

By the time Fearless and I arrived back home it was close to two a.m, and we immediately settled in for some sleep.

"Good night *(breath)*, Spunk," Fearless yawned. "Sleep well."

"I'll sleep better after we find Amanda."

Sweetie purred. "You'll find her, I know you will, Spunk. Everything is going to work out fine. You'll see."

Sweetie —always the optimist.

CHAPTER 18

Sleep was sweet, but much too short. Within the hour, Fearless was batting my ears.

"Spunk, wake up, Ollie's outside. (*Breath*). They found something."

"Okay, buddy, I'm awake. Let's go."

Outside I paused, looked around, and softly barked, "Ollie, where are you?"

Two hoots told me he was in the large maple tree near the barn. Fearless and I ran over to him.

"Ollie, what did you find?" I asked.

"Not me, Spunk, Goliath. He thinks he found the kidnapper's house. I came to show you the way."

"Okay, let's go." I said.

Fearless paused and interjected, "Wait a sec. Hey *(breath)*, Ollie, would you be so kind to please remember *(breath)* that Spunky and I can't run as fast as you can fly *(breath)*? Plus we have obstacles down here *(breath)*, and you don't have any up there."

"No problem, Fearless, I'll fly low, slow, and stick to the path."

Once again my friend was looking out for me. He had said, "*We* can't," when in truth it was I who couldn't. My old joints were more limiting than my friend's breathing issues. You gotta to love the guy.

We set off through the woods. Ollie looping and swooping between the trees was a remarkable sight. He looked like a fighter pilot weaving his way through a maze. I gained a new level of respect for his aviation skills. I sure wouldn't want that big boy chasing my tail!

When we reached the road in front of Gifford's farm, Goliath was waiting for us. "Spunky, I'm not sure what we've found exactly, but follow me."

He walked straight down the road and then, after several minutes, turned left down a narrow dirt lane.

"See that house tucked in the woods back there?" Goliath asked.

"Yeah."

"Well, this tiny, white, fluffy little ball standing here beside me is named Tiny. She says the man who lives in that house has been acting weird, plus he has a black car locked in his garage."

I leaned in toward Tiny and asked, "Acting weird how, Tiny?"

The moment I opened my mouth, Tiny jumped and hid behind Goliath.

"Sorry, Spunky," said Goliath. "She's a shy one. She told me the man came home the day before yesterday with a young woman. Tiny's been living in these woods for more than three months, and has never seen that girl before. The man's usually outside a lot, working in the yard, fixing the house, taking out the garbage, stuff like that, so Tiny sees him every day. But since he returned with that girl, he hasn't left the house even once. Plus, before the girl arrived, the man put out kibble for Tiny every day, but since then her bowl's been empty. Something ain't right."

"Are they still in the house?" I asked.

"We think so. It's stayed quiet and dark inside, and the car is still in the garage."

"Come on, then. Let's go see."

We walked quietly onto the front porch. Using a rocking chair as my platform, albeit a moving one, I looked in through the front window. From this vantage point I could see into the living room and dining room. After studying the interior, which was shrouded in darkness, I jumped off the rocker and went to sniff around the front door.

"It's not them," I announced.

"How do you know?" Goliath asked.

"Goliath, am I correct that you didn't look inside?"

"That's right. I waited for you. Why?"

"Go take a peek."

Goliath jumped gracefully onto the rocker, put his paws on the windowsill, and put his nose to the glass. A few seconds later he shook his head from side to side and said, "Oh, yeah, I see what you mean. I doubt a kidnapper would do that."

Tiny was anxiously prancing from one paw to another. In an elfin voice matching her name she said, "What do you see? How do you know he's not the bad guy?"

I explained what I had learned. "For one thing, the scents by the front door don't match the ones I found at the crime scene, which you and Goliath couldn't know. For another, but inside the house there's a huge banner that reads 'Congratulations, graduate!' In addition, there are fresh flowers and balloons everywhere. I'm thinking maybe a dad brought his daughter home, and they had themselves a big celebration. Tiny, I'm sorry about your kibble, but with all their celebrating maybe the man just forgot. I bet things will be back to normal by tomorrow."

Tiny again took refuge behind Goliath. "But, Spunky," she insisted, "I'm telling you that girl doesn't live here!"

"Maybe she's been away at a college. In any case, I'm sure this isn't the bad guy's house. Tiny, tomorrow, if you act sweet and cute, the girl might even let you inside."

For a moment, Tiny forgot her fear and stepped closer. "You think so, Spunk?"

"Could be. A lot of women are suckers for a fluffy little cutie like you. If you rub against her ankles and purr a lot, I'll bet she'll fall in love with you. Besides, didn't you tell me the man was living by himself, and no other woman was living here?"

"Yup, until the other day it was only him."

"Maybe that means the girl's momma is gone. Translation: Your extra loving might go a long way to warm her heart."

Tiny began prancing again. "But you're absolutely, positively sure this guy isn't the kidnapper? Spunky, I want an inside home with all my heart, but not with a kidnapper."

"My nose is sure. It's not him. Besides, over past few months, he's already shown you kindness. He cares about you. I think you'll be fine."

Goliath stepped forward. "Sorry for the false alarm, Spunk."

"That's okay Goliath, I'd rather play it safe."

"I should have looked inside myself before I called you. Next time I'll do more poking around."

"I seriously doubt the next one will come equipped with a banner! Please don't hesitate to roust us out again. Come on, Fearless, let's head back home. Are you coming, Ollie?"

"Naw, I'll stay at this end. They might need me to go get you again—unless, of course, you two would feel safer having me fly a long."

"Thanks, Ollie, but we'll be fine."

As Fearless and I headed home, we were both grateful for the slower pace.

CHAPTER  19

I was having a wonderful dream involving juicy pork chops when Fearless once again batted my ears.

"Huh? Now what?"

"Sorry, Spunk. *(Breath.)* I hate to wake you so soon *(breath)*, but Ollie's outside. Goliath sent him *(breath)* to get you again."

"Goliath must be certain he's got something this time. He'd hate to be wrong twice. Come on, we'd better get a move on."

Once again we followed Ollie back to Gifford's farm. There we waited while he flew off to ascertain the exact location of our spies. A few minutes later he was back, and off we went. He led us to Goliath, who was waiting on the far side of the farm. Standing next to Goliath was a scraggly, battle-scarred, yellow-striped male bobtail with half of his right ear missing. Next to this ragamuffin stood two stunningly beautiful, dainty, shiny-coated female felines; one was pitch black, and the other pure white.

Goliath stepped forward. "Spunk, this is Hobo and his lady friends, Black Velvet and Lady Crème. They live in

Mr. Gifford's barn and keep the mice out of the apple bins. Hobo has lived in these parts for over ten years, and knows everybody around here. He says a man by the name of Mr. Whitehead lives in that house over there on the other side of the road. According to Hobo, he teaches at the high school. Every day, Monday through Friday, he leaves the house at precisely seven a.m., returns at noon for lunch, leaves again at twelve-fifty and returns home promptly at five p.m. Hobo says you can set your clock by him. Well, at least you could until two days ago. Hobo didn't actually see the man come home, but he says the car is in the garage, and it hasn't moved in two days. The man hasn't gone to work. I told Hobo maybe the guy was sick, but Hobo said he's seen the man take out the garbage and walk to the mailbox, and he didn't look sick at all. I thought maybe he's on vacation or something like that. We tried to get a peek into the house, but all the blinds are shut tight. Hobo says that's odd, because this time of year the man usually keeps his windows wide open, and he never shuts his blinds, even at night. When Hobo told me that the car in the garage was black, I thought you'd better see for yourself, even if I can't get a peek inside."

"You're right, Goliath," I said. "I need to do some sniffing around." I ran to the front porch and gave the door my nose test, but didn't find what I was seeking. I paused, then ran around the house to check the back door.

"Ah-ha! Boys, I smell the rat! It's them! He and the girl went in through the back door."

"But how are we going to see inside?" said Goliath.

"Good question." I sat on my rump and sucked up a snootful of the night air. "Hey, where are the raccoons?"

"They're here," said Goliath. I can smell them too. Hobo, do you know the racoons?"

"Of course I do, it's my territory, isn't it? The ringleader is Roxie. Do you want me to go get her?"

Her? The head of the raccoons is female? Now, that was one gal I definitely wanted to meet. "Hobo, do you know where she is right now?"

Hobo looked at me as if I were seriously deficient. "Can't you see her? She and her young-uns are standing right there by the woodpile."

Ah, the challenges of older eyes! I turned my head toward the woodpile and took in another snootful of night air. "Okay, I've got 'em now. Would you go ask her if she and her friends would be so kind as to help us? I want them to knock over those garbage cans and make a huge ruckus, but I need them to wait for my signal. Okay?"

"Sure. I'll go tell her. Be right back." Hobo headed to the woodpile to talk with Roxie.

Fearless leaned over and whispered. "Roxie must be *(breath)* one tough lady if she's the *(breath)* leader of the raccoons."

I nodded. "Yeah, a momma can be a force to be reckoned with."

Behind me Einstein whispered, "I'll second that."

Hobo returned and said, "Roxie said she'd be glad to help. She's getting the big boys together, and they'll head over to the cans to wait for your signal."

Goliath leaned in and asked, "What do you have in mind, Spunk?"

A few minutes later, everyone knew their assignments. Fearless and I positioned ourselves to the left of the front door, while Einstein hid behind the flowerpots on our right. Goliath, Hobo, his lady friends, and the others headed to the backyard. We couldn't be sure which door might be used, so we needed to cover both exits.

I issued a short yip, and the raccoons set to work. The nighttime peace vanished with the sound of crashing cans and fighting raccoons. They put on a great show! After only a moment the front porch light came on.

I whispered, "Get ready, boys."

The door swung open and a man came running out. As I hoped, he left the door open, and Fearless and I ran inside. Once we were in, my nose led me to a room in the back. I whined softly and scratched at a closed door. The door opened.

"What in heaven's name? Where did you two come from?"

We had found Amanda!

She knelt down to pet me, and Fearless rubbed against her leg. "Aren't you the two sweetest things?"

An angry voice shouted, "What's going on?"

Amanda jumped. "I don't know how they got in here, honest I don't." The man who was coming at us was not the warm, welcoming type. I turned and claimed the ground in front of Amanda. I growled deeply, raised a lip, and bared my teeth. Fearless arched and hissed. I growled again viciously.

The man backed off. Then I barked, giving the prearranged signal to Goliath. On cue, he and his crew launched the next stage of our plan by hurling themselves against the back door. There was no way the man could ignore such a clatter.

"Now what in tarnation is that?" he cried. Keeping his eyes locked on us, he backed down the hall, then turned and headed to the back of the house.

I gently grabbed Amanda's pant leg and pulled. She said, "What is it girl?"

I pulled again. "No, doggie, let go," she said. "I can't go with you. Go now, go quickly before he comes back and gets angry. Go, doggie, run!"

The ruckus at the back door ceased, and the man's the footsteps pounded in our direction.

"Come on, Fearless." I said. "We can't get trapped in this house."

We ran toward the front door. "It's shut, Spunk! *(Breath.)* Now what?"

"Quick,—under the table, and be quiet."

The man's agitated voiced boomed. "Where did those critters go? How did they get in here? Where are they?"

He started up the stairs. I barked three times, causing him to turn abruptly and at the same time telling Goliath's team to start another assault on the back door. Simultaneously, Einstein heard his cue and attacked the front door.

"Amanda, get back in that room and don't make a sound!" the man shouted. He slowly advanced to the front window and peeked out. Given the location of the window, I figured he saw that no human was on the porch, but he couldn't see low enough to determine what was causing the horrendous screeching and rapid, thunderous blows to the bottom of his door. He picked up a hockey stick, opened the door, and stepped onto the porch. Fearless and I bolted through the open door as Einstein became a blur leaping off the porch.

The three of us ran for the woodpile with the man yelling right behind us, "Get! And don't come back. Ya hear me? Get!" Once the darkness had swallowed us, he returned to the house and slammed the front door behind him.

Einstein hissed, "Spunky, we did it! We found the rat!"

I snarled, "Found, yes, trapped, no."

CHAPTER  20

There was no time to waste. Fearless and I raced for home, while Ollie, the raccoons, and the free spirits stayed behind. They would attempt to delay the rat if he tried to escape. If he did manage to get past the critter blockade, Ollie would track him from the air.

By the time we reached home and charged into Mom's bedroom, Fearless and I didn't have enough breath left to sound an alarm. The boys immediately saw our dilemma and issued it for us. As soon as they began yowling, Mom shot up in the bed, "Hey! What's going on?"

She turned on the light and saw that Fearless and I were breathing hard. She jumped out of bed exclaiming, "What in heaven's name? What happened?" Her voice and her own rapid breathing told us she was frightened. Fearless rubbed against her leg while I patted her foot with my paw. She knelt down. She had gotten the message. "Okay, I understand, you're both all right. But what the heck is going on?"

Just then Bobby demonstrated a streak of wisdom way beyond his young years. Knowing our mission, seeing our current state and that we had awakened Mom, he drew the correct conclusion. He leaped onto the side table and grabbed Frank's sock. He shook it vigorously, dropped it and then yowled so loud we all jumped. Mom's head jerked around. "Is that it, Spunk? Do you want me call Frank again?"

I nodded and nudged her hand with my nose.

"Lord of mercy, what the heck do I tell him this time?"

Still shaking her head in disbelief, she went ahead and made the call. "Frank, please don't be angry. I'm so sorry to wake you, but Spunky and Fearless just woke me. They're sweaty, breathless and, from what I can tell, determined to see you. I don't have a clue where they've been, or what they were up to, but you'd better get over here fast."

Luckily Frank knows Mom to be a levelheaded woman, otherwise he might not have reacted so quickly. He arrived in record time, albeit without his socks.

"I called Tony. He's on his way. Have you figured out what they want?"

"No. It took a while for them to get their breath back, and they needed some water and a little rest, but now Spunky's pacing back and forth at the front door. I went ahead and put on her harness, since I reckon she wants you to take her somewhere. But don't ask me what Fearless is thinking. He's just sitting there, eyes shut, completely calm, with his tail wrapped around his feet."

Fearless meowed softly. "Cats don't waste energy. *(Breath.)* That's how we sustain nine lives."

I snorted. Enough of all this jibber-jabber, we had a rat to trap. I barked loudly and jumped against the front door.

"Frank, it seems you're going for ride," Mom said.

"We need to wait for Tony," said Frank.

Oh, no we don't! I barked loudly three times and again jumped against the door. The message was clear: Listen up, Frank, we're not waiting for anyone!

Mom intervened. "Apparently Spunky doesn't agree. I think you should leave right now. I'll call you when Tony gets here and you can tell us where you are."

Frank paused. "No. Maybe it's better if you don't ring my phone. I'm not sure where Spunky is taking me or what we're getting into, and my phone ringing unexpectedly might not be good. Tell Tony to head toward Gifford's farm, and I'll call him when I know more."

"Gifford's farm?"

"Well, that's the last place Spunky took us, so I'm assuming we're headed in that direction again. I'll call Tony if I'm wrong. Come on, Spunk, let's go." He opened the door and I bolted for the car. Fearless was not about to be left behind and quickly darted out the door behind me.

Frank looked down. "Looks like Fearless is coming with us. Does he need a harness too?"

Mom laughed. "Putting a harness on Fearless can be tricky. Don't worry, he'll stay close to Spunky. Besides, unless you're going to next county, I'm sure he can find his way back if he has to." Then she added, "But if you do end up going far, don't let him out of the car, okay?" Mom was hedging her bets. If she only knew how far her cats actually traveled some nights, she'd be the one having kittens!

Off we went. Luckily, Frank remembered his previous driving lessons and was an obedient chauffer. Given the hour and the empty roads, I was able to direct him quickly to the kidnapper's house.

When we arrived it was still before dawn, so all Frank could see was a darkened building. When he trained his flashlight on the house, he exclaimed, "Holy cow! What's going on?" The front porch was wall-to-wall critters—cats intermingled with raccoons, plus one very large owl. Literally, my cohorts had things well covered! As Frank approached the house, everyone but Goliath and Einstein ran (or flew) off, but I knew they'd stay nearby.

Goliath and Einstein already knew Frank from our last adventure, so they had no reason to fear him. They stayed to give me an update. Goliath nuzzled me and meowed softly, "Spunk, after you left, all the lights went off. The house has been quiet ever since. They're still in there."

Frank turned, headed back toward his car, and whispered. "Hang on, Spunk. I have to let Tony know where I am."

He placed the call, speaking quietly. After he hung up he slapped his thigh and whistled softly, and I went to see what he wanted. He knelt and spoke in a whisper.

"I need to wait for Tony. He's only a few minutes away. I sure wish you could tell me why we're here. Look, Spunky, I know you'd never intentionally put me in danger, but I'm not about to go knocking on the door of a dark house without backup."

I snorted and gave him a hard stare. He laughed. "I know, you're right; you and those critters are more than enough backup. But I'd be hard pressed to get a district attorney to understand why I relied on a bunch of cats and raccoons instead of waiting for my partner. Tony will be here any minute."

We waited.

CHAPTER 21

Well, I should have said "Frank waited." The cats and I used the time to devise our plan. Then Fearless went to update the gang stationed at the back door, while Einstein headed off to round up those who had fled. We needed everyone to be armed and ready.

A few minutes later we saw headlights coming down the street. Frank stepped into the road, waving his arms, and Tony came to a silent stop. Which was good, because this wasn't the time for screeching brakes. Tony leaped out of car, his hand on his gun, ready to rumble.

"What have we got, Frank?"

"Slow down, partner. See that dark house over there?"

"Yeah."

"Well, when I drove up, the porch was covered with cats, raccoons, and an owl."

"An owl?"

"Yup, one very large owl. My best guess is that Spunky thinks this is the kidnapper's house, so it's possible Amanda is inside. We need a plan."

I snorted twice. "We already have a plan." But the detectives paid me no heed.

"Question," said Tony. "Are we supposed to treat Amanda as a hostage, or a suspect?"

"Good point. The lab confirmed her prints are on the knife, so that makes her our prime suspect. But let's not forget she's just a kid. I think we should consider her potentially dangerous and act with caution until we know more."

"And the 'kidnapper,' if that's what he is, must be in there too, right?"

"Right. Maybe he kidnapped her, maybe not; but at the very least he aided and abetted our murder suspect."

"So we have no proof that the girl was actually kidnapped," said Tony. "In fact, we don't even know if she's in this house. It might be the milkman's house, for all we know. We can't just break down the door."

"Okay, how about this: We knock on the door and tell whoever answers that we're scouting the area looking for the missing girl. We'll see how they act, and play it by ear. We can always back off and regroup if it doesn't work."

"Okay, but from what I can see, there's nothing suspicious going on here, except maybe some health code violation for hoarding cats. No judge is going to think we had legal grounds to search the house because a dog tipped us off. We have to do this by the book."

"Agreed. But first I want to go around back and see if anyone could skedaddle out that way and not be seen. Hang on a minute."

Frank walked around to the back, but he quickly returned, chuckling.

"Fear not Tony, in order for anyone to escape that way, they'd have to get past Fearless, twenty cats, and three raccoons. Sneaking out the back is not an option."

Tony and Frank approached the front door. Again Tony cautioned, "Remember, Frank, by the book." Frank nodded.

Tony knocked. Frank stood off to the side, holding his gun down by his leg. Meanwhile, Goliath, Einstein, and I positioned ourselves behind Tony.

There was no response from within the house. Tony knocked again. Nothing. He pounded harder. Finally a light went on, and the voice of the man we had already seen shouted, "Who is it?"

"Clearwater Police. Open the door, sir."

The porch light went on, the latch turned, and the door slowly opened. The man pulled the door inward, but only wide enough so he could see out. Tony identified himself, showed his badge, and then placed his hand flat against the door.

"Yes, officers," said the man. "What can I do for you?"

"We're canvassing the neighborhood asking if anyone has seen a teenage girl who's gone missing," said Frank.

"You're canvassing at this hour? It's still dark! No, I haven't seen anyone around here."

"Would you mind if we come in and take a look around?"

"Yes, I'd mind! The sun isn't even up yet, and I have a right to my privacy." He paused and then said with a smirk, "Of course, if you have a warrant I'll certainly let you in. Do you have a warrant, officer?"

"No, sir, but we..."

From my viewpoint, this "by the book method" was getting us nowhere. We had to get inside now. I looked up and verified that the man eyes were on Tony, not us. I quickly assessed the width of the door opening. It was definitely narrow, but Einstein's skinny frame might just get through. I jerked my head and gave him the go-ahead.

Einstein silently slipped his scrawny body through the opening. Now we were ready. I barked the command, and Einstein immediately launched his attack. The man screamed, Tony pushed on the door, and in he went, with Frank right behind him.

Goliath and I followed on Frank's heels, but quickly skidded to a halt. The man was still screaming and dancing a painful jig as he tried to dislodge one very unfriendly kitty. Einstein's legs were wrapped tightly around the man's lower leg, and his claws were embedded in the man's blue pajamas. The man hopped, yowled, and shook his leg, but Einstein hung on like a child clutching the pole on a merry-go-round horse. I swear that cat was smiling!

Now that's the way to bust a rat!

Frank pointed his gun at the man and yelled. "Okay... er...you...cat...let him go!" Einstein didn't bat an eye. Ferals don't obey humans, even if they're cops. I barked once, and Einstein looked toward Goliath. Ferals aren't known for obeying dogs either, especially when they're having this much fun. Goliath hissed, and Einstein released his prey. The man stumbled toward the couch, cursing a blue streak, with blood running down his leg.

There was no time to waste. I barked twice and ran toward the bedroom. Frank kept his gun on the man and said, "Tony, follow Spunk, but be careful, there could be more than just this one."

I stopped at the closed bedroom door and barked again. Tony yelled, "Amanda, are you in there?" Silence. I barked again and scratched at the door. Tony now commanded. "Police! Whoever's in there, come out with your hands up! Now!"

The door slowly opened. There stood a terrified Amanda with her hands in the air. Her cheeks were soaked with tears, and her lower lip was trembling. With a quivering voice she said, "Don't shoot. I didn't want to kill him. I had no choice. He was abusing me. I had to stop him. I had no choice."

CHAPTER  22

Once the handcuffs were in place, Frank got a towel and wrapped it around the man's bleeding leg. He then made a call, and two patrol cars arrived with their lights flashing and sirens blaring. Right behind them, two more detectives arrived with their lights and rooftop sirens piercing the night. Guess Tony wasn't the only small town cop to use any excuse for lights and sirens, but what was with all the hoopla? We'd already done the hard part.

The arrested man confirmed that his name was Harold Whitehead. Once Frank read him his rights, he stopped talking. They loaded him into a patrol car and told the officers to take him to the hospital to have his leg treated, then take him in for booking.

As the patrol car pulled away, Frank asked Tony in a whisper, "Can a cat be charged with police brutality?" They wisely agreed to not to even ask.

Out of an abundance of caution, Tony took Amanda to the hospital too. Who knew what she might have gone through in the last two days? Frank stayed behind to get the other detectives started on searching the house. But before he herded Fearless and me back to the car, he gave us a few minutes to conduct our own investigation. Frank can be a very wise man.

When we arrived back home, Mom had the coffee ready and breakfast started. "Did you find Amanda?" she asked.

"We sure did!" said Frank. "Spunky led us right to her."

Mom smiled proudly at me, then she quietly asked Frank, "Is Amanda okay?"

"Physically? There were no obvious injuries, but…"

"Yes, I know." Mom cut him off and knelt down to love on us. "Come on babies, Momma has a special breakfast for her investigators extraordinaire. Frank, can you stay and eat?"

"Sure can! It smells wonderful. I'm starving."

"Good. Frank, I'm not ignoring what you said, but let me feed these two and finish fixing our breakfast, then I'll be able to listen more closely to what you have to say. Go ahead and pour yourself a cup of coffee." Mom gave me my regular food, but graciously topped it off with some cooked chicken. Fearless got his kibble with a small side of fresh fish. Now if I could just snag some of that bacon, all would be perfect!

Once Mom and Frank were settled at the table she said, "Okay, now I'm all ears. If you'd be so kind, please start at the very beginning."

Frank told Mom all about our adventure. I was impressed by how skillfully he related the events; he even remembered to mention the raccoons. When he finished the story, Mom sighed deeply and then asked, "Was there any physical evidence of abuse?"

"Tony called me while you were fixing breakfast and said Amanda told the doc she wasn't raped and she wouldn't allow a rape kit to be done. But there were fresh bruises on both of her upper arms. They looked like some large, strong hands made them. Other than that, the doc found no injuries."

Mom shook her head slowly and said, "Frank, that girl is going to need a lot of help. I know she's a murder suspect, and that limits what you can do; but I'm telling you I think the truth could be buried deep. All may not be as it appears."

"Well, we'll soon know if she is even going to talk to us at all."

"Doesn't her mother have to be present when you talk to her?"

Frank sat back in his chair, and playfully shook his finger at Mom. "Shame on you, Hannah. Do you think I'd try to railroad a minor?"

"Of course not, Frank! I'm sorry if it sounded that way. Honestly, I'm just curious how it works."

Frank smiled. "Fear not, my dear. As soon as we arrested her we called the captain, and he notified Children and Family Services. He decided to err on the side of caution, since we don't know anything about Amanda's relationship with her mother. I'm sure a rep has already been assigned, and we'll let them decide how to handle it. We won't question Amanda unless they're present or tell us what to do."

Mom was quiet, her face a mixture of sadness and anxiety. Frank leaned forward and gently placed his hand on her arm. "What's really worrying you, Hannah?"

"I'm not sure, Frank, but I've got a really bad feeling about this one, and I honestly don't know why it's so strong.

I'm worried about that girl. Promise me you'll let me know if there's anything I can do to help her."

"Sure, Hannah, I'll let you know."

"Do you promise?"

"I promise."

CHAPTER  23

Our next update came several days later when Frank stopped by for coffee. He now knew Mrs. Pederson had mentally relinquished custody of Amanda years ago, and said she did not want custody now. The judge decided to play it safe and abide by Mr. Pederson's Last Will and Testament, which named his sister, Lucinda, as Amanda's guardian. Aunt Lucinda had arrived from Houston to take custody of Amanda, but given that Amanda had allegedly killed Lucinda's brother, it was now doubtful if Lucinda was the best choice. Amanda's uncle Alfred, her mother's brother, had flown in from Chicago, and Frank had spent time talking to both of them. He said neither one believed Mr. Pederson had ever abused Amanda, although Mom reminded him that all too often family members are the last to know or accept that abuse is happening. Since Amanda couldn't leave the state because of the case against her, and since neither Lucinda nor Alfred could stay here indefinitely, they agreed to let Amanda remain under state guardianship until they knew more. Frank said his impression was that the aunt and uncle were so shocked and befuddled by the whole affair that they seemed grateful not to have any responsibility for Amanda.

Frank also conducted several interviews with Amanda's mother. "Now that's one strange lady," he said. "She might just qualify as one of the most narcissistic people I've ever met. She spent most of the time talking about how this was affecting her, instead of the effect on her daughter, and she's only been to the jail once to see Amanda. She didn't argue at all about the state being granted guardianship over her daughter. In fact, she said she wished she had never come back to this town. I avoided asking her why she didn't want custody. Truth is, I found myself wondering if Amanda isn't better off away from that woman."

Mom listened intently and silently. Perhaps she was unusually quiet because Frank hadn't asked for her opinion, but that had never stopped her before. After Frank left, her face told me she was troubled, but I didn't have time to find out more. We had to rush to get ready for Samantha's next therapy session.

Today Samantha wasted no time with chitchat. She didn't even say "Hello." Instead she immediately made a jolting announcement. "I've decided to go back to Florida and turn myself in."

Mom's eyebrows shot up. "Whoa! That's a mighty big decision. Don't you think we should discuss it first?"

"Why? You said I should turn myself in."

Mom frowned, her cheeks puffed out, and she exhaled loudly. Her voice dropped as she spoke slowly and deliberately. "Now, wait just a minute. I said you *could* turn yourself in, I never said you should or shouldn't do it."

"Okay, okay! But you do think I should turn myself in, right?"

Mom took another deep breath and let it out slowly. "Samantha, I do believe you need to stop running from the law; and yes, you need to take responsibility for your actions. Yes, turning yourself in is the responsible thing to do, but you can't just try to solve this whole thing in one fell swoop. You have a child, and you have to consider her well-being. If you—"

Samantha interrupted. "Oh, I've taken care of that. Lisa is going to take care of Caroline until I get out."

The furrows in Mom's brow deepened as her left eye squinted shut and her right eyebrow arched. "What about Caroline's father? And who is Lisa?" I could understand Mom's frustration. Trying to keep up with Samantha's thought processes was like trying to catch a hyperactive frog.

Samantha spoke rapidly. "Oh, I kicked Robert out three days ago. Lisa and I have been friends for years. She lives here, is about my age, has no kids, and works as a waitress over at Johnny's Rib Shack. She lives with her Aunt Lucy, who raised her. Caroline has been a part of their lives since she was born, and both of them adore her. I talked to Aunt Lucy, and she's willing to care for Caroline while Lisa is at work. So that part is all set."

"Wait a minute. Slow down. What about your job? How will you get to Florida? Do you have a lawyer? And what about your furniture and belongings here? There are a lot of questions that need to be answered."

"I gave my boss notice. I'm leaving my car here with Lisa. I'll take a bus to Florida. No, I don't have an attorney.

I can't afford one. I'll ask for a public defender when I get there, and I'll store what I can at Lisa's and sell the rest." Samantha sat back, took a breath and smiled.

Mom sat quietly watching her for a few moments, then said, "We'll it appears you do have a plan."

"Yes, ma'am. I told you, I've always taken care of myself."

"So you did." Mom began tapping her lip with her index finger. She was trying to decide whether she wanted to say what she was thinking. She scratched the side of her head, another telltale sign of hesitation. Would she keep her thoughts to herself, or not?

Finally she spoke. "Samantha, I have a friend I'd like you to speak to. He's an attorney. You should have some legal counsel before you turn yourself in to the authorities."

"I can't afford a lawyer."

"I know. I think I may be able to get him to see you for free. I really think you need professional advice."

"Okay. If you say so. When can I see him?"

"I'll call him today and let you know. Now, I think we should talk about how you feel about going to jail and leaving your daughter…"

When the session ended, Mom called Tom Mackey, an attorney and a longtime friend. He had helped Mom with clients in the past, and vice versa. One could say they belonged to the same mutual admiration society.

Mom put Tom on the speakerphone, explained the situation, and then said, "Tom, this girl really can't afford an attorney, and you know I've never done this before, but if you'll agree to see her, I'm willing to pay your fee."

"I'd be more than willing to work out a payment plan with her," Tom objected.

"I know, but from all I can tell she can barely keep food on the table and a roof over her head. Besides, I'm afraid she won't agree to see you if she has to pay anything. But she definitely needs legal advice before turning herself in, and an overworked public defender in another state isn't going to cut it. Could you meet with her and see what you can find out? If it turns out her case is too complicated, maybe we won't be able to do anything, but at least I'll know we tried."

"Okay, Hannah. For you, I'm willing to see her *pro bono.*"

"I sincerely thank you for that offer," said Mom, "but I want you to be paid. If I myself were between a rock and a hard place, I know you'd help; but that's not the case this time." She chuckled, "Besides, I might need a freebie in the future, so this time let me pay. But I know Samantha wouldn't want to be in my debt for anything, so I prefer she not know that I'm paying. I know we don't have a lot of time to figure this out, but I'll trust your decision. Would you be willing to let her think you're seeing her as part of your regular *pro bono* work?"

"Sure. But you understand that once she talks to me, I won't be able to tell you any details of our discussion."

"I know. That's fine. I don't need details, I just need to know she's gotten some sound counsel. But Tom, when you first meet her, please don't make the same mistake I did and judge her too quickly. I know it's a terrible thing for a psychologist to admit, but that's exactly what I did. Her story sounds so flakey that it makes her sound flakey too.

Her life really has been quite strange, but overall I think she's remarkably sane. I grant, she may not be in the best emotional health, but she's definitely sane."

"Fair enough, Hannah, I'll keep it in mind. Would you see if she can come here tomorrow at ten a.m.? I'll go ahead and put her in the book, and she can call my secretary to confirm whether or not she'll be here."

"I'll call her right now. And thanks, Tom, I truly appreciate it."

Tom laughed. "We'll see how you feel after you get my bill."

CHAPTER  24

Hooray, we were going to see Quincy! My buddy and I hadn't seen each other in days, because he had been stricken with a stomach bug and wasn't allowed out to play. But earlier today Jacob called to tell us Quincy was all better and needed a good romp. Mom and I headed out the door with plenty of time to spare.

"It's such a beautiful day," Mom said, "I think we'll take the long way around. It'll do us both good."

I certainly didn't argue with her plan. Taking the longer route meant we would go through one of my favorite places, the pine forest. Most humans don't know that pine trees emit negative ions, creating a naturally uplifting atmosphere. Mom always feels better after a walk through the pines and the smell is unlike any other. It makes for a peaceful, beautiful walk for both of us.

Today, however, there was a very loud exception. A pileated woodpecker was relentlessly drilling into a tree and making the most terrible racket.

"Look Spunk," said Mom. "He's beautiful—extremely noisy, but beautiful. But why is he here? Woodpeckers live in deciduous trees. I've never seen one hammering away on a pine tree. That's very strange! I would think pine sap might be problematic for a wood pecker."

As we got closer, Mom saw her answer. "Ah-ha! It's not the pine he's working on. There are two oaks in the middle of those pines. He's definitely not in his usual habitat, but he's hard at work on the right tree."

I wasn't sure about all that, but I did know his loud hammering wasn't enhancing Mom's ionic experience. I barked. Mom jumped. She told me to hush, which I did, eventually, but not until I was sure that noise box had been told to clear out. As he flew off, a thick blanket of silence descended over us.

"Ah, that certainly is much better," Mom said. "He was beautiful to see, but thanks for booting him out."

My pleasure. I'm not happy when anything or anyone messes with my Mom's peace.

We continued on our way, and by the time we reached the park we were both nicely mellow. Jacob and Quincy were already there waiting for us.

Jacob smiled and said, "Thank goodness! I didn't want to start without you, but I wasn't sure how much longer I could make this big boy wait for his run. Days without any park time hasn't been easy on either of us."

Mom laughed. "I understand completely! Go ahead, turn him loose. Spunky will give him a good run for his money."

Had the woman lost her mind? A young Labrador always has energy to spare, but trying to keep up with one who hadn't run for days would be like trying to keep up with a rocket. The moment Quincy was unhooked I said,

"Go, my friend, run—and run a lot! Don't come back to get me until your tongue is all rubbery!"

"Are you sure, Spunk? I hate to leave you."

"Believe me, I'm sure. Now go, but run in big circles so they can see where you are and won't worry." Quincy took off, and I jogged slowly after him. He ran full-out to the top of the hill, then turned and ran back. His throttle was wide open.

Jacob laughed, "Look at that boy go! It does my heart good to see him feeling better."

"Did Dr. Steve come up with a diagnosis?" Mom asked.

"Not really. All the tests came back negative. He said Quince must have eaten something off the ground that his gut didn't like, but nothing showed up in his tests. The medication and chicken-and-rice diet finally settled him down. Obviously, he's feeling a whole lot better."

No fooling! Even after Quincy finished a fourth circuit, his tongue was barely drooping, and when he skidded to a halt beside me he was barely out of breath. "Okay, Spunk, I'm ready to play."

"I don't know about that. From what I can see, your tongue is not one bit rubbery."

"It's okay. I blew off enough steam so I can tone it down now."

I knew Quincy's word was good, so off we went, sprinting across the field. While the pine forest has great benefits for Mom, the best tonic for me is a good romp with my pal. We certainly had ourselves a splendid frolic. By the time we headed back home, my tongue was rubbery, and Mom and I were both in high spirits.

When we reached our driveway, Mom's cell phone rang.

"Hi, Frank, I sure hope you feel as good as I do right now."

Mom listened for several seconds before saying, "Sure, come on by. We're just getting back from our walk. Okay... see you in an hour."

As she put the phone back into her pocket she shrugged, "I'm not sure what that was all about, Spunk, but Frank sure sounded down. I think he needs a supersized pine forest. Maybe a good dinner will cheer him up. Let's go see what we can come up with."

By the time Frank arrived, the enticing smell of Mom's homemade spaghetti sauce wafted through the house. The effect was not lost on Frank.

"Hannah that smells wonderful! I didn't think I was hungry, but you just changed my mind."

"Good! The pasta is almost done, and the salad is ready. If you'll spread the garlic butter on that bread over there, I'll pop it under the broiler and we'll be ready to eat in no time at all."

"Hannah, you're a godsend. This is just what I needed. Want some wine?"

"Sure, the red would be nice. Pour me some while I put the food on the table."

As he poured the wine, Frank began to hum. Maybe spaghetti sauce also emits negative ions.

CHAPTER  25

"Hannah, this is delicious," Frank said between mouthfuls of spaghetti and salad. It's been a long time since I've had homemade sauce. I always use that stuff in a jar."

"Well, bottled sauce is certainly faster, but nothing tops that fresh-cooked taste."

She paused and then asked, "Frank, are you up to telling me why you sounded so down on the phone, or would you prefer to eat in peace?"

"Truth? I'd love not to think about work for a while. Would it be okay if we talk about something else?"

"Sure. Reprieves are good for the soul. Should I tell you about my day?"

Frank smiled and nodded. The meatball in his mouth preventing him from actually speaking.

Mom began her monologue. Over the last few years she's become more proficient at lighthearted chatter. As a psychologist, her job requires serious in-depth discussions, and she tends to carry that over into her social life. Previously, Dad was the one who carried the bulk of casual conversation with other people. Seven years ago, when Mom became a widow, she had to learn new skills.

About twenty minutes later, Frank pushed his plate away. "I can't eat another bite. Thank you, Hannah, not only for a delicious dinner, but also for the mini mental vacation. You were right; it did my soul good."

"Good. Now, how about we take our coffee out onto the patio? It's a beautiful evening, and we can watch the sunset, if the bugs leave us alone."

"Sounds great. Want me to do the dishes first?"

"You're a good man, Charlie Brown. Sure, you can start on them while I make the coffee."

Ten minutes later we were all outside. Mom was right, it was a nice evening. The temperature was in the high sixties and the crispness of early autumn hung in the air. Mom and I shared the lounge chair, while Sweetie curled up on Frank's lap. The rest of the boys stretched out on the patio. The concrete still held the warmth of the day, which must have felt good on their bones.

Frank took a sip of coffee and then said, "Okay, Hannah, I'm ready to talk about why I called you."

Mom smiled. "What? You mean you didn't come over just to partake of my scintillating conversation and wit?"

Frank chuckled and raised his eyebrows. "Of course, that's always on my list of reasons for wanting to see you. But today I need your advice on how to handle Amanda."

Mom leaned toward him and said. "What's the problem?"

Frank dug in his pocket and pulled out a dollar bill. He laid it on the table and said, "Doc, I'm experiencing a lot of anxiety about this case, and I think I need counseling."

Mom smiled and nodded as she tucked the dollar into her pocket. "Sir, you just hired yourself a therapist."

Some time ago, Mom and Frank had come to an understanding. If Frank paid for her services, then legally he was her client, and this protected their conversation under doctor–patient confidentiality. Although Frank knew Mom would never divulge the details of the cases he discussed with her, the exchange of a dollar prevented their discussions from coming back to haunt him if the any of the cases went to trial.

He began talking. "Amanda now has a lawyer as well as a guardian, Mrs. Jackson, assigned through Children and Family Services, but she's chosen to ignore their advice and is talking to us. That part is good for us, but the problem is she keeps saying the same thing over and over. She says, and I quote, 'I'm sorry. I'm so sorry. I had no choice. I had to kill him. He was abusing me. I had to stop him. He was coming after me again. I didn't want to kill him. I had no choice. I'm sorry. I'm sorry.'"

"And which part of that bothers you?"

"Everything about it feels off. When we ask her a question about her early childhood, she responds like a regular person. Even despite that mother of hers, it sounds like she had a good life and was a happy kid. But the moment she starts talking about stabbing her father, something inside her shuts off. All emotion vanishes, and she just recites the same words over and over. She sounds like a robot, or a stuck record. We've tried going at it several different ways, but when she gets to the stabbing, she says the same thing, the same way, in the exact same tone."

"Frank, you know as well as I do that people who have been abused can sometimes block all emotions related to those traumatic events. They can also distort what actually happened."

"I know, I know. But Hannah, this girl doesn't even change her words. She literally repeats the same phrases again and again. Her guardian keeps trying to get her to take her attorney's advice and hush up, but she refuses. She says she stabbed her father and she should be punished for her crime. Over and over, she recites the same mantra."

"What about Mr. Whitehead? What does he say?"

"He's not talking now. But right after we got him to the station he told us a few things."

"Such as?"

"He said he didn't do anything wrong. He said the day before Pederson's death Amanda confided in him that her father was abusing her, so the next morning he went to their house. He wanted to confront Mr. Pederson. But when he got there, there was no answer to the bell, and he thought he heard crying; so he tried the door, and it was unlocked. He walked in and went straight to the kitchen, where he found Amanda standing over Mr. Pederson's body. Her hand was on the handle of the bloody knife stuck in Pederson's chest. Her father was obviously dead."

My head jerked upward. What? That's not right. My nose had already proven that Mr. Whitehead first went into the living room and sat on the couch. Since Pederson's and Amanda's scents were as fresh as his, they were all in the living room at the same time. Furthermore, I'd followed all three of their scents from the living room to the kitchen—but

Whitehead was claiming when he first saw Pederson, he was dead.

Dead men don't walk to the kitchen!

Mr. Whitehead was lying!

Mom continued, "What did Mr. Whitehead say happened after that?"

Frank rubbed his temple and said, "Whitehead said he told Amanda to follow her regular morning routine. To go on to school with that kid in the car and try to act like nothing happened. That way, he said, she would have a witness to testify that she had gone to school as usual. He said he knew Amanda couldn't keep up the façade for long, so he promised he would pick her up around the corner from the school shortly after she got there. He says he was trying to protect her. He thought if he got her out of the house, maybe the police would think an intruder had stabbed Pederson. Later he realized he hadn't wiped her prints off the knife, but it was too risky to go back, so he simply hoped that no one would believe she could do such a thing."

Mom asked, "Do you believe his story?"

"Hell no! Everything about the man tells me he's lying, and both of their stories sound too rehearsed. Problem is, Amanda corroborates his story. She says she begged him to pick her up and to hide her."

Mom thought for a moment and then asked, "In your experience, what does a teacher usually do when a kid tells them they're being abused by a parent?"

"They report it to the principal or guidance counselor."

"Did Whitehead do that?"

"No, but when I asked him why he didn't, he said Amanda threatened to harm herself if he told anyone."

"So he decided to handle it himself?"

"That's what he claims."

"I guess that's possible—not smart, but possible. All right, let's go back to Amanda's story. How many sixteen-year-old female alleged murderers have you interrogated over the years?"

"None. I did arrest a young adult for murder once, but he was a male."

"So it's possible your instincts could be off a little because she's a girl. But you're a good detective, Frank. What does your gut tell you?"

Frank paused, closed his eyes, took a deep breath, and said, "Honestly? I think she's lying. I don't think she stabbed her father." He opened his eyes. "Problem is, I don't have one shred of evidence that says anything different from what they're both telling me. Her prints are on the knife, she says she did it, he says she did it, and they're both sticking to the same story." He paused and slowly shook his head. "Something is off. But why would a sixteen-year-old girl confess to killing her father if she didn't do it?"

Mom paused before she said, "I'm sure there are a multitude of answers to that question, Frank, but we don't have a clue yet as to what *her* answer might be. What I can tell you is this: if she is lying, then the *reason* she's lying is at the heart of this thing. Whatever secret she's safeguarding, she believes it's worth more than her own life. The key is to figure out what that secret is. Can you arrange for me to see her?"

"I'll talk to the caseworker from D.C.F.S. and ask if she'll allow it. But in the meantime, can you give me some guidance on how to gain Amanda's confidence?"

"I can give you some techniques, but none of them is going to change the fact that you're a cop. In her mind you're the very person she has to lie to. Maybe you could ask the caseworker if she'd agree to let Amanda have psychological counseling to help her deal with the trauma of stabbing her father. No decent caseworker should refuse help for a traumatized client, since doctor-patient confidentiality is guaranteed."

"She'll turn it down real quick if it's not in her budget."

"You know I'll do it for free."

"But, Hannah, if *you* see her and it's confidential, how do *I* uncover anything new?"

Mom smiled. "If I'm successful, Amanda might stop lying. Since I'd have to act in her best interest, I can't promise I'd recommend that she tell *you* her truth; but I might get her to tell *someone*."

Frank sighed. "In all honesty, Hannah, being able to discuss the case with you helps me. I don't want to burn that bridge. If you're her therapist, does that mean we can't discuss the case?"

Mom nodded. "I agree, it could get complicated. Yes, we could still discuss the case, but of course I couldn't tell you what she and I discussed. And since you just hired me, a conflict already exists. Unless, of course, you fire me." She sighed again. "You're right, it's already getting complicated. It would be much easier if we used another therapist and left me out of it."

"Why don't we sleep on it and see what we think tomorrow." Frank's eyes twinkled. "Now, my dear, how about a nightcap before we retire? Perhaps after that, I'll give you another opportunity to take my mind off of work."

Mom smiled. "Now, that's one challenge I could easily enjoy."

CHAPTER  26

The next morning Mom was up early. As she puttered around making the coffee and frying bacon, she sighed repeatedly. Something was amiss. When she stopped and stared out the window, I took the opportunity and nudged her with my nose. She looked down and smiled. Then she sat down and patted her lap, and I jumped up onto the throne.

"Good morning, sweet girl. How are you?"

I gave her a little kiss, then turned and gave her my back. Something was troubling my mom, so I had to forego the prolonged, loving face wash I would have liked to give her.

As she stroked my sides, her words began to tumble out. "I don't know what's wrong with me, girl. I just feel down. Maybe it's all this mess with Amanda, but I don't think that's all it is...."

"Morning, Hannah." Frank's voice interrupted our privacy.

My head jerked up and my face showed my displeasure. The man's timing was terrible.

"Morning, Frank." Mom gently lowered me to the ground and stood up. "How about two eggs over easy, bacon, and toast?"

"Sounds wonderful. But why did you get up so early? I could've stopped at the diner on my way to work."

"I know, but I like cooking, and besides I wanted to talk to you some more about Amanda. Pour yourself some coffee while I cook your eggs."

Frank poured himself a mug and settled in at the table.

As they began to eat, Mom said, "Frank, I've tried to look at this from many sides. It would be fascinating to delve into Amanda's psyche, but we've already seen how that would cause problems. Plus, after more thought I realized I may not be the best qualified for the job."

Frank quickly interjected, "Why not? You're a heck of a lot better than any police shrink I've ever worked with."

Mom smiled. "Thank you, kind sir, but I think Amanda might react better to a male."

"What? The girl admits she murdered her own father! If you ask me, she seems a tad hostile toward males."

Mom smiled. "True, it seems that way, but humans can have a distorted sense of security in something that others think they should hate. For example, why do some abused women stay with their abuser?"

"Because their fear of the unknown can be greater than the fear they already know," said Frank.

"Correct. Even though their lives are terrible, they know what to expect; so, in a twisted way it's easier to live with that than the thought of being alone. Since we have no way of knowing what's actually going on in Amanda's mind, maybe we should stack the deck in our favor and start with a male. Seeing how she reacts to a male who isn't a cop might tell us a lot too."

"Do you have someone in mind?"

"I think Joe Hoffman would be perfect. He has the advantage of all the work he's done with people who suffer from PTSD, and his personality would be an asset. He's kind, calm, and pretty unflappable. The only problem I see is that he doesn't have the credentials you'd need for an expert witness in court."

Frank sat back, wiped some egg yolk off his face, and thought for a moment. "Right now I'm far more interested in unraveling the truth than I am in the court case. Besides, if Joe could get Amanda to open up, and it turns out I'm right that she's innocent, then maybe she wouldn't go to trial after all. On the other hand, if she does go to trial and if the D.A.'s office wants expert testimony, then they can get their own shrink."

"Okay, so what's our next step?"

Frank swallowed the last of his coffee and rose from his chair. "Talk to Joe and see if he'll agree. I'll talk to Amanda's guardian and see if she'll allow it. I'll call you later." He kissed Mom goodbye. "Thank you, kind lady."

Then he smiled and said, "Thanks for *everything*. Please feel free to send me the bill."

Mom laughed. "Believe me, Frank, I plan to collect payment in full for every service rendered."

Mom's tone may have sounded light and sweet, but hovering right below the surface there was sadness.

CHAPTER  27

As soon as Frank left, Mom called and made an appointment to see her special friend Dr. Joe Hoffman. He has a doctorate in American history and is a tenured professor at the college. He is also a Vietnam veteran and after overcoming the disabling effects of his own post-traumatic stress disorder, he became a certified PTSD counselor.

He also has been a buddy of Mom's for decades. They met on a picket line years ago when Mom, Dad, and Professor Hoffman were demonstrating against Clearwater's lack of racial and ethnic diversity. Back then Professor Hoffman was one of only two African-American professors at the college. Over the years Clearwater has become more diverse but like many small mid-western towns, it is still more than eighty-percent Caucasian.

Mom arranged to meet Professor Hoffman at his office at lunchtime. She told him she'd pick up some food so that they could avoid a noisy, crowded restaurant. That was partly true, but she also had an ulterior motive. She was planning to take a special gift to Professor Hoffman, one she couldn't take into a restaurant.

Professor Hoffman loves people and he loves teaching, but he loves Sweetie even more. He's always been great to me and to all of the felines, but his heart belongs to Sweetie. It's been that way for years, and none of us knows exactly how it happened. The special bond between them is obvious to all, including Mom. Today she was bringing Sweetie as a special treat.

A little before noon we headed out the door. We arrived on campus after stopping at Subway. Mom let me carry the sandwich bag. She knows I take great pride in helping her, and that I'd never abuse her trust—although at the moment the wonderful aromas wafting up my nose were not easy to ignore. The moment we entered Professor Hoffman's office, Mom held up Sweetie's crate and asked, "Joe, which would you like first—your sandwich or your treat?"

Professor Hoffman clapped his hand together as his face lit up like a child's on Christmas morning. "Sweet lady, you already know my answer."

Mom opened the door to Sweetie's crate and said, "Go on, Sweetie, say hello. There's no sense in us trying to accomplish anything until he's had his fill of your loving."

Meowing loudly, Sweetie ran across the room. He leaped onto the desk and began rubbing up one side of the professor's face and then the other. I wasn't sure who was purring louder, Sweetie or the professor. Mom took the sandwich bag from me, sat down, and began scratching my ear. "Ah, Spunk, isn't love grand?"

No doubt about it, they were something special.

Finally the professor began spitting out cat hair. He pulled back and said, "Okay, my friend, enough face-rubbing." He pushed his chair back and patted his lap. Sweetie stepped forward, turned, and settled in. "Okay, Hannah," said Professor Hoffman, "now we're ready for lunch."

Mom laughed. "Don't think I didn't notice that you said '*we're* ready for lunch.' That's one reason I didn't bring you tuna. The other is that since you like ham and Sweetie doesn't, I know one of you will stick to his diet."

Professor Hoffman laughed. "Party pooper!"

After setting out the food Mom explained why she'd asked to see the professor. To avoid any conflict of interest, she told him to consider this a hypothetical case, and as she told Amanda's story she avoided referring to anyone by name.

Mom halted when Professor Hoffman held up his hand. "Is this the case I read about in the paper last week?" he asked.

"Remember, this is entirely hypothetical," Mom said. She cocked her head to one side and her eyes got bigger as she added, "Besides, the girl in my story is a minor, so the police wouldn't release all their information to the press, right?"

Professor Hoffman frowned momentarily as he pondered what Mom had just said. Then he nodded. "Okay, I get it; the newspaper may not have had all the facts. Go ahead with your hypothetical case."

By the time Mom finished her story, the sandwiches and chips were just a memory. Unlike Sweetie I love ham, and Mom was generous with the tidbits. I also love chips, but she says they're not good for me so she keeps them all for herself. I agree with Professor Hoffman: Mom's a party pooper!

Professor Hoffman settled back with a cup of coffee and sighed. "I don't know, Hannah. If this girl's telling

126

the

truth, then putting her with a male therapist might shut her down even more. What was the nature of the abuse?'

"Not a clue. The hypothetical girl refuses to say, but she denies being raped and refused a rape kit. There were no signs of sexual trauma, and in fact she says she is still a virgin. But there was recent bruising on her upper arms. Hypothetically, of course."

"Since as you say there are no significant problems in school or other signs of disturbed behavior, whatever happened to make this hypothetical child stab her own father must have been extremely traumatic. Why do you think she'll trust a male now?"

"Because she already has."

Professor Hoffman cocked his head and frowned deeply. When the answer came to him, he raised his eyebrows and nodded. "Ah-ha. The male teacher."

"Exactly. She demonstrated trust when she first told him about the abuse, and then again when—according to her—she willingly left the school with him."

"Good point. Do you think I could see a hypothetical case file before talking to this hypothetical girl?"

"If her caseworker agrees to counseling, and if the girl agrees to see a counselor, then hypothetically you could."

"And, hypothetically, would I have to testify?"

"If the police don't hire you, then you're not their consultant, so I'd say no. Besides, the police prefer a consultant to specialize in a relevant field, in this case, adolescent psychology. PTSD hasn't been mentioned in her case, let alone diagnosed, so I doubt you'd ever be called to testify—hypothetically speaking, anyway."

Professor Hoffman laughed. "See? One more good reason to not pursue a doctorate in psychology."

"You mean one more excuse! So, what do you think? Do you think you might be able to help this girl?"

"I'd be willing to try—hypothetically, of course."

"Good. I'll let you know if we can turn the hypothetical into reality. Now, would you like me to leave Sweetie here while Spunky and I run some errands?"

Professor Hoffman and Sweetie both began to purr simultaneously. The professor smiled and said, "I believe, once again, you know the answer—and it's absolutely not hypothetical."

CHAPTER 28

I love when Mom takes me along on her errands, especially on those days when the weather is cool enough for me to stay in the car with the windows partially open. Of course, if it's too hot, Mom leaves the air conditioner running. She'd never put us at risk like some thickheaded humans do. How could anyone think their animal or their child would be comfortable—let alone safe—in a hot car without the air on? I'm telling you, if critters ran the world, people would be required to pass a test before being allowed to have a child or a pet!

On second thought, if we ran the world, guess who would be the pets?

Of course, Mom would pass that test with flying colors. For example, on a cool day, how far she opens the windows depends on where she parks. If she isn't sure about the neighborhood, or if she can't see the car from inside the store, then she opens the windows only a crack, so that I can't stick my head out and no one can reach in and do me any harm. Of course, I don't know why anyone in his right mind would be foolhardy enough to stick an uninvited hand into *my* car.

Today offered the perfect situation. The weather was cool, so that the windows could be down far enough for me to stick my head out; and our first stop was Harry's Grocery. Mom says Harry has the best meats in town, and his register is by the front window. He's always happy to keep an eye on Mom's car and her critters while she shops. Mom said it would cost less to go to Wally World, but she likes to support the local businesses. Besides, Harry's critter hospitality is priceless. Mom went inside.

"Well, hello there, Ms. Spunky. How are you this fine day?"

Harry! I wagged vigorously as I licked his hand. When Harry isn't too busy, he comes out to say hello.

"I don't see any cats in there with you. Do you have your Mom all to yourself today?"

I softly woofed my confirmation.

Harry laughed. "Well, that makes you special, doesn't it?"

I woofed again. When you're right, you're right!

"Well, I think a special doggie deserves a special treat," Harry said. He glanced back toward the store. "I know your mom doesn't mind if I do this, but let's keep this our secret, okay?"

I snorted very softly. After all, he did say it was a secret.

"Good girl, no sense alerting your mom, because then she might decrease your dinner, and we wouldn't want that." When I licked his hand it opened to reveal a small but juicy chunk of raw beef. I gently took it and dropped it inside the car, then returned to the window and gave Harry plenty of wags and kisses. Good manners dictate that one say thank you before gobbling one's treats. But as soon as Harry returned to the store I hunkered down and had myself a delicious snack. Mom was right; Harry did have the best meats in town!

After Harry's we made several other stops, which resulted in even more treats. Shirley, the bank teller, sent me a biscuit through that tube contraption at the drive-through machine, and Pete, the hardware man, was super-nice and gave me a free rawhide treat. It was bonanza day, and I was making out like a bandit. With so many admirers spread all over town, I could have scored many more times, but too soon Mom announced we were done with our errands, and we headed back to the college pick up Sweetie.

When suppertime rolled around, was it any wonder I wasn't very hungry?

CHAPTER  29

Later that evening, Tom Mackey, the attorney who had offered to help Samantha, called. Mom put him on the speakerphone as she straightened the papers on her desk.

"I'm glad you warned me that Samantha's story might sound kooky," he began. "I had trouble just keeping up with the cast of characters."

Mom chuckled. "I agree, it's a challenge."

"Thank goodness you're her therapist. I doubt many therapists would have gone out of their way to get her legal counsel."

"Well, it seemed like the right thing to do."

"I think it was too. First, let me say that I have Samantha's permission to call you and give you an overview, so legally I'm free to tell you a few things. After she and I talked, I made a few phone calls and located a former fraternity brother of mine, Stewart Dunlap, whose law office is fairly close to the town in Florida where Samantha jumped bail. He's agreed that when she turns herself in he'll represent her, *pro bono*, as a favor to me."

"Oh, Tom that's great news! Now she'll certainly have proper counsel." Mom hesitated and then asked, "That's true, right? This frat brother of yours was a good student, right?"

Tom laughed. "Fear not, Hannah, Stewart graduated higher in the class than I did! But as we both know, people can change. I've kept up with him over the years, but just to be sure I made a few calls to check him out. Both he and his practice are highly regarded, and he said he'd keep me informed every step of the way. So I think it will work out fine."

"What do you think will happen to Samantha?"

"It's too soon to tell. Stewart said he'd pull the case file, read the facts, and see which judge heard her case. Some judges take bail-jumping personally. The biggest problem may well be that she did all of this in Florida, which is not the best state in which to forge a check. It's an automatic felony there. When she jumped bail, Samantha knew that she was facing a year's jail time. For now, we'll just have to let things play out and see what happens. But Stewart is sharp, and I think he'll do everything he can for her. He'll try to expedite getting her on the docket, which shouldn't be hard since there's a warrant out for her. He wants her to go down there in two days so that she can be available to go to court at a moment's notice. I told him we'd pay for her motel room, which I assumed would be okay with you. He's hoping to minimize any jail time."

"That's perfectly fine with me. It sounds like a wonderful plan. I'm sure Samantha was relieved."

Silence.

"Tom?"

"The truth is, Hannah, I found it close to impossible to tell exactly what Samantha felt about anything. The woman laughs at all the wrong times. She's headed to Florida in just two days so time is very short, but I sure wish you could cure her of that behavior *before* she goes up before a judge."

"Maybe I still can. I can certainly try. I'll call and ask her to see me tomorrow."

Samantha's true feelings may be hard to read, but right now Mom's were easy. When she hung up, she was smiling from ear to ear.

Then her smile got even wider.

Frank called and gave Mom the good news that Amanda's guardian had granted her approval for Professor Hoffman to begin counseling Amanda. The whole process had been fast-tracked because DCFS had used him numerous times for kids whose parents suffered from PTSD. His reputation preceded him and paved the way for their quick approval.

Mom then called Professor Hoffman, who was pleased and said he'd go to the jail tomorrow to have his first meeting with Amanda.

Mom went to bed a happy camper.

CHAPTER 30

Samantha had agreed to an extra session, so the next day after she signed on they began discussing her visit with Tom Mackey. Samantha said she was relieved to know she would have a lawyer in Florida.

Then Mom broached the subject of Samantha's inappropriate laughing.

"Samantha, Mr. Mackey and I share a concern that we need to discuss. We've both noticed that you often laugh when you say something that isn't at all funny. I think you laugh when you feel uneasy, or when talking about something that's painful or difficult. Unfortunately, the laughter makes it appear that you aren't taking the subject seriously, and that might be a problem if it happened in front of a judge."

"Well, there's nothing I can do about it," said Samantha. "It just happens."

"I see how you might think that, but I believe we can change it."

"Why does it matter? I'm turning myself in, aren't I?"

"Yes, but the judge will be forming an opinion of you based on what he sees as well as what you say. Inappropriate laughter makes you seem insincere. For example, if you tell the judge you're sorry for what you did, he won't believe you mean it if you laugh when you say it. Does that make sense?"

"Yeah, I guess so, but I can't stop it, especially when I'm nervous."

"I think I can help. Here is what I want you to try. Put your hands together in your lap, with your fingertips touching. That's it. Now I'll pretend to be the judge, and I want you to answer me the way you'd answer him in court, keeping your eyes on me the whole time. If you feel the urge to laugh, I want you to press your fingertips together in sequence: start with the thumbs, then the index fingers, then the middle fingers, then the ring fingers, and finally the two pinkies. When you get to the pinkies, start the sequence over again. Hopefully that will help you focus on your fingers and forget to laugh. Are you ready?"

"Okay, but this feels really stupid."

"Just give it a try. Okay, here we go. Remember I'm acting like a judge.

"Ms. O'Brian, you broke your bond agreement and fled the state. Tell me why I shouldn't just send you back to jail."

Samantha hesitated and looked down at her hands.

"Samantha, keep your eyes on the judge," Mom said.

Samantha's head jerked up and she said, "Because judge…I'm…really sorry…for what I did…and I…have a…daughter…back home…that I…need to…take care of." She spoke in a halting cadence, matching the action of her fingers. She then threw her hands in the air and said, "This is stupid! I sound like I'm mentally deficient."

"That was just your first try, but at least you didn't laugh."

"Great, so my choice is either I can laugh and sound insincere, or I can sound like an idiot!"

Mom chuckled. "Try it a few more times. You'll see, I think it will get easier to move your fingers and speak normally at the same time. Go ahead, give it a try."

Samantha repeated the same phrase several more times, and after the fourth run she smiled. "Hey, I did it!"

"You certainly did. Congratulations! Now I'll ask you some more questions, and I want you to keep doing the same thing. We'll keep practicing until you can do it without thinking, just like breathing."

By the end of the session, Samantha was able to respond to every question Mom asked without laughing. Mom also had Samantha practice using the same technique with only one hand, one finger at a time against her thumb, as a backup plan in case she needed to use the other hand to do something like when she raises it in court to affirm she'll tell truth.

Samantha would be leaving tomorrow. Mom told her that if she needed to talk while she was in Florida, she should feel free to call her. I couldn't see Samantha's hands, but she must have been pressing her fingers together because she didn't even smirk when she said, "Thanks, Doc, for all you've done. Thanks for not giving up on me. I don't know what's coming, but thanks to you and Mr. Mackey I don't feel so alone."

Mom smiled at success. Obviously, she had practiced my rule number six: Tenacity and creativity will always serve you well.

CHAPTER  31

Two days later, early in the morning, Mom got a call from Tom Mackey. I didn't need the speakerphone to know it was good news. Mom pumped her fist upward and danced a jig as she exclaimed, "Oh, Tom, that's wonderful! I'm so happy for Samantha. No repercussions? No fine? No jail time? The judge vacated his previous order *and* expunged her record? Your friend must be one great attorney! Now Samantha has a real chance to make a new life for herself. I can't thank you enough for making this possible."

Mom listened for a moment, and then she laughed, "My friend, that's one bill I'll be delighted to pay. Thank you again. Let me know when I can return the favor."

When Mom hung up, she scooped Bobby into her arms, hugged him to her chest and danced around the kitchen. "Can you believe it guys? Florida is an hour earlier so it's like it just happened! She only got down there yesterday and they heard her case first thing this morning. The judge let Samantha walk! No fines! No jail time! He told her he was impressed that she was trying to do the right thing by turning herself in, even though she has a young daughter back home. And her attorney told Tom Samantha didn't laugh even once! She acted like a mature adult—well, at least she did until the judge said he was dismissing the charges, then he said she let out big 'Yippee!' And Tom said he didn't think it hurt one iota that the judge has a daughter about Samantha's age. That's a blessing if I ever heard of one. The right judge, the right timing, and the right answers. And Tom's attorney pal said he'll help Samantha start legal action to get her son back! Also *pro bono*! That's a miracle all by itself!"

Bobby finally let out a loud meow to let Mom know that in her joy she was squeezing him pretty hard. Mom got the message and plunked the boy down. She looked around for another candidate to scoop up, everyone had fled the scene.

Mom laughed. "Okay, you chickens, see if I care! Spunky will dance with me."

I stood on my hind legs, and Mom and I danced our own jig. Mom was beaming from ear to ear. I loved seeing her this happy.

Shortly thereafter Professor Hoffman stopped by for coffee, and unfortunately her smile quickly dimmed. He had come from his third session with Amanda, and he certainly wasn't dancing any jig.

"I've seen Amanda three times now," he told Mom. "I've counseled a lot of traumatized people over the years, and by now, ninety percent of the time I have found a way to get them to open up, even if it's only a smidgen. But this gal has built a solid brick wall around herself. I haven't made an inch of progress. Not even a crack."

"But, Joe, it's only been two days."

"I know, but if you could see her face, especially her eyes, you'd understand what I mean. She seems bound and determined to not open up. It's eerie. I don't see anger, or even fear, just cold, quiet resolve. Keep in mind, she's already spent a week locked in a cell. She's been before a judge, pled guilty, refused bond and a trial, and she'd probably already be sentenced if not for her guardian and Frank convincing the judge to hold off until a psych evaluation can determine whether she understands the consequences of her actions. As far as I can tell, Amanda is one-hundred percent determined not to help herself."

"Didn't you get any hints as to why?"

"Guilt? Remorse? I don't know, but with all the evidence pointing to her killing her father, maybe she just wants to be punished for what she did."

"Can you tell me anything about what you two talked about?"

"You know I can't give you specifics, but in general we talked about her mother, her childhood, her father, and her school. I covered all the routine topics, and I didn't find any red flags until I got to the subject of being abused and stabbing her father. Then she immediately froze over."

"Did you see a negative reaction to the fact you're a man?"

"No. In fact, the first time we met I sensed a softening compared to what she gave Frank."

"So what does your gut tell you?"

Before answering, Professor Hoffman took in a deep breath and released it slowly. "Hannah, I can tell you this: I'm not at all convinced she killed her father. I know she says she did, and I know her prints are on the knife. But what bothers me is this: If she did stab him, and if she wants to be punished for it, then why is there no emotion when she talks about doing it? There's no sign of remorse, or sadness, or anger—nothing. Frank was right when he said she uses the same words over and over. Her story doesn't change. It is as if she memorized her lines and she's sticking to the script."

"What are you going to do?"

"I'll keep seeing her. Maybe she'll slip up or let her guard down just enough that I can learn something. If nothing else, at least I can be supportive. She's undergoing evaluation by the court's psychiatrist, and Frank said he thought that could take another two or three weeks, so I have some time."

Mom leaned over, laid her hand on Professor Hoffman's arm, and said, "Joe, just do your best. Give it a few more sessions, and maybe you'll see something. All you can do is try, my friend. That's all any of us can do."

CHAPTER  32

After Professor Hoffman left, Mom went outside. She sat in the lounge chair and patted the cushion, inviting me to join her. I jumped up and settled in next to her thigh. The big oak tree protected us from the sun, while the warmth of the day was comforting. Nevertheless, Mom's anxiety was palpable.

"From the first moment I heard about this girl I've been deeply troubled," she said, "and I don't know why. I think it's time to relax, shut off my mind, and hopefully get some insight into all this."

Mom took control of her breathing, forcing it into a deep, steady, slow rhythm. As her eyes closed I heard her mutter softly to herself—not words that I could understand, but murmurings. She refers to this as her "prayer language." She tells patients that "self" can often get in the way of discerning truth, and if you can detach from your own thoughts, your own knowledge, and become peaceful, you may hear the voice of your spirit and receive new insight. As she stroked my back, the tension in her body began to melt away, and we began our peaceful journey.

Critters don't measure time like humans. We stay in the moment, so I admit I lost track of time. But sometime later Mom shifted in her chair, and I became aware that a cooler breeze now stirred the oak.

Mom rose and said, "Come on, Spunk. I need to call Frank. But before I do that, I'm putting on the kettle. While we were out here it sure cooled off." We went inside and Mom filled the kettle and turned on the stove. She pushed the speakerphone button, punched in Frank's number, and while it was ringing she located her favorite teacup.

"Hello?" said Frank's voice over the speaker.

"Frank, it's Hannah. Did I catch you at a bad time?"

"Nope, but I am heading to a meeting soon. How are you?"

"I'm fine, thanks. Listen, Frank, the last thing I want to do is to screw up your investigation, so I thought I should run my idea past you before I do anything. As you know, Joe Hoffman has been talking with Amanda, and you and I have agreed I shouldn't see her, which is fine. But I'd like to go and talk to some of her friends to see if I can learn anything from them. Would that be okay?"

Frank hesitated and then asked, "Why? What do you think you might find? We've already talked to the kids who were immediately involved."

"I know, I know, but I want to talk to the friends we don't know about yet. I'm trying to fill in some of the blanks."

"I appreciate you asking me first. I think it would be fine. So long as you don't present yourself in any official capacity, I can't stop a private citizen from talking to another citizen."

"That's me, Frank, just plain Jane, private citizen."

Frank and I both knew Mom was no plain Jane.

She hung up and sat down with her tea and her favorite dog and said, "Spunk, it's time this plain Jane started doing a little detecting of her own."

Now, that's my mom!

CHAPTER  33

As she sipped her tea Mom pulled out her address book, looked up a number, punched the speakerphone button again and then punched in a number.

"Clearwater High," came a voice. "How may I help you?"

"Hello, this is Dr. Hannah Richards. I'd like to speak to Principal Ames, please."

Principal Ames and Mom met years ago when he first referred a student to her for counseling.

"Hi, Hannah! How have you been?"

"Just fine, Richard, and you?"

"A long holiday would be wonderful, but I can't complain. Listen, I want you to know the Anderson boy is still doing well. I'm glad his parents agreed to let you see him."

"That's terrific. It has been months since our last session so I am glad to hear he is still doing well. He seemed like a good kid who hit a big bump in the road and didn't know how to get back on track. He was willing to do the work, which we both know makes all the difference."

"True, but you were the right person at the right time. Now, what can I do for you?"

"You've read about Amanda Pederson in the paper?"

"I sure have, but I wish I hadn't. She's a sweet kid. I can't believe she stabbed her father. Is there anything I can do to help her?"

"Maybe there is. I agree, parts of the story don't make sense. I'd like to talk to some of her friends to see if I can find some of the missing pieces. Do you know who she hung out with?"

"Can you hang on a minute?"

"Sure." While she waited, Mom grabbed a paper and pencil.

"Thanks for waiting," said Principal Ames after a short pause. "You have your methods of getting to the truth, and I have mine. Don't tell anyone, but my secret weapon is my secretary, Mrs. Mitchell. That woman knows more about what goes on in this school than I do, and she has the memory of an elephant. She can tell me who hung out with whom, back to when they were freshmen! Her motto is 'To know what a kid is really like, check out who they hang with.' Anyway, she gave me the names of Amanda's closet friends, do you have pencil?"

"Sure do."

"Amanda was tight with four girls. Sally Anderson, Pamela Watkins, Mary Copeland, and Nancy Evans. If you come by the school I can point them out to you, and you can take it from there. I trust your judgment and I don't see why you can't approach them yourself and ask if they want to talk to you."

"That would be terrific. When would be a good time?"

146

"Well, it's almost eleven thirty, and lunch period starts at twelve-thirty. None of them are cleared to leave the school, so they should be in the cafeteria. Can you make it by then?"

"I can be at your office by twelve fifteen. Will that work?"

"Perfect! I'll be expecting you."

After Mom hung up she closed her eyes and sat quietly for a few minutes. She then sighed and said, "Now to accomplish the second thing I need to do." She picked up the receiver and punched in another number.

"Judy? Hi, it's Hannah. How are you? Great. I'm calling to see if you can come over for dinner tonight? Terrific! How about five-thirty? Nothing fancy, just you, me, and some hamburgers, is that okay? Wonderful! See you then."

Oh boy! Judy was coming tonight! Judy Rodgers has been Mom's best friend longer than I have. Mom loves to see her, and so do we critters. Still, today there was a significant decrease in Mom's enthusiasm. Something was amiss.

CHAPTER 34

Several hours later Mom returned from the high school, but we learned nothing because as soon as she came in the door she changed her clothes and began cleaning the house.

"Whoa, Spunk, Mom is giving that vacuum cleaner one vigorous workout. That doesn't bode well, does it?"

"You're right, Sweetie—not good, not good at all."

Mom tries to stay ahead of the fur balls, which is a never-ending task in our hairy family, but no one would call her a clean freak. She pulls out the vacuum several times a week, and her usual tempo is slow and steady. But when she's upset or trying to work through something, she can become a cleaning whirlwind. We've found a direct correlation between the degree of her anxiety and the intensity of her cleaning. Given the force we were seeing behind that vacuum, something had Mom very upset.

From his safe zone up on the table, Sweetie asked, "Do you know what's up with Mom?"

"No, but I do know something's been gnawing at her for several days now."

"Is it about that girl?"

"Until this morning I would have said that could be it. But today Mom launched into action over that one. Once she actually starts doing something about a concern, her agitation diminishes. So unless something happened at the school that we don't know about, this isn't about Amanda. Nope, I think this is something entirely different. I don't have a clue what it is, but considering how much fervor we're seeing, I can tell you one thing—change is a-coming, Sweetie, change is a-coming."

CHAPTER 35

Judy was on time and brought cat treats. But that doesn't mean she forgot about me. She knows these cats, with their finicky palates, turn up their noses at dog treats. I, on the other hand, have never met a cat treat I didn't find tasty. Judy knows that all hearts can easily be won with only one bag.

While we were enjoying our special appetizer, Judy helped Mom finished getting the hamburgers and fries ready. They then settled in to eat and began catching up on each other's lives. For the first hour we heard the usual banter between two close friends. But when they got to the coffee and cheesecake, the tone changed.

"Judy, I'm struggling with something."

"I was wondering how long it would take you to tell me what's bothering you."

Mom chuckled. "That, my friend, is why we're so close. You read me well, and your patience is vast."

"So what's going on?"

"Frank."

"Okay, what about Frank?"

"You know I care a great deal for him. I love the man, I really do, but things have changed." Mom paused and looked down at her cup. "Don't get me wrong, Frank is a wonderful man—and before you ask, because you will, yes, the sex is terrific. That's not the problem. My quandary is that we've morphed into a couple. In some ways it's like we're married couple, but we're not married—and please note, I have no desire to be married again, at least not in the foreseeable future."

"Does Frank want to get married?"

"I don't think so. I think he's happy with the way things are."

"But you're not."

"Apparently not. I thought I could be a liberated, progressive woman and have an active sex life with no commitments. But it turns out I'm not wired that way. I love what Frank and I share, but it's really bothering me that we've turned into a couple."

"Why does it bother you? Do you want to date other men?"

"Not particularly, but neither do I want to be told I *can't* date another man."

"Did Frank say that?"

"No, we've never discussed it. And if I'm honest, it wouldn't matter anyway. I'd never be comfortable being sexually involved with two men at the same time. If Frank and I weren't having sex we would be two friends having a great time together. We wouldn't be a 'couple.' But if we weren't having sex I doubt Frank would stick around. Of course, if he did leave we'd no longer be a couple, but neither would we be having a great time together. See my dilemma?"

Judy cocked her head and said, "I get it. But, my dear, the age-old question remains: Can a man and a woman be close friends without being intimate?"

"I'd say that's extraordinarily difficult when two people are attracted to each other. Of course, it's much easier if one's gay and the other one is straight."

"And Frank isn't gay."

Mom raised her eyebrows, shook her head, and said, "Definitely not gay."

Mom sighed. "Even though Frank and I have never talked about commitment, once you become sexually involved with someone, haven't you automatically made a commitment? Otherwise, why are you having sex with them? I don't know, Judy, maybe young folks can just hop into bed without any attachments, but I can't be sexually intimate without first being emotionally intimate; and to be emotionally intimate, you have to get to know and trust a person. First you care about them, then you trust them, and if you develop deeper feelings then you start sleeping together; and before you know it—*poof*—you start acting like a monogamous couple. How do I know we've become a couple? Because today I was actually uncomfortable telling him I couldn't see him tonight because I was having dinner with a friend."

"But why would you feel uncomfortable about that?"

"Because we're a couple!" Mom laughed, "I know, it's crazy, right?"

"Hannah, maybe this commitment is starting to pinch and you don't like how it feels."

"I've thought of that, and maybe that's part of it. But the question is, where do things go from here? I have no desire to get married, but it's not about marriage. For me, this isn't a legal or moral issue. If I'm in a sexual relationship, it has to be the real deal. I need a relationship where we're free to tell each other exactly what we want and need, free to explore fantasies and dreams; where we have no secrets, and where we both know we want to share a future. Bottom line, I want and need more than just sexual intimacy. I need soul intimacy. I can't achieve that unless I know I'm going to be with a man for a very long time, maybe the rest of my life. I can't reach that level of intimacy while wondering whether or not he'll be gone in a month. As time goes by, whether you talk about it or not, the level of commitment increases."

"And does that commitment scare you?"

Mom paused, rubbed her face, and said, "Scare me? Maybe, but I really don't believe fear is the driving force behind my hesitation." She took in a deep breath, let it out slowly, and then said, "If I'm truly honest, I think it's doubt."

"Doubt?"

"Yeah, doubt. I don't think Frank's the one."

"But you said you love him."

"It's not hard to feel love for a person. I love you, but that doesn't mean I'm a lesbian. People fall in love all the time. The question shouldn't be do I love him, but rather do I want to spend every day of the rest of my life with him? You can deeply love, respect, admire, and trust a good friend, just the way I do Frank. Any friendship can deepen as the years pass, but don't forget, friends also spend a lot of time apart and alone. They don't wake up together every day, they don't eat meals together every day, they don't keep a budget and pay bills together, they don't even see each other every day. They may not even talk to each other for a whole week! It's no wonder friendships survive better than marriages. The real question isn't do I love Frank, but do I love him enough to want to spend the rest of my life with him?"

"Doesn't it take time for that kind of love to develop?"

"Maybe. But when I started dating Adam it only took a few weeks before I knew I'd stay with him forever. I never thought a man like that would be with me, but I knew I'd follow him anyway. Of course, I didn't tell *him* that right away, but I still knew it. I've told you before, for years I figured that one day he'd wake up, look at me, and wonder how he ever got there. I truly believed the day would come when he'd leave, but that didn't change the fact that I knew I wasn't going anywhere." Mom laughed. "Luckily, as it turned out, Adam didn't want to go anywhere either!"

"Hannah, your Adam was a remarkable man. All of us who knew him knew he was one of a kind. Don't you think it's unfair to expect to feel the same way about Frank?"

"I really don't think I am expecting that. Frank's a completely different type of man, and I love who he is. I don't want him to change. But as much as I love who he is, it doesn't mean I can envision a life with him. I doubt I'll ever feel what I felt for Adam for any other man, but I do expect to be able to love another man enough to want a lifetime with him—albeit a different life. Maybe you're right, maybe it does take time for all that to develop. But it's also possible that it just isn't there and it never will be."

"Maybe you need to lower your expectations. Being alone for the rest of your life wouldn't be good."

"The fear of being alone is a lousy reason to settle on someone."

"A lot of people do exactly that."

"And a lot of people regret it."

"Maybe you need to give it more time. You don't have to have all the answers right now."

"Maybe, but I can't stay in this state of limbo for long. I know myself, and the fact that I'm even telling you about my doubt means it's no longer a minor reservation. It means there's a deeper root, and I think I need to do something. Do you think that's wrong?"

"There is no wrong or right. This is about how you feel."

"So what do you think I should do about it?"

"Oh no, my friend, you'll have to answer that question on your own. The real question is, what do *you* think you should do?"

Mom sat quietly for a few seconds and exhaled a big breath before she said, "I think I need to go back to being single."

Sweetie's head jerked in my direction. "You were right, Spunk. Change is definitely a-coming."

Indeed it was, and a big change at that.

CHAPTER  36

Three days later, Samantha was back for another therapy session. Today, after recounting what had happened in court and talking about the fantastic *pro bono* offer from Stewart Dunlap to help with getting her son back, Samantha raised the inevitable question.

"Do you think I need to continue therapy? My friend says the changes in me are amazing and that I no longer act like a crazy person. I really don't want her to have to keep paying."

"Well," Mom said, "while I think you certainly could benefit from continued therapy, I understand your finances; and I agree with your friend that you've made great progress. You should be proud of the work you've done. But you'll have new challenges with the battle for custody of your son. So what about this idea? I know a group therapy program through a local church, and it's free. It has absolutely nothing to do with religion. Two social workers who attend that church started it as a way for people to get free support, and they're both excellent therapists. I think they might let you join the group if I refer you, and that way you could suspend your regular sessions with me, but still have support and continue doing the work. But still, I suggest you make a commitment to your friend that if she sees you deteriorating, you'll heed her advice and at least call me. Of course, you can always restart with me on your own at any time. How does that sound?"

"I'm willing to try it."

And so Mom and Samantha finished their final session.

Saying goodbye to a client is bittersweet. Though Mom strives to maintain professional detachment, some clients touch her heart more than others. Samantha turned out to be an unexpected surprise, but a nice one. Samantha benefitted greatly, but so did Mom. Next time Mom has a strong, negative reaction to a new client, she may remember Samantha and be slower to judge.

CHAPTER  37

Mom went to the school to interview Amanda's friends for three days. But we critters still knew nothing, because each time she got home she went right back to vigorous housecleaning. She cleaned out closets, rearranged the kitchen cabinets, and organized her files. She even shredded her old tax returns. Today, after she returned, she had beaten a batch of dough to within an inch of its life, she baked two loaves of bread and then made an apple pie. Over the last few days she had talked to Frank several times on the phone and said the usual things, but she had avoided seeing him.

She also spent time each day being quiet and listening to her spirit. When she's in the middle of a struggle, peace does not come easily. It's something she has to work at. I know this because most of those time I'm lying on her lap while she takes her quiet time. As she gently strokes my body, she enters a zone in which our rhythms meld, and in this zone my sense of what she's experiencing expands. Of course this is much easier when she talks out loud as a way of processing her thoughts, as she often does.

We all knew Mom cared deeply for Frank. Her conflict seemed to be between a sincere desire not to hurt him and her increasing belief that she could no longer be in an intimate relationship with him. She remained stuck on trying to figure out how Frank would react if she told him how she felt. She acted out several different scenarios, rehearsing different speeches to see how they sounded. Much to my delight, she finally got sick of going 'round and 'round the same mountain and accepted the fact that she couldn't be all-knowing. She certainly knows this, but sometimes she doesn't want it to be true. Today, however, she was finally able to separate herself from her emotions by realizing if one of her clients had the same problem, she'd tell them to be honest and talk to their partner about it.

When she had settled it within herself she called Frank, and he agreed to come by around eight in the evening. Before he arrived, the boys and I had a lengthy discussion about how we might be able to help.

The moment Frank walked in the door it was obvious he knew all was not well.

"Hannah," he said after they sat down together on the sofa, "I don't need any detective training to know something is wrong."

"True, Frank, true. There's no easy way to do this, so I'm just going to say it, and then we can talk about it for as long as we need to."

Mom took a deep breath and said, "I know you're really overworked with the Pederson case, and my timing stinks. I wish I could put my feelings on hold, but that would necessitate lying to you, and I refuse to do that. So here it is. Lately I've had some serious questions about where we're headed and whether or not our relationship should stay the way it is. Quite simply, I don't want to get married, and I don't think you do either. I don't see us heading toward a permanent life together, and I'm not comfortable staying in a casual sexual relationship any longer. In all honesty, I truly don't know what we're going to do about it, but I need to tell you what I'm feeling."

Frank stiffened, anger flashed across his face, and he stood up. Before he could utter a single word, I jumped against his leg and tried to distract him.

His voice reflected his anger. "Not now, girl. Hannah, I—"

I whined softly and once again jumped against his leg. This time he actually yelled at me. "Spunky, I said not now!"

Mom's tone held caution and an unspoken warning, "Frank..."

Frank sighed. "Okay, okay, Spunk, here I'll sit back down."

As soon as Frank sat, I jumped onto his lap. I gave him two quick licks on his cheek and then quickly turned around. I knew what needed to happen, and it did. Frank began stroking my sides. Now I was in a much better position to influence his mood. A moment later, his touch began to soften.

Frank sighed again, "Okay, Hannah, I'll be honest and tell you that your feelings aren't a shock. I've known for a week or more that something was gnawing at you. I should have been brave enough to ask you about it. Maybe I didn't want to risk having this very discussion. I got angry just now because I felt rejected; but now, after taking a few breaths, I'll admit that I too have been feeling a bit uncomfortable."

"Am I correct that you're not anxious to be married again either?"

"Yup, that's a fact. I love being with you, and I do love you, but I simply have no desire whatsoever to get married. Maybe it's us, or maybe it's just me, but I don't want to be married."

Mom smiled and said, "Believe me, I know exactly what you're talking about. Even though I love you too, I have absolutely no desire to get married again. Do you think there's something wrong with us?"

Frank laughed. "You're the shrink, not me! But no, I think we're boringly normal." He paused and then continued, "Hannah, not many people would have the guts to start this discussion, and I'm grateful you did. I don't like it, but I'm grateful. And you're right, our relationship would definitely be damaged if we started lying to each other or trying to fake it."

"You're a wise man, Frank. So tell me, what do we do?"

Frank wiggled his eyebrows and with a chuckle jokingly said, "I guess heading into the bedroom is out of the question, right?"

Mom's spontaneous laugh was spontaneous and sincere. "Good deduction, Sherlock."

Frank then became more serious. "Hannah, look, I wouldn't mind one iota keeping everything just like it is, but we wouldn't be having this discussion if that was okay with you. Besides, if I'm brutally honest, I've met one or two women and if I wasn't in a relationship I would probably have asked them out to dinner. So the question is, can we continue to be 'friends with benefits'?"

161

"That's sounds grand in theory," said Mom, "but the truth is I think I need to return to being single again—without benefits. I know it'll be awkward, but I love being your friend, I love doing things with you, I love working with you on the Pederson case—in fact, I love working with you, period. Maybe if we focus on the case for now, and not our relationship, it can evolve into something we can both live with. What do you think?"

"I really would hate to lose you as a friend, so I'll give it a try. Now, how about we go out and get us some coffee and dessert and discuss Amanda."

"Better yet, I just baked an apple pie, and my coffee is way better than the diner's. How about we head into the kitchen and get caught up."

As they headed to the kitchen, Sweetie leaned in to me and whispered, "Nice move, Spunk, Nice move."

CHAPTER  38

Once the coffee was brewed and the pie warmed, Mom and Frank sat down and she related what had happened at the school.

"Several days ago, I asked Principal Ames to point out to me the four girls Amanda regularly hung out with. Their names are Pamela Watkins, Sally Anderson, Mary Copeland, and Nancy Evans, and I was able to observe them in the cafeteria at lunchtime. They were chatting and laughing like any other teenage girls, but it soon became obvious that Pamela is the leader of the pack. She was always the first to speak, and then the others responded. Three of them, Pamela, Sally, and Mary, are what some would call—stereotypic cheerleader types—pretty faces, long blonde hair, fair skin, delicate features, and bodies that unfortunately are probably the envy of their classmates."

Frank asked, "Unfortunately?"

Mom shrugged and said, "My first impression was that those three are way too thin to be healthy. I'm sure a lot of boys would call them 'hot' but to me their size-two bodies were anything but attractive. True, not every thin girl has an eating disorder, but what bothered me about these three was their weight in proportion to the rest of their bodies. They weren't just skinny, they were emaciated, and in fact when I got to talk to Nancy later, she told me that those three routinely purge. Anyway, I'll tell you more about that later, but Nancy was noticeably quieter than the others. She seldom spoke and mostly just nodded her head. Personally, I'd call her naturally beautiful, but she makes herself unattractive with way too much makeup. She did look a lot healthier than other three, but if she were standing next to them my guess is people with judgmental eyes would call her pudgy."

"Could you hear what they were talking about?"

"I got myself a cup of coffee and found an empty seat a few tables away. I couldn't hear every word, but enough to say that most of their conversation was normal teenage stuff, with every other sentence involving boys. But what was unsettling was Ms. Pamela. She would stop in the middle of the conversation, point to some kid walking by, and make a really cruel comment—and believe me, she made sure she said it loud and clear. Every time it happened, Sally and Mary giggled, but Nancy lowered her eyes and looked away. I had no warm and cozy feelings for those three bitchy princesses. They acted like spoiled-rotten bullies.

"Before the lunch period ended, I walked over to them and knelt down between Pamela and Mary. Before Pamela could open her mouth, I introduced myself and said that I was hoping they could help me help Amanda Pederson. I told them I'd heard they were friends of hers, and I asked if that was true.

"Right then every eye shifted to Pamela. She informed me, in a very snotty tone, that yes, they knew Amanda all right, and she did occasionally hang out with them, but she certainly wasn't a friend. When I asked why not, you should have seen that girl's face. It immediately turned mean and cold. She said, 'Duh! Amanda's a wacko, that's why. She stabbed her father! No friend of mine would do that. That girl's crazy!' Mary and Sally kept their eyes locked on Pamela the whole time and nodded in agreement like two bobbleheads. But then when I asked Nancy if she was Amanda's friend, her eyes stayed on me, not Pamela, and she actually began to tear up. But then darling Miss Pamela loudly cleared her throat, and Nancy immediately lowered her head and mumbled, 'No, ma'am, we're not friends.' When the bell rang I discreetly followed them down the hall. The three princesses went into the restroom, but Nancy hung back. I approached her, gave her my business card, and said if she wanted to talk about Amanda she could call me anytime and it would be our secret. Then I hightailed it out of there before her royal highness returned.

"The next day I went back. I didn't approach them, but I stayed within visual range. I know Nancy saw me, but she completely ignored me. But today, when the three princesses went into the restroom, Nancy looked right at me and then headed down the hall by herself. I followed her, and when she was out of range of the restroom she waited for me to catch up. She told me she had lied, and that Amanda was actually her best friend. She said she didn't have a clue how she could help, and that Pamela would make her life hell if she ever saw us talking, so we agreed to meet after school at the college library.

"She actually showed up, Frank. She's a sweet kid. Sure, she has identity issues, and her self-esteem is extremely low, but she seems like a good kid, and I think she really cares about Amanda. Apparently they've been friends since first grade and pretty much did everything together. She told me that at the end of last year Pamela said something to Amanda in gym class, and shortly after that Amanda started hanging out with them. Amanda wouldn't tell Nancy what Pamela had said, but she didn't abandon Nancy either. Nancy said that Pamela lied about them and Amanda only occasionally hanging out together. They were always together. Amanda always took Nancy along, and eventually the three accepted Nancy as the tag-along. According to Nancy, Amanda said she hated Pamela's guts, but the price of ending up on Pamela's shit list was too high. Apparently Miss Pamela wields way too much social power. Nancy said she never felt particularly threatened by Pamela because she didn't have much to lose, and besides she thought Amanda would always have her back. But about a month ago, she said, Amanda abruptly changed. According to Nancy, Amanda became withdrawn, secretive, and stayed away from Nancy and the group. Nancy said she thought Amanda might have a secret beau, because several times she saw Amanda get into a car with a guy parked down the street from the school. Nancy never got a good look at the guy, but she thought he looked older. But she said Amanda knew a lot of guys from her church, and sometimes they'd pick her up after school. Nancy had gone with them several times to get burgers, but she never went with this guy. Amanda kept him a secret."

"That's interesting," Frank mused.

Mom continued, "When I asked Nancy about the other three girls, she smirked and said, 'If you like girls who are shallow, bitchy, and obsessed with how they look, then you'd love those three.' Then she said something very telling. She said sadly, 'But lousy friends are better than no friends.' She went on to tell me that the three girls work out all the time, and purge when they think they've eaten too much, which according to Nancy is now pretty much all the time. Nancy said she tries to ignore all the mean stuff they say about her weight, and Amanda did too, at least she did until this summer. But according to Nancy, when Amanda returned from visiting her mother in New York she was upset, but again she wouldn't tell Nancy what had happened. Nancy said she started to worry, because shortly after that she began to wonder if Amanda had started purging too."

Frank shook his head slowly. "To tell you the truth, Hannah, purging is something I've never understood."

Mom sighed. "An eating disorder can be hard to identify, and the reasons behind it multifaceted; but when it turns into an addiction, the related behaviors parallel every other addiction. Alcoholics abuse booze, others abuse drugs, and a person with an eating disorder uses food in a destructive manner by restricting, binging, or purging. Like other addicts, they're seeking a way to escape or have a sense of control over a life in which they feel powerless. Regardless what their drug of choice is, they all experience a high. You and I may have difficulty comprehending that high, but addicts will destroy their lives in order to get it one more time. Every one of them is on the same path, a path of destruction. But each person's journey and how it began is as unique as they are."

"Do you think these girls are at risk now?" Frank asked.

Mom shrugged. "That's like asking someone how long can you safely play Russian roulette? If you're asking me if there's enough obvious physical damage to support legal intervention, I would have to say no. Where their parents are in all this is unknown, but sadly the law would rule they are not yet damaged enough."

Frank went back to the issue at hand. "Given what Nancy said, that Amanda came back from New York upset, not just bored like her mother claims, then something happened."

"Agreed."

"Did Nancy ever learn the name of the guy who picked Amanda up from school?"

"Nope."

"Did she see him again after Amanda was arrested?"

"I asked, and she said no."

"Did Amanda say anything to Nancy about her father?"

Mom sighed deeply before responding. "Yes, I'm sorry to say, she did. She told me that several weeks after Amanda's abrupt change, she called Nancy one night in a rage. She was crying and yelling at the same time about how furious she was with her father. She wouldn't say why, but Nancy kept pressing the issue. She told me she wished she had just shut up."

Frank asked, "Why?"

"Because when she kept pushing, Amanda started screaming into the phone, 'Shut up! I told you already, I can't tell you. All you need to know is he's a bastard! I hate him! I hate him! I wish he'd drop dead!'"

CHAPTER 39

The next morning, Professor Hoffman stopped by to give Mom an update.

"I still haven't made an inch of progress," he said. "In fact, I may have actually moved backwards."

"Backwards?" Mom frowned and asked, "Joe, what happened?"

Professor Hoffman took a sip of his coffee before he spoke. "I've seen Amanda three more times since we last spoke, and still every time I bring up anything about the stabbing she immediately begins reciting her mantra. The reason I say I may have gone backwards is because today she actually started saying it before I even finished my sentence. That's not good, Hannah. When I leave here I'm on my way to see her again, and I'm at an impasse. I feel like all I'm doing is helping her rehearse her lines. I can't see that I've gained one ounce of her trust. I'm going in circles and getting nowhere."

Mom leaned over and placed a loving hand on his arm. "Joe, what I do know is that you are terrific at handling damaged people. I've seen you do it over and over again.

If Amanda won't open up to you, then maybe she's just too damaged to trust anyone. She may have built so many walls that no one can get in."

When I heard that, my head popped up at the exact same moment Fearless sat upright. We stared at each other. We were in accord. That first night, when Amanda opened the bedroom door and saw both of us, her heart softened. Maybe she was too damaged to trust a human, but what about a critter?

Fearless jumped up on the table, startling both Mom and Professor Hoffman.

"Fearless, what are you doing?" said Mom. "You know you're not supposed to jump up here when there's food on the table."

Fearless head-butted Mom on the chin.

"Okay, okay, I love you too. Now get off the table, please."

But Fearless plunked his rump down right in the middle of the table. Of course he made sure he missed the plate of cookies.

"Fearless, I said off!"

Fearless tilted his handsome, crooked head even further and meowed his best plea. At the same moment, I pushed my way up onto Mom's lap.

Mom laughed. "Okay, you're both adorable and hard to ignore, but…" Her words fell away the moment she started stroking Fearless, and a smile tugged at the corners of her mouth.

"Joe, I just had an idea. What if today you took Sweetie and Spunky with you to see Amanda?"

Fearless had concentrated on Sweetie's name because he knew Sweetie could influence Professor Hoffman more than he could. In turn, this then might increase the chance for a successful critter intervention.

Joe's face lit up. "That's a terrific idea, Hannah. I always said you were one smart woman."

Yup, one smart woman with two very smart critters!

CHAPTER  40

Shortly thereafter, Sweetie and I were off to visit Amanda in jail. Mom had already talked to Frank, who in turn had talked to Captain Swenson, who in turn was delighted that I was coming to see him. The man is a diehard dog-lover. Although he's always kind to any animal, he doesn't adore felines. The cats say this must be the result of some mental defect, so they don't hold it against him.

The captain and I had a joyous reunion. The last time we saw each other was months ago at Mom's shindig celebrating the successful conclusion of our last case. The humans could see that he was meticulously dressed, but I especially enjoyed his German shepherd "cologne." He has four of those big boys, named Sergeant, Lieutenant, Commander, and Rookie, the youngest. I know from my visits to his house that he loves to get down on the floor and wrestle with his best buds. His wife is highly proficient with a clothes brush, but thankfully, she can't brush away their scent. Today the captain was gloriously drenched in Eau de Shepherd. Add to that his expert back-rubbing skills, and I was in pure bliss. The man should have been a doggie masseur!

Finally he said, "Well, Spunk, I guess it is time for you to go to work. Your mom and Frank are hoping you'll be able to work your wonders on Amanda. To tell you the truth, this one may be too much even for your talents. That girl is one tough nut. I doubt even you can crack her."

I licked his nose. Oh, ye of little faith!

The captain then showed Professor Hoffman, Sweetie, and me to an interview room and left us there. The room was bare concrete walls with a metal table and four chairs. There was a mirror on one wall which I knew from Mom was two-way. Professor Hoffman took Sweetie out of his crate, and we settled in. Before long the captain returned with Amanda. Her head was down and her shoulders bent. She was a walking zombie. She gave no sign that she saw us. She looked like she had aged ten years since I last saw her. I went over to greet her. When I jumped against her leg, she came out of her trance and her face lit up. She knelt down.

"Well, look at you! You found me again, didn't you?"

She moved to the chair, sat down, raised her head, and made eye contact with Professor Hoffman. "Good Morning, Dr. Hoffman. How do you know this cutie?"

Professor Hoffman smiled. "Spunky and I have been friends for years. She lives with a very good human friend of mine."

I jumped into Amanda's lap, and she smiled, "Your name is Spunky, huh? Sounds like the perfect name for you. And who is this beautiful cat?"

Sweetie walked across the table and touched his nose to Amanda's in a gesture of friendship. He then rubbed against Amanda's extended hand.

"You're not the same cat that was with Spunky the last time I saw her," Amanda said.

Professor Hoffman intervened. "That's right. This is Sweetie. The cat who was with Spunky when they found you is named Fearless. He really wanted to come and see you again, but as a favor to me he let Sweetie take his place. "

"As a favor to you?"

"Yes. Fearless knows Sweetie holds a special place in my heart. By letting him be the one to come today, it gave us some extra time together." Sweetie's purr increased, and his contentment radiated outward.

The effect was not lost on Amanda. "Well, listen to that. You certainly have a loud purr motor, don't you?"

Sweetie moved forward and rubbed his head against Amanda's cheek. Amanda giggled, "That tickles."

Professor Hoffman smiled. "It's wonderful to hear you laugh, Amanda," he said.

Instantly Amanda pulled back, and the door to her soul slammed shut. Her hands dropped into her lap, she lowered her head, and she quietly said, "I shouldn't laugh. I don't have any right."

Professor Hoffman sighed and then gently said, "You may not feel like it, but you…"

The litany began, "I stabbed my own father…"

Professor Hoffman tried several times to redirect the conversation, but Amanda wouldn't give up her monologue of guilt. Finally he said, "Listen, Amanda, I really need a cup of coffee. I'll be right back. Would you keep an eye on these two while I'm gone?"

Amanda nodded.

"Do you want me to bring you something?"

Amanda spoke softly. "Water would be fine, thank you."

Professor Hoffman left the room, but we knew he wasn't leaving the scene. He was joining Mom in the observation room on the other side of the mirror. Before we set out this morning, he had Mom sign a confidentiality agreement specifically for this meeting. They both knew that her contract with the police department contained a provision that said that if she had a separate confidentiality agreement connected to a particular case, she was exempt from standard police reporting requirements. She had asked for this stipulation so that she would be free to help someone on her own terms. Today, Dr. Hoffman wanted Mom to be there so she could translate our behavior, but he also had to protect Amanda.

For the first five minutes after Professor Hoffman left the room there was absolutely no need to protect her. She didn't say a word, but even though she was silent she was communicating nevertheless. Every stroke of her hand down my back was full of sadness and despair. I wanted to turn and kiss her nose, but I resisted and stayed at my post. Today my job was not as a comforter, but a conduit. Sweetie was the designated therapist, and my job was simply to keep Amanda as tranquil and open as possible.

Sweetie moved forward, lowered his head, and rested the top of his head against Amanda's chest. He didn't rub. He didn't move. He just leaned into her. In the feline world, this is the ultimate hug. I felt the effects of his purring as they passed through Amanda's body and into her hands. Over and over, the waves of Sweetie's love and serenity flooded into Amanda. As she pressed back softly against him, she reminded me of a frightened child falling into the reassuring arms of a loving parent. She kept one hand on me as her other hand stroked Sweetie's head. Our circuit was now complete.

A wet tear fell on my back.

More tears dropped, and then Amanda said, "Oh, if only you two could stay here with me. It wouldn't be so terrible. I wouldn't be all alone."

Sweetie pressed in more firmly.

Amanda sobbed, "What am I going to do? If only I could tell someone the truth. If I could just tell one person, then maybe I wouldn't feel like I'm going to explode." She gulped in air. "But, that can never happen. Not ever. I can never tell anyone, not a soul. No one can ever know!"

Sweetie's purr swelled in volume, and again the effect was not lost on Amanda.

"Oh, you *are* a sweetie, aren't you? I know, I know. I know you'd understand. I could tell you. You'd never tell anyone, would you?"

It's a good thing Mom had signed that agreement. The truth was about to be revealed.

Amanda dropped her face close to Sweetie's ear and whispered.

Sweetie and I heard Amanda speak the truth.

Unfortunately, we were the only ones.

CHAPTER  41

A dog's ears are about twice as sensitive as a human's, but cats are the hands-down winners. Their ears are five times more sensitive than humans' ears, and their funnel shape are great enhancers. Though Sweetie and I had heard Amanda's truth very clearly, we knew that her softly whispered words never made it across the room, let alone through the two-way mirror to the observation room where Mom and Professor Hoffman were listening.

Amanda pulled back and sighed. "Thanks guys. It felt good to be able to say it."

Jeepers! Amanda had finally revealed the truth, and not a single human heard it. Now what?

Sweetie gently rubbed against Amanda's face to reassure her of his acceptance and love. After a heavy dose of special loving, he made his next move. He rose, turned, walked to the middle of the table, and lay down. He stretched out a paw, and Amanda leaned forward to reestablish contact. But since I was still on her lap, she couldn't scoot her chair closer to the table. Even at this distance, Sweetie and I could easily hear her whisper, but Sweetie was betting that

Amanda would instinctively raise her voice to compensate for the increased distance.

Sweetie cocked his head and gave her look as if he were confused.

Amanda saw the questioning look. "I don't know how it all happened, Sweetie," she said. "Everything went so wrong so fast."

Not the answer Sweetie was seeking.

Sweetie raised his purr volume another notch, and I felt a strong wave of love radiate over Amanda. I, too, increased my focus and sent my own wave of affection upward through her hands. Amanda's body softened. She said, "I love you guys."

Once again tears fell on my back, but no words were uttered. Twice Sweetie got up and leaned into her, but Amanda wasn't talking.

Finally the humans conceded defeat, and Professor Hoffman returned to the room. He gave Sweetie a sweet, loving kiss. He knew his friend had touched Amanda's heart.

He handed Amanda a bottle of water and quietly sat down. Perhaps now she might open up a little more to him. But she stayed silent.

"Amanda, you seem very upset," Professor Hoffman said gently.

Amanda began reciting her mantra. Sadly, despite her softening to us animals, her response to human intervention remained unchanged. Professor Hoffman wasn't able to get a thing out of her, and after a few minutes he reluctantly gave up.

On the way home Mom babbled, "What did she say? If only we knew what she told you. What else could we have done? Tell me Spunk, tell me."

I licked her hand. For the moment, that was all I could offer.

CHAPTER  42

When we got back home Mom called Frank to fill him in on our visit to the jail. She turned on the speakerphone, then went to fill the kettle. Initially her voice revealed that she was still uneasy starting a conversation with Frank, but once she got talking about Amanda and our visit, she quickly returned to her former ease.

"Do you believe it, Frank? It looked like they got Amanda to tell the truth, but we couldn't hear a single word! If I had known that would happen, I would have taped a hidden microphone to Spunky's collar!"

As the words fell out of her mouth, Mom heard her own idea for the first time. Her eyebrows shot upward and she asked, "Hey, Frank, why not? Could we do that? Do they make a tiny mic like that?"

Frank chuckled, "I'm sure they make a microphone small enough for a dog collar, but you know as well as I do that we can't secretly tape her! Even if we did ignore that legal detail—which we won't—no judge would ever allow a doggie wire! The one who wears a wire is required to testify in court to verify the evidence. Unfortunately, even Ms. Spunky wouldn't be able accomplish that feat."

Mom chuckled. "I guess a paw on the Bible and three barks isn't acceptable, huh? But I wasn't thinking of using a wire for your benefit, but for Joe Hoffman's. If he could learn the truth, maybe he'd be able to help this poor child put the pieces of her life back together. That's pretty much impossible when he's flying blind."

"I know," said Frank. "But Amanda isn't just a therapy patient, she's also a murder suspect in our custody, and the rules can't be bent. She agreed to therapy with Joe, and he informed her in advance that periodically an associate of his would be observing, so what happened today was all legal. But we can't push it any further."

"I know, I know. Of course you're right. I'm just completely at a loss as to how we can get her to repeat what she told Spunky and Sweetie. That girl needs a friend!"

My head shot up. "Hey Sweetie," I said. "Mom just gave us the answer."

Sweetie meowed, "Spunk, what are you talking about? Frank said 'no' to you using a microphone."

I snorted, "The answer isn't microphone, Sweetie. The answer is a friend!"

CHAPTER  43

Later that day I held a planning session with the boys. First, I laid out the basics.

"Okay, we now know that Amanda has been lying to the cops. She didn't kill her father. We think she knows who did, but we couldn't get her to tell us. She trusts us, but we need to transfer that trust to a human. So far, Professor Hoffman hasn't been able to make that connection, but from what Mom's told us Amanda does in fact have a friend—Nancy. They've been friends since childhood, and even when Amanda joined that new pack she made sure Nancy was included. Amanda didn't abandon Nancy, so maybe we can use that bond to our advantage."

Fearless used his own experience to illustrate. "Yeah, like when I was a kitten and got injured *(breath)*, the momma cats carried me here to Mom *(breath)*, so then you guys became my new clowder."

I don't know if there is actually a scientific name for our blended pack of cats, a human, and a dog. I simply call it—family.

Fearless continued, "Even though I hadn't seen the free spirits for years *(breath)*, once our paths crossed again *(breath)* we were automatically connected by our past. *(Breath.)* If Amanda and Nancy have that kind of bond *(breath)*, maybe it can help us *(breath)* help her."

Bobby butted in, "Great, but how do we find this Nancy character?"

Silence filled the room. We knew about Nancy, but we didn't know who Nancy was.

But I was not about to be deterred. "Rule number eighteen: Every problem has a solution if you're willing to see it. The fact that we can't see it right now doesn't mean a solution doesn't exist. Let's review what we know about Nancy."

Sweetie was the first to chime in. "Mom described Nancy's pack of friends: three scrawny, malnourished blondes, plus Nancy, a healthier-looking brunette who wears too much makeup."

"That's right," I said. "What else do we know?"

Bobby jumped in. "Well, we know where to find them during the week—at the school."

Fearless provided the next piece. "If they're a pack, they might leave school together. *(Breath.)* And we might see them. *(Breath.)* How many packs can there be that contain *(breath)* three skinny blondes and a plumper brunette?"

Fancy-Pants was not about to be left out of this discussion. "Even if we see several packs like that, we could split up and track each pack. We only need to get close enough to hear what they're saying. Eventually one of them will call another by name, and since Mom already told us their names we'll know right away when we've found the right pack."

Yahoo! We were on a roll! I added, "Then, once we've identified the right pack, we can follow Nancy to her house. And once we know where she lives, we can make contact on our terms."

Then Bobby introduced an obstacle. "Okay, say we do find her, fine. How are we going to get her to the jail to see Amanda?"

Obviously, Bobby is not a terrier. But I am, and I'm all about tenacity. "We'll figure that part out later, Bobby. Believe me, brother, if we find Nancy she's going to the jail one way or another."

How was I going to make that happen? I didn't have a clue, but today I didn't need to know how, only that I would.

Rule number three: You may not see the solution to a problem, but never stop believing you'll figure it out. Keep the faith and move forward.

CHAPTER  44

When school ended the next day, we implemented stage one of our plan. In order to determine how many packs of girls we might have to track, the four cats and I hid in the bushes outside the school's main entrance. Since one of the girls might remain after school, we looked at packs that had three skinny blondes but no brunette, or ones that had a brunette and at least two skinny blondes. When the dismissal bell rang and the doors opened, it was a shock to see such an abundance of skinny, malnourished blonde girls.

By the time the main rush dwindled we had counted twenty packs that met our criteria. There was no way we could follow them all. But even before I voiced the obvious problem, Fearless supplied a solution. "I'll run over to the college and tell the Campus Cats *(breath)* we will need trackers tomorrow."

The next day we had more than enough trackers. But keeping twenty-plus cats inconspicuous was another challenge. Our feline phone line wove its way between the bushes and behind the trees. Fearless and I lay at the head of the line, closest to the door. When a qualifying pack of girls appeared, I'd nod and Fearless would pass it down the line. Then the cat at the end of the line would break away and follow them. Within a matter of minutes, our well-choreographed routine resulted in one tracker following each pack of girls, and we still had three trackers to spare.

Later that evening, when all the trackers had reported back, we'd narrowed the prospects down to ten possible packs. The others were dropped because their tracker had heard them use the wrong names. But we still hadn't heard anyone use the *right* names.

The next school day we were back at it. Whenever one of our ten candidate packs emerged, their previously assigned tracker followed them. Each tracker secretly hoped to be the one who had been assigned to the coveted prize.

Fancy-Pants won! His assigned pack contained a suspect brunette and one less blonde than the day before. He set off behind them, and after only fifteen minutes he hit the jackpot. They went down several neighborhood streets and past many houses before the brunette veered away and started up a walkway to one of the houses. She turned her head back toward the group and said, "See you tomorrow, Pamela." One of the blondes then replied, "If you say so, Nancy."

Bingo. Fancy had found Nancy's house!

CHAPTER  45

After dinner, Fearless and I took a leisurely stroll out to the barn.

"There are too many unknowns in this puzzle," I said.

"Like?"

"First, who is the unknown man who Nancy said picked up Amanda after school? Why didn't Amanda tell Nancy about him, and where did he go? Second, why did the teacher Mr. Whitehead say that he walked into the kitchen and found Amanda standing over her father's body? My nose says he was in the living room with both Amanda and Mr. Pederson. So, why did he lie? Third, what is it with Amanda's mother? That woman is one strange momma dog. Why doesn't she defend her daughter?

"Fourth, and most importantly, why is Amanda lying? We now know she didn't kill her father, so why lie? Who is she protecting? I swear, Fearless, the deeper we dig, the more questions we uncover."

"But Spunk, how many holes *(breath)* do you have to dig when you're looking for *(breath)* your special bone?"

I chuckled. "My friend, I have to dig a lot of holes, because I always forget where I put my bones!"

"Okay, *(breath)*. But you never stop digging *(breath)* until you find it."

"True, true. My terrier brain doesn't know how to quit." I paused, then said, "So maybe we should dig a little deeper into one of the existing holes to see if we missed a bone."

"Huh?"

"Mr. Whitehead, my friend. I think we need to dig some more in that hole. And we still need to figure out how to get Nancy to the jail to see Amanda. That'll take some doing."

Fearless shrugged nonchalantly and said, "The Campus Cats can help us with Mr. Whitehead *(breath)*. Meanwhile, getting Nancy to the jail *(breath)* may not be as complicated as it appears."

"You've always been a clever fellow," I said. "And the solution is…"

Simultaneously, we both said, "Mom!"

I snorted. "Dang, Fearless, you're good. Yeah, Mom needs to talk to Nancy about the importance of befriending Amanda again. But have you also come up with how we get Mom to do that?"

"Getting Mom over to Nancy's house *(breath)* won't be a problem. But first we have to get the idea *(breath)* to use Nancy into her head, and *(breath)* I know only one way to accomplish that."

"The zone!"

"The zone" is a special place a human mind can go when they stroke an animal and allow themselves to relax. Over the years we've given Mom a lot of practice at this. When she enters that peaceful state, she shuts off the voices in her head; and I believe that's when our thoughts can filter through and mingle with hers. Of course, it's possible that all we actually do is increase her tranquility, but I do know that time after time she emerges from "the zone" with a new idea that matches an idea we wanted to plant in her mind. We now needed to get her into that zone ASAP!

An opportunity arose later that evening. After Mom finished the dishes, she went and sat in her favorite chair, picked up a book, and started to read. But before long her sighing and fidgeting told us she was having difficulty concentrating. Seeing my cue, I jumped into her lap.

"Hey, Spunk, did you come for a visit? I sure don't mind the interruption; I'm having a hard time getting into this book."

Fearless jumped onto the arm of the chair.

"My, my both of you! What did I do to deserve such a gift?"

I kissed her nose. Many things, Mom. You're the best! I turned around and presented a proven mediation-enhancer, my back. Fearless rubbed against Mom's shoulder, then settled in beside me.

"Ah, the perfect peace combo." Mom leaned back, closed her eyes and said, "Now if only you could make my anxiety about Amanda disappear." With one hand on each of us, she began stroking our bodies. Gradually the strokes became softer and more rhythmic. Her breathing deepened, and her body began to relax. As she drifted into the zone, Fearless and I focused on one word: Nancy.

190

Within a few moments Mom softly muttered, "But how…?"

I envisioned our answer.

Mom drifted deeper into the zone. Unfortunately, however, a less desirable outcome occurred. Mom began to snore. Apparently we had done our job a little too well!

CHAPTER 46

While Mom slept, we headed out in search of the Campus Cats. Luckily for us, Goliath was spending a quiet evening sprawled on the grass outside his home.

"Evening, Goliath, how come you're not out gallivanting?"

He snorted. "Heck, Spunk, cavorting is for the young."

I grinned, "Ain't that the truth! Where's Einstein tonight?"

Goliath smirked. "That boy will never admit he's too old for anything! Sit down a spell and enjoy the cool grass."

"Thanks, but I'm afraid this isn't a social visit. We need your help again."

"No problem. Your adventures keep me young. Whaddaya need?"

Fearless chimed in, "Mr. Whitehead *(breath)*. We need to learn more about the man."

I added, "The problem is he just goes to school, comes home, and doesn't seem to do much else. How can we learn anything about the man if he doesn't go anywhere except the school and home?"

Goliath said, "Well, a predictable routine does make it easier to know where he'll be."

"Yeah, but we can't see behind walls."

"He's a teacher at the high school, right?"

"Right."

Goliath slowly nodded his head. "I have associates at the school. They might be willing to spy for us, if the price is right"

I exclaimed, "Cats live at the school?"

"Well, yeah, in the basement. But they'd be in big trouble if they were caught upstairs during school hours. No, the allies I'm referring to are mice."

"Mice! You have a friend who's a mouse?"

"Quite a few, to be precise. The mice at the school have an arrangement with the basement cats, who, in turn, have an arrangement with me."

"Huh?"

"A few years ago, the school had a serious rodent problem. The maintenance supervisor, Mr. Johnson, didn't want to use poison around the kids, so he adopted two cats from the shelter and made them a lovely home in the basement. At first the cats did exactly what cats do, and annihilated a mess of mice. But then the chief mouse, Tito, whom I've known since he was a young-un, came to see me, and I helped negotiate a truce. We agreed that the mice would limit their colony to a specified number and wouldn't roam around during school hours, except at designated intervals when certain mice go out on daytime missions in order to be seen by the teachers. Tito always lets me know in advance when such a sighting is scheduled, and then one of my crew catches a field mouse and hands it over to the school cats. After the teachers report a sighting to Mr. Johnson, the cats deposit the dead field mouse on the stairs for Mr. Johnson to find. That makes Mr. Johnson happy, and it reinforces the importance of the cats in the basement, which helps assure that their living situation will continue. As payment for their protection, the mice bring me and the school cats tasty cheese tidbits from the kitchen. And I can call on the school cats for help when I need it."

"Very impressive," I said. "A win-win for everyone!"

Goliath groomed his whiskers. "Spunk, you know as well as I do, a treaty only works if all sides get something they want."

"Do you think Tito would be willing to help us?"

"I do. He's always imagined himself a bit of a detective. Let me talk to him and see what I can work out."

As we headed back home I said to Fearless, "I think Goliath could negotiate anything, even world peace."

Fearless snorted, "Sadly, Spunk *(breath),* too many humans view compromise as a weakness *(breath),* not a strength."

"Poor foolish souls."

CHAPTER 47

Mom was already in bed reading the same book when we arrived home.

"Aw, there you two are," she said with a smile. "I knew you'd be fine, but I couldn't fall asleep until I knew you were home for the night."

Mom drifted off to sleep right away, and we were again denied any "zone" activity. But the next morning, as Mom sipped her coffee, we saw our seeds begin to sprout.

"It was the weirdest thing, Spunky," she said. "Last night I dreamt about Nancy. Why she popped into my head is beyond me, but it gave me an idea. If I could get Nancy to visit Amanda, maybe—just maybe—Amanda might confide in her. If nothing else, at least Amanda might not feel so alone. But I have no idea how to get to Nancy. I suppose I could hang around the school and try to talk to her, but those girls seem to travel in a pack, which isn't very conducive to having a discussion. Or I could try to get her alone, like before, but that might take a while. I even thought about asking the principal to give me her address, but that would be unethical so that's a no-go. I thought about hanging around outside the school and following her, but I'm sure the rest of the herd would spot me. Besides, an old gal like me hanging around outside the school would look pretty dumb, even creepy. So I'm stumped. Any ideas?"

Although we knew Mom was only talking to herself, we weren't about to pass up the opportunity. I barked twice.

Mom jumped. "What? I certainly wasn't expecting an answer."

Seek and yea shall find, Momma! I jumped off her lap, went to the back door, pulled my leash off the hook, and returned with it hanging out of my mouth.

"What? You want to go for a walk now?"

Well, not exactly. Fearless leaped onto the counter, and before Mom could work up a reprimand, he snagged a claw around Mom's key ring and dropped her keys onto the floor.

Mom quickly linked the clues. "Okay, you want me to drive you somewhere, right?"

I barked an affirmation, and right after breakfast we were on our way.

Fearless sat quietly in the back seat, confidant that I could handle directing Mom to Nancy's house. Of course, when we got there Mom had no idea why we made her stop in front of that particular house. She assumed the answer must be inside so she got out and rang the bell. Luckily, Nancy's parents weren't home; Mom would have had trouble explaining her presence if a stranger had answered the door. And of course Nancy was at school; so no one answered the door at all

When she got back in the car, Mom said, "Now what is this all about? Obviously you wanted me to come here, right?"

I snorted and licked her hand.

"But there's no one here. So now what?"

Fearless jumped into the front seat and placed his paw on the dashboard clock. I joined in by pointed at it with my nose.

"The clock? Okay, I see the time. Do you want me to wait for something?"

We didn't budge. We stayed silent.

"Okay, not that. Do you mean this is the wrong time?"

That earned her a bark.

She looked at both of us intently. Her mental wheels were turning, and she verbalized her thinking process. "Okay, before you got me here we were talking about Nancy. Do you mean to tell me this is Nancy's house?"

Another bark!

"How could you possibly know that?"

We ignored her question and swiveled our heads toward the house. "Okay, okay," Mom said. "Who knows how you two ever figure out half the things you do! But if this is Nancy's house, then she's in school, so…you want me to come back later. Is that it?"

Two happy barks sealed the deal.

All the way home Mom kept muttering, "How in heaven's name do you know where Nancy lives? How could you possibly know that?"

Mom, some things in life must remain a mystery!

CHAPTER  48

Later that morning, Mom met with a new client on line. Her name was Lucy, and her very first question set her apart from all the others.

"Excuse me, Dr. Richards, but are you a Christian therapist?"

Mom, though startled, quietly answered, "I don't claim to be one."

"But are you?"

"Would you tell me why that's important to you?"

"Because I'm a Christian, and I need to know your beliefs. Are you a Christian?"

Mom paused. She may have been thinking about how much she should or wanted to reveal. She then said, "Lucy, even if two people are both Christians, their religious beliefs can vary greatly."

Lucy paused, "Okay, valid point. So what church do you attend?"

Even I knew this was a step too far. Mom let out a breath. "If you're looking for a therapist who has the same religious beliefs as you, wouldn't it be better to get a referral from your church or your pastor?"

"I already did that," Lucy said, "and quite frankly both of the therapists they recommended were sweet and nice, but not at all helpful. I don't need someone quoting the Bible to me. I need someone to help me. So please tell me, what do you believe?"

Mom said gently, "Lucy, I honestly don't think it should matter what a therapist's religious beliefs are. Their religious, political, or personal beliefs shouldn't determine how they conduct themselves as a therapist. My job isn't to judge you, but to help you process and problem-solve your life based on what *you* believe. Your beliefs are part of what makes you who you are. My question to you is, if I were to give you advice that went against your beliefs, why wouldn't you just tell me that you disagree?"

Lucy dropped her head and mumbled, "Because I'm suppose to accept the guidance of those in authority over me."

Mom sat up straighter, squared her shoulders, frowned slightly, and said, "Lucy, accepting guidance and blindly obeying someone are two very different things. I can tell you this: no therapist should claim to have that authority over you, or try to impose it on you. In fact, *no one* has the right to absolute authority over you. A boss may have authority over how you do your job, a parent has certain authority over a minor, and I grant that different religions recognize varying levels of spiritual authority. But how much authority you grant to anyone is completely up to you. A person always has a choice to accept or reject someone's guidance or instruction. Anyone who asks that you give up that choice, or requires blind obedience, I believe is wrong and may even be dangerous."

Lucy looked up, cocked her head and said, "But what about the Bible? Isn't that the ultimate authority we all have to follow?"

Mom smiled and gently said, "Lucy, when the good Lord returns, maybe then humans will finally agree on which interpretation of the Bible is correct. Until that time, I operate under the premise that God, in all His infinite wisdom, opted to leave man his free will, and so do I."

"But then how do you know if what an elder tells you to do is right?"

"That question has many answers. Some Christians might say you should pray, ask for wisdom, listen to your spirit, and try to discern if that guidance confirms what you already know to be the truth. I happen to believe wise counsel brings peace, not condemnation."

Lucy leaned in, "How can you tell…"

Mom knew it was time to redirect the conversation. She held up her hand, "Lucy, I'm not a pastor, and with all due respect, this isn't a Bible class. We could have a lengthy discussion about my beliefs versus yours, but that isn't what therapy is about. The question is why do you think you need help?"

"Because I've been fired twice for trying to save everyone."

"That could make it difficult to earn a living," Mom said gently.

"Do you think you can help me?"

Mom paused before she said, "If you're asking me to resolve a religious conflict for you, then no, I can't help you. A pastor should be able to do that for you. But if you want to find a better balance between your religious beliefs and the practicalities of living in this world, then yes, I may be able to help you. But I need to make something clear. It doesn't matter to me if my client is an atheist, a Jew, a Muslim, or a Christian. I believe the main goal of therapy is to improve a person's ability to function in this world. What god people choose to believe in is entirely up to them. I think therapy should affect what a person believes about himself, not the deity he believes in. Make sense?"

Lucy nodded. "Yes, but if you're an atheist, how can you understand my beliefs or my world?"

"Every client has a unique set of values and beliefs. Some beliefs come from religion, some from ethnic groups, some from families, and some from one's own sense of self-worth. My job is to help people explore the impact of those beliefs on their lives. If one or more of those beliefs causes so much conflict that it leads someone to seek help, then the real issue may not be the belief, but why the belief is causing them distress. My goal is to try to help people answer that question."

Lucy sighed. "You make it sound easy."

"No, I wouldn't say it's easy. It can be challenging for people to look at themselves honestly, but I sincerely believe that if people have the courage to explore who they are and why they do what they do, then they can move forward."

"How does one begin?"

Mom's face softened as she said, "By talking, taking it one step at a time, and you deciding for yourself if you feel comfortable and can trust me."

For the first time Lucy smiled. "I think I'd like to begin."

Mom nodded. "Then we shall."

CHAPTER  49

Later that day Mom drove us back to Nancy's neighborhood. She was smart and parked on the opposite side of the street and a few doors down from Nancy's house. That way she could see anyone walking toward the house from the school.

We waited.

Mom didn't know that we already had an alert system in place, in case Nancy didn't come straight home after school. While Mom was busy counseling Lucy, Fearless had collaborated with Goliath on a plan. As a result, Fancy-Pants and Lion King were waiting outside the school. Goliath and a bunch of other cats had already formed a line from the school to Nancy's house, with Goliath in the last position, nearest the house. When Nancy left school, Fancy-Pants and Lion King would follow her. The cat chain would send us updates as to their position, and we would know if she veered off course. The pairing of Lion King and Fancy-Pants was the key. Although Fancy-Pants was the one who could identify Nancy, many of the cats didn't know him. On the other hand, every cat out there knew Lion King, so the combination of the two made reporting their location foolproof.

Twenty minutes later, one very large, furry feline landed with a thump on the hood of Mom's car.

Mom jumped. "Oh my gracious! Who the heck is that?" She paused, leaned forward, squinted, and said, "Wait a minute, I know that cat. That's Goliath, right?"

A soft woof told her she was correct.

Fearless meowed twice to inform me that this meant Nancy had veered off course and was not heading home. Mom got out of the car and approached Goliath slowly. "Well, hello there, handsome. Are you okay? What are you doing here?"

Goliath already knew Mom from our previous adventures, so he tucked his head down and rubbed against her outstretched hand. Mom graciously accepted the honor and gently scratched his head.

"Given past events, I assume you're not here by happenstance. You're working with those two, correct?" Goliath purred louder and knocked her hand with his head. Mom smiled. "So now all I have to do is figure out why you're here. Would you excuse me for a minute?"

Mom stuck her head back into the car. "Okay you two, Goliath showing up like this means you want me to know something, correct?" I nodded and snorted.

"Odds are you knew that if Goliath landed that hard on my car I'd get out to make sure he was okay, which I did. Getting out of the car would expose me to being seen, and since I don't see Nancy anywhere down the street, does this mean she isn't coming?"

Boy, Mom was getting good at this! Once again, I nodded and gave her a snort.

"Okay then, we go home and try again tomorrow. Is that what you want me to do?"

That won her a clear affirming bark.

She offered Goliath a ride, but of course, he declined. A free spirit never willingly climbs into a car.

CHAPTER  50

On the way home Mom went past Judy's house. When she saw Judy's car in the driveway she stopped. Given Mom's own dislike of doorbells startling her, she phoned first.

"Hi there! The critters and I are in your driveway. Do you have time for a coffee?"

I guess the answer was yes, because Mom parked the car and we headed inside.

"Your timing is perfect," Judy said. "I was about to take a break."

Once the coffee was poured and we were given some chicken tidbits, Judy and Mom settled in at the table.

Mom began, "I had an interesting new client today. She led off the session by asking me if I was a Christian therapist."

"That's a first. Did you tell her you're a Believer?"

"Nope."

"Too personal?"

"Maybe, but I don't think that was my real reason. You and I both know there are so many different Christian doctrines out there that any two Christians could be worlds apart on the rules to live by. Besides, I don't believe therapy should be a platform for a religious debate, nor a Sunday school class."

"Amen to that! But knowing you and the strength of your beliefs, I marvel at how you can keep those beliefs to yourself with some of the people you treat."

Mom chuckled, "Believe me, I have to do my own work right along with my clients, and yeah, there have been a few, in fact one very recently, who pushed my buttons."

"What do you do when that happens?"

Mom chuckled again. "I pray, my friend. I pray a lot." She took a sip of coffee, then said, "Actually, if I have a strong reaction to someone, it's my job to figure out what triggered it. More times than not, the answer is that I need to get over myself. It's not my job to change them; they have to do that for themselves. Well, at least I try to remember that, anyway."

"Do you ever think about becoming a Christian counselor?"

Mom raised her eyebrows, tilted her head, smiled, and said, "Last I heard the Spirit is right there with me all the time. Sometimes I receive nuggets of wisdom that I know darn well don't come from my brain. I guess one could say that I am a Christian who's also a counselor, so I am already a Christian counselor. In truth, I don't really understand why going to a 'Christian counselor' is so important. A good therapist should help you sort out your beliefs without imposing their own, and a good pastor should teach you what your religious beliefs are all about."

Judy smiled at that. "From the stories I've heard, some 'Christian counselors' act like frustrated preachers and use therapy to guilt-trip people into adhering to the Bible."

"From my point of view, counselors like that are *mis*using therapy to try to get people to follow a set of religious doctrines."

Judy laughed. "And there, my friend lies the rub. This is where law and grace diverge."

"How true, how true! In all fairness, though, I've known a few good Christian counselors—and some lousy non-religious ones. Unfortunately, most people feel more comfortable firing a lousy plumber than a lousy therapist. My question is would you rather have an exceptional counselor who may or may not be a Christian, or an ineffective one who happens to be an outstanding Christian?"

"For my money and mental health, I'll take the former any day of the week." Judy then cocked her head. "Hey, on a different subject, how are things going with Frank since you became single again?"

Mom chuckled. "I wouldn't call seven days much of a test, but I think we're managing fairly well. The fact we have Amanda's case to talk about helps a lot. Maybe we should wait until Frank starts dating another woman to see the true strength of my resolve."

Judy nodded. "To use your words, how true, how true!"

CHAPTER 51

About one a.m. Fearless woke me with a gentle head-bop. "Spunk, Goliath sent word *(breath)* he wants to see us. *(Breath)*. Tito's with him. *(Breath)*. He wants us all to meet."

I sighed. "I wish cats and mice kept daytime business hours! Come on, let's get going."

When we arrived, Goliath was sitting by the tree in front of his house.

"Good evening—oops, I mean good morning, Goliath," I said. "I heard Tito was here, but I don't see him."

"Sorry to roust you so early, Spunk. I know you dogs need your beauty sleep."

I chuckled, "If we keep having these early meetings, my friend, I certainly might grow a few more grey hairs."

Fearless said, "I smell Tito *(breath)*, but I don't see him either."

Goliath smirked, "Oh, he's right here. Come on out, Tito. These are the friends I told you about."

The fur on the back of Goliath's neck began to move. It looked like a small tumor was growing out of his fur. Then a minuscule gray head with big eyes appeared, followed by a sweet, squeaky voice.

"Hello!"

"Tito says my neck is the safest spot in the whole world," said Goliath. "Tito, meet Ms. Spunky and Mr. Fearless."

Tito waved and squeaked, "Hi, guys!"

I snorted, "My, my! I've seen some unusual things over the years, but I've never seen a mouse emerge from the back of a cat. That's one for the books!"

Goliath nodded, albeit slowly so as not to dislodge Tito. "A mouse in cat territory faces many dangers, but my gang knows Tito is protected, so they don't mess with him. In fact, my guys would fight to protect him, but we never know if an interloper is lurking about who doesn't know the rules and might do him harm. So when Tito needs to see me, he sends word and I dispatch an escort team to fetch him."

"It's great to be escorted by two friendly cat guards," said Tito, "but up here is the coziest, safest place of all. I plan on retiring right here!"

Goliath laughed a deep belly laugh. "That, my friend, will cost you a heck of a lot of cheese! Now, tell Spunky what you learned about Mr. Whitehead."

My jaw dropped. "You know something already? It was only yesterday that we asked Goliath for help."

Tito stood up as tall as he could on his hind legs, clasped his tiny hands across his puffed-out his little chest, and said, "Ms. Spunky, when Tito's Detective Agency is on the case, we do not rest. But I admit this one did present some challenges to my sleuthing skills. First, let me say that the easiest part was observing the man in his classroom. His room is on the second floor, and we have dozens of ways to get into the crawl space above it. It only takes an easy nibble on that flimsy foil ductwork and, *voilà*, we have free access to the ceiling vents, which make great observation posts. I didn't see anything weird going on in his classroom—apart from the fact I had to endure too much human history. Mr. Whitehead acted fine. He was kind to the kids, and he's very patient. Well, I should say he's patient with the kids. I can't say that with regard to critters."

"What do you mean, Tito?"

"Mr. Whitehead is well known to us mice. When we're out on a planned teacher sighting, we avoid him at all costs. Most of us head to Miss Gatsby's room. We love taunting that poor dear. You should hear her shriek! Loud, yes, but so adorable—plus, she's absolutely harmless. Mr. Whitehead, on the other hand, yells, curses, throws books and erasers and anything that isn't nailed down. The man is a mouse bigot!"

Fearless nudged me. "As I recall *(breath),* he wasn't particularly fond of cats and dogs *(breath)* either."

"So you learned nothing we can use?"

Tito shook his little finger at me. "Patience, Ms. Spunky, patience. All will be revealed. As you know, Whitehead goes home every day for lunch. A good detective stays with his subject, and I wasn't about to let him out of my sight, so I needed to follow him to his house. That was a bit tricky because of the car and all, but I had a plan. Early this morning I sent my team out to the parking lot to watch for Mr. Whitehead's arrival, and they told me where he parked. As soon as the lunch bell rang, I ran downstairs and out one of our many secret exits. Then I waited behind the tire of his car, and when he opened the door and got in, I jumped in right behind his seat." Tito laughed and smacked his tiny thigh, "He never saw a thing!"

I was impressed. "Wow, Tito, you're amazing!"

"Hey, being my size does have a few advantages. So, off we went to Mr. Whitehead's house. Of course, I'd never been there, so I didn't know if he had a cat or some other mouse monsters. I couldn't smell any cat odor in the car, but I knew I might be heading into a war zone. I also knew that the odds of being seen would be much greater if I tried to run into the house with him. This was where a certain weird behavior of his paid off. As every mouse knows, Mr. Whitehead is never separated from his briefcase. He takes it with him everywhere, even to the bathroom. Weird, huh? Today was no exception. His briefcase was sitting right there on the passenger's seat, so while he focused on driving, I crept along the floor to the far side of the car, climbed into the passenger seat, and hid behind his briefcase. The tricky part came when we arrived at his house. He turned off the motor, reached over and grabbed the case with his right hand, and immediately turned away as he stepped out of the car. I was counting on him not looking closely at what he was doing. Sure enough, he never noticed this tiny mouse hanging on to the soft leather folds at the back of his case.

"I got a safe but bumpy ride all the way inside. Once there, I sprinted to safety under his desk, where I could assess the environment for danger. While Mr. Whitehead was making a sandwich, I scoped out the terrain and determined

212

it was only the two of us. That makes sense, given his apparent dislike of four-leggeds."

"He took his sandwich and a glass of milk into his office, and sat down at his computer. Now comes the interesting part—interesting, but creepy. The whole time he was eating lunch, Mr. Whitehead looked at pictures of young girls on the computer."

My head jerked up. "What? Are you saying he's one of those creeps we all want to sink our teeth into?"

Tito scratched his head. "Well, not really. None of the girls was naked, thank goodness. That would have been more than my sensibilities could bear. It was more like he was looking for something or someone in particular."

"How do you know that?" I asked. "No offense intended, but what do mice know about computers?"

The sweetest little laugh sprinkled out of Tito. "No offense taken, Ms. Spunky, but you forget, I live in a school! There are computers everywhere. My personal favorite is in Mrs. Langston's home economics class. She has food shows playing all day long. Some nights she forgets to turn the computer off, and it goes to sleep mode; so all we have to do is jump on the enter key and wake it up. With a few clever dance moves around the keyboard, we have a whole night of mouth-watering entertainment!"

Goliath cleared his throat, reminding Tito to return to the matter at hand.

"Sorry, I digress. Anyway, I saw Mr. Whitehead log on to several different websites. He already had his own passwords, so he's been there before. And it seemed like the pictures were there waiting for him—and every one of them was of a teenage girl."

"I don't like the sound of that," Goliath grumbled.

I nodded. "Yeah, sounds creepy to me too. Did you see anything else?"

Tito shook his head. "Nothing important. Other than that he eats bologna sandwiches and doesn't leave leftovers—not even crumbs!"

Fearless smiled, then asked, "How did you get back *(breath)* home?"

Tito beamed. "Same way, my friend! I took the briefcase express back to the car, and Mr. Whitehead's taxi service brought me right back to the school."

I was sincere when I said, "Tito, you were extremely brave to get into that car with a known mouse-hater. I can't thank you enough for helping us."

"Thanks, Spunk. Should I keep up my surveillance?"

"I certainly don't want to put you at any further risk." I paused, then asked, "Tell me something, which way was his computer facing?

Tito smiled and raised his little index finger. "Ah, I see where you're headed. The computer faces the east window; and yes, his back was to the window."

"Were the blinds shut?"

"Nope. In that room he has curtains, and they were pulled back. I know because I was hiding in the folds."

"Great! Goliath, would you find out whether Hobo and his lady friends are willing to do some surveillance work for us?"

"Sure thing, Spunk. I'll bet we can also get the raccoons to help, if he leaves those drapes open and works at night."

"Good idea! Tito, again, I can't thank you enough. I don't have a clue what it all means, but I do think you've uncovered some important information."

Tito's tiny little chest swelled. "Thanks, Spunk! I'll maintain surveillance of the subject at the school. Let me know if there is anything else the mice can do for you."

As we headed back home I said to Fearless, "Tito may be little, but he sure has some big *cojones*."

"Yeah," Fearless said. "Plus he's so freakin' *(breath)* cute!"

CHAPTER 52

Later that day Mom drove us back to Nancy's house. The rest of our crew returned to their assigned posts from the day before. After about twenty minutes, Fearless meowed an alert and turned to face the window. Coming toward us were four cats walking in a group. Well, I should say that the four cats weren't merely walking, they were strutting their stuff. The one in the lead, a fluffy white gal, held her tail high and sashayed her booty with attitude. The two directly behind her mimicked her every move, while the fourth shuffled along like a sad sack with her head and tail drooping. She looked like a deflated balloon. The message was clear: We couldn't yet see them, but we knew exactly who was headed our way—three blondes and a Nancy.

I waited until I saw the girls come into view, then I nudged Mom's elbow and pointed my nose down the street.

Mom turned and said, "Okay, I see them. Shoot, the three nincompoops are with her. How will I get to talk to her if they stick around?"

Fear not, we had a plan for that. As soon as the girls passed our car I nudged Mom again, but this time I had my leash in my mouth.

"What? You want to go for a walk *now*? If those three see me it will ruin everything."

I nudged her again and stared at her with a hard eye. She studied my face.

"Okay, you're right. I forgot, you're the one that got me here in the first place, so you must have a plan. What do you want me to do?"

I dropped the leash, turned, and pawed the door handle. Mom got the message and quietly opened my door. I slid out onto the sidewalk, but not before receiving a stern warning. "You better watch yourself out there, missy, or you'll be in big trouble."

That was a given. To ease her mind, I plunked my rump down on the sidewalk so Mom could see me through the open door. No sense pushing my luck unless I had to.

The pack of girls stopped at Nancy's gate and stood there talking. Nancy pointed at her house and said something, and the girls turned and walked toward the front door.

Time to move. After checking for traffic, I ran straight through a muddy puddle and made a beeline for the blonde with the most arrogant walk. I jumped against her leg and deposited some artistic though very dirty paw prints on her pants. She squealed, "Argh! You little shit, look what you did! These are my Calvin Kleins!"

I quickly turned and jumped on blonde number two and gave her a nice big pair of paw prints. Additional paw-painting on blonde number three proved unnecessary, as they were already headed down the street. They were cussing a blue streak, threatening to call animal control and yelling that they had to get home to wash off the muck before it ruined their pants.

Gee whiz, it was only mud!

I turned around and cocked my head at Nancy. She chuckled. "Well, that was fun! I wish I could splatter them with mud and get away with it!" She knelt down and gave me a fine head scratch. "Now, who do you belong to?"

"That would be me."

Nancy's head jerked upward. "What? Dr. Richards! What are you doing here?"

Mom smiled and said gently, "Sorry if I startled you. That smart little dog is Spunky, and she ran off Pamela and the girls so that I could talk to you without them seeing me."

Nancy laughed. "Well, Ms. Spunky, you certainly made my day!" Then reality registered, and Nancy's eyes darted down the street toward the girls. She looked down at the ground and mumbled, "What do you want?"

"Would it be okay if we sat on the porch?"

"We should probably go inside, in case they come back to yell at me for letting a dog to do that to them."

"Why would they blame you for that?"

"I didn't say it had to make sense. They blame me for stuff all the time that isn't my fault. It's just what they do. Do you want to come in? My mom's still at work."

"Yes, thank you. That would be nice. Would it be okay if Spunky comes in too, or should I put her back in the car?"

Nancy pulled a tissue from her pocket. "No, she can come inside, as long as her paws are clean. My Mom would have a fit if she saw muddy paw prints—but we'll be careful, won't we Spunky?"

Nancy was good people. She wiped my feet, then I licked her hand, and we went inside.

The house smelled like a bottle of Pine Sol! It looked more like a display home than one where real people lived. Everything was sparse, in its place, and void of any human clutter. Nancy took off her shoes at the door. "Please wipe your feet."

"I'll do better than that." Mom also took off her shoes. "Spunk," she said, "you stay off the furniture, understand?"

Nancy smiled. "Thanks."

We went into the kitchen. Everything gleamed. I'll bet no one dared to drop any food around here!

After Mom and Nancy sat down at the table, I jumped against Nancy's leg and begged for her lap. Nancy patted her permission, and I took full advantage. I turned and gave her my back to scratch.

Mom explained why we had come, but before she could finish Nancy interjected, "I can't go see Amanda."

"Why not?"

"If Pamela found out, she'd make my life a living hell." Nancy mumbled.

"I understand your anxiety, but we could go on Saturday or in the evening, if that would make you feel safer. I don't see how they would know."

Nancy sighed. "Amanda doesn't want to see me."

Mom cocked her head. "I seriously doubt that. She seems very depressed. I think she could really use a friend, and you're the only person I know of who qualifies."

Nancy stared Mom in the eye, and then in a slow, firm voice said, "I don't believe for one second that she killed her dad. I don't care what anyone says."

"See, what I mean? She needs someone who believes in her."

"But the cops will be listening."

"I promise you I'll try to make sure that doesn't happen, but if I can't be certain then I'll tell you in advance. Is that fair?"

"Yeah, I guess so."

"Nancy, think for a moment. How would you feel if the roles were reversed?"

"I can't. It's too terrible!" She paused and then said, "I guess I could try. I owe her that much."

"Thank you. I do believe it will be a good thing."

As Mom and Nancy talked some more, I narrowed my focus to one thought. Then as if on cue, Nancy asked, "Could Spunky come with me? I'd feel braver if she did."

Mom smiled. "She does have that effect on people. Since Amanda's already met Spunky, she could be a great icebreaker. Of course, she can go with you."

They set a time on Saturday for Mom to pick Nancy up and exchanged phone numbers in case there was a problem. Then as Mom was leaving, she turned, opened her arms, and said, "Would you mind if I gave you hug? I'm very proud of you for having the courage to see Amanda."

Nancy's immediate response was to step back, but then she smiled and stepped into Mom's arms. I watched Nancy slowly melt into Mom's hug.

I've seen scared puppies act the same way.

CHAPTER  53

The next morning Goliath not only waited until the sun was up, he personally came to our neighborhood. I expressed my gratitude. "It certainly was kind of you to wait for daylight and come all the way over here yourself. Not necessary, but definitely appreciated."

Goliath smiled. "The time and place for a meeting depend on how many felines are involved. Today it's just me, so no problem. Actually, it was just after midnight when Hobo and the raccoons reported in to me, but I thought it would be okay to delay bringing you the update.

"Do you remember early on when Hobo said it was odd that Mr. Whitehead's blinds were drawn tight, because this time of year he usually keeps them all open—day and night?"

"Yeah, that was one of the things that tipped Hobo off that something was amiss."

"Well, as Tito said, this guy is a creature of habit, and luckily for us he went back to his old ways. Last night every blind and curtain in the house was wide open again. Hobo sat on a garbage can outside Whitehead's window and had an excellent view of the computer screen. After the sun went down he started getting bleary-eyed so he asked the raccoons to take over. They reported that Whitehead spent hours on that computer last night, doing the exact same thing Tito saw him do."

"Looking at pictures of young girls?"

"Yup, and the raccoons said the only girls he spent time really focusing on were white teenagers. He printed out several photos and put them in his briefcase. He looked up some other stuff too, but the raccoons weren't sure what it was all about."

I said, "Something stinks."

"I agree. The man apparently has no life apart from school and that computer, and he hangs on to that briefcase as if his life depended on it. Something is not right. Do you think we should keep the peeping Toms in place again tonight?"

"Maybe for a night or two, but I'm not sure we'll learn much more. As you said, he's a creature of habit, so he'll probably just keep doing the same thing. Maybe Hobo can keep an eye out and give you a heads-up if he sees anything different. Please thank all of them for being such good spies."

After Goliath left, Fearless summed it up pretty well. "Like I've said before *(breath)*, if a man hates critters *(breath)*, look for a deeper problem."

"I agree, my friend. But the question is how deep, and how dark?

222

CHAPTER 54

When we pulled into Nancy's driveway on Saturday she was waiting on the porch. As Nancy walked toward the car, Mom rolled down the window and asked, "Is your mother home? I'd like to meet her. I'm sorry I do not know her name."

"No ma'am, she's at work. Her name is Susan. Susan Evans" answered Nancy.

Nancy got in the car and Mom asked, "Is she okay with me taking you to see Amanda?"

"She said it was up to me, but..."

"But? Does she have any objections I should know about?"

"No, she said it was fine. She's more worried about the dirt and germs in the jail than anything else. It's okay. That's just the way she is."

"Does she suffer from germaphobia?"

Nancy nodded. "Yeah. She's always been that way, but it got a lot worse after Dad died."

"I'm so sorry to hear you lost your dad. When did that happen?"

Nancy turned her head away and looked out the window. "Ten years ago. He was in a car crash."

"Oh, that's terrible, and so sad! You would have only been—"

A loud meow came from the back seat. It startled Nancy, and she swung her head around. "What was that?"

Mom chuckled gently. "Sorry, I forgot to tell you. I decided to bring along an extra critter. That's Sweetie back there. He's quite special. Amanda's met him too, and they shared a very sweet moment together, so I thought she'd be happy to see him again. Do you like cats?"

"Not as much as dogs," Nancy said.

I licked her hand. Obviously, the girl had good taste! But she hadn't met Sweetie yet, so I knew her opinion of cats was about to change.

Mom tried to ask more about Nancy's family and the death of her father, but Nancy only shrugged and began asking questions about Sweetie and me. She obviously didn't want to discuss her family any further, which is exactly what Sweetie had just said. Mom may have missed Sweetie's clue, but she didn't miss Nancy's. She retreated and kept the conversation light.

When we arrived at the jail, Captain Swenson was there waiting for us. After allowing the appropriate amount of time for a proper meet and greet, Mom introduced Nancy. Captain Swenson shook her hand and in a kind voice said, "Dr. Richards tells me you're a friend of Amanda's, and you're worried about your visit staying private. I want to assure you, no one will be listening. You'll see a security camera in the room, but I have set it to visual only, no sound. For everyone's protection we are required to monitor when a prisoner has a visitor. But what you and Amanda say will be completely private."

Nancy smiled and nodded. "Thanks."

Captain Swenson escorted Nancy, Sweetie, and me into a visiting room. He put Sweetie's crate on the table and opened the door, and gave Sweetie a fine scratch behind the ears. He showed Nancy a button to push when she was ready to leave, or in case there were any problems. As he left he gave me a smile and a knowing wink.

Nancy patted her lap and I took my place. Sweetie walked across the table and lay down within petting distance, but was respectful of Nancy's personal space. Being a gentleman, Sweetie never crowds a non-cat person. It's bad manners. But he did turn up his purr volume to send a warm and welcoming message. Nancy couldn't help but notice. She smiled and tentatively reached out one finger. Sweetie lowered his head as an offering of friendship, and Nancy gave it a rub.

"My, my, Sweetie you sure purr loud! I must admit, you're a very handsome cat—though not nearly as cute as Ms. Spunky."

As I said, good taste.

The door opened. Nancy raised her head as a guard accompanied Amanda into the room. Neither girl spoke. They reminded me of two dogs reuniting after a prolonged separation—tentative, guarded, and with no eye contact. Amanda sat down and stared at the floor.

The guard left, but the silence remained.

Sweetie decided it was time for the silence to end. He walked across the table to Amanda, leaned in and rubbed against her, which made Amanda look up and focus. "Well, hello to you too! What a wonderful surprise. I didn't know you'd be here today."

Not wanting to be rude, I woofed softly. Amanda looked over at me, which meant she also had to look at Nancy. "Hello there, Ms. Spunky." Her eyes and voice then dropped as she said, "Hi, Nance."

I felt Nancy's breath on my back as she, too, dropped her head. "Hey." she said softly. "How are you? You don't look so good."

Amanda actually laughed. "That's a heck of thing to say to a friend!"

Nancy mumbled softly, "Am I? Am I still your friend?"

Amanda sighed and her voice softened. "Nance, I'm so sorry for the way I acted. You didn't do anything wrong, and I pushed you away. I hated hurting you. I was lashing out at everyone. When they told me you were coming today, I was happy. Really, I was."

Nancy puffed out her cheeks, exhaled her anxiety, and then raised her head. Her face was now beaming. Then she began babbling, "Oh, thank God! I was so scared you'd never speak to me again. I thought I'd lost my best friend. I didn't know what to do. I thought—"

Amanda reached across the table and laid her hand on Nancy's arm. "It's okay, Nance, we're fine. Really, we are."

Nancy sniffled, and a tear dropped onto my back. "Thank God." Then her anxiety level increased again, and she lowered her voice. "Are you sure they can't hear us? That captain guy said no one would be listening, but—"

Amanda interjected, "Captain Swenson's been very kind to me. You can trust him."

All the same, Nancy scooted her chair, and me, closer to Amanda. When she was up close and personal, she whispered, "How are you really doing?"

Amanda pulled Sweetie closer, leaned in, and snuggled her head against his body. Her voice was sad. "The worst part is being all alone."

Nancy whispered, "I know you didn't do it. Please, tell me you didn't."

Amanda leaned back and put her arm around Nancy. She said softly, "It doesn't matter whether I did or didn't. I have to say I did."

"Amanda, we've been friends forever," Nancy whispered. "I swear, I won't tell a soul. But I have to know the truth. Please, please tell me."

Amanda paused, studied Nancy's face, and nodded. Maybe she didn't really trust Captain Swenson as much as she claimed, because she put her lips right up to Nancy's ear and whispered.

Nancy's body sagged with relief.

Nancy now knew what we knew. Amanda had not killed her father.

Nancy turned and whispered quietly, "Then who did?"

Amanda's hands flew to her face and covered her eyes. "Please, please don't ask any more questions! I told you the truth. I can't tell you anything more. Please, just let it go." Tears began rolling down her cheeks.

Nancy gently took one of Amanda's hands in hers. "Okay, okay. I won't push. Please don't cry. How about we talk about something else? Want to hear all the weird stuff Pamela's been up to?"

Amanda wiped away her tears as she chuckled and said, "Yeah, that would be really great."

For the next thirty minutes the two girls laughed and shared all kinds of important nonsense. Sweetie and I watched as a special bubble formed around them, and for a brief time two lifelong friends escaped to a magical place and got a reprieve from reality.

****

It's almost impossible to get a human to babble on command. On the ride home, Mom tried every polite approach she could think of to get Nancy to divulge what she and Amanda had talked about, but Nancy's lips were sealed. She was polite, and thanked Mom for taking her to see Amanda. She said that if Captain Swenson would allow it she would like to go again as soon as possible. When we arrived at her house she kissed the top on my head and then turned to the back seat and said, "Bye, Mr. Sweetie. You're awesome!"

See? I told you, Sweetie is an attitude changer!

After Nancy left we witnessed the opposite truth about babbling: once a human starts, it's hard to find the off switch. The moment Nancy was out of earshot Mom started hammering us with questions, and the barrage continued all the way home. But once again she failed to understand my answers, so I gave up and went to sleep.

Later that day Professor Hoffman called. He reported that Amanda had told him she loved seeing Nancy, and that she seemed less depressed. On the other hand, she hadn't given him a smidgen of new information.

Phooey! We had hoped that softening Amanda would produce a better payoff. But apparently Amanda's lips were as tightly sealed as Nancy's.

"Now what?" I asked Sweetie. "The humans still don't know the truth."

"Don't worry, Spunk," said Sweetie. "At least one two-legged now knows what we know. That's progress."

"Yeah, but that two-legged ain't talking. Gee whiz, getting this truth into the light is going to be tricky."

Sweetie grinned, "No problem, Spunk. Tricky is your specialty."

Ah, Sweetie and his blind faith! The problem was that at the moment all I felt was blind.

CHAPTER  55

After church on Sunday Mom invited Frank over for lunch. There were a few awkward starts and stops, but once they began eating the tension plummeted. Humans need to occupy their hands and mouths. Eating seems to be their number-one method of accomplishing that.

Mom filled Frank in on all that had transpired, including Nancy's visit to Amanda in jail. Frank loved the part about how we managed to get Mom to go to Nancy's house.

"Hannah, I swear, your critters can find people faster than Google!" His mood then abruptly shifted. "It's great that you got Nancy to see Amanda, but Amanda still hasn't opened up to anyone about what really happened." He paused and then shrugged. "Well, that may not be true; we don't have the slightest idea of what Amanda told Nancy, or even what they talked about. We couldn't even hear what Amanda whispered to Sweetie and Spunky the other day!"

Simultaneously, both of their heads dropped and their eyes bore down on me. I barked twice.

Hey, don't look at me like that! I told you—she didn't do it!

"Too bad I still can't understand 'woof,'" said Mom, "but I know one way or the other Spunky will figure out a way to get the truth to us. She always does."

Boy, talk about pressure!

Mom then asked Frank, "What's happening with Amanda's mother?"

"Ruth? She's still in town. She was staying at the Westin with her brother and sister-in-law, but when I told them it would be a while before we could release Mr. Pederson's body, the relatives headed home and Mrs. Pederson moved back into the Pederson house. Given all we heard about the woman, I doubt that is what Mr. Pederson would have wanted. And it sure would give me the creeps to be cooking in the same kitchen where my spouse was just murdered. But the forensics team finished processing the crime scene and she's still legally his wife so there wasn't anything I could do to stop her moving in. She wanted us to let her leave town, but I got permission to treat her as an out-of-town witness, so she gets her expenses reimbursed, including meals. Once she got some money, she backed off."

Mom's brow furrowed. "Didn't Mr. Pederson leave the house to Amanda?"

"Yeah, but all that's in legal limbo. In this state you can't inherit if you murder your benefactor, so if Amanda is convicted Pederson's assets will probably go to her mother. I'm guessing Pederson never thought Amanda wouldn't inherit, so he didn't name a second beneficiary. In that case, his wife would get everything."

"Do you think she has anything to do with Mr. Pederson's murder?"

"Do I have any evidence? No. But there's something she's lying about, and I can't for the life of me figure it out. And unfortunately time is running out. I've only got about one more week, and if we don't uncover anything new, I'll have to cut her loose—unless of course, in the meantime someone makes it a criminal offense to be a cold-hearted mother. Then I've got her dead to rights!"

"I'm afraid the jail cells would be quite full if they ever passed that law. Besides, cold-hearted doesn't automatically mean a bad mother. But I know what you mean. From what I've heard, she may be guilty of both cold-heartedness and bad mothering. But we don't know what we don't know. She may be an alcoholic, which wouldn't be a minor detail."

Mom then switched topics and asked, "And what about that guy Nancy saw picking up Amanda? Any leads on him?"

"Nope. I asked Amanda about him, and she said he's just a guy she met at church. She claims they're just friends and he knows nothing about any of this. She says she won't give me his name because she doesn't want us to bug him. So I checked with the pastor and youth leader at her church, and they said Amanda socializes with a lot with the young people, both guys and girls, but no one in particularly stuck out. We thought about interviewing every boy in the congregation, but that's a lot of kids and we don't even have a clue what he looks like, since only Nancy saw him and that was from a distance. Anyway, we've already identified the pertinent prints at the scene, so I don't see any reason to put manpower into finding someone we haven't even linked to the crime."

"Sounds like a lot of dead ends."

I yawned. Okay, enough lollygagging. It was time for them to start down a new path. The boys were right beside me waiting for a tidbit to drop, so the conditions were perfect for us to generate an intense mental beam. The humans may have heard a few indistinct snorts from me, but the boys received the message loud and clear. Simultaneously, all eyes stared up at Mom with the same name emanating from each brain.

Mom suddenly changed the subject. "I still have a bunch of unanswered questions about this Mr. Whitehead character. Like, why did Amanda choose him to confide in? Why not someone else? Why not a woman? And don't you find it odd that Whitehead risked confronting a father on sexual abuse based solely on the story of a girl he sees only forty minutes a day in his history class? True, anyone hearing about abuse should take it seriously, but most people would report it to the authorities. From what we know, Whitehead never told anyone, nor did he try to get Amanda to talk to the school counselor. He simply decided to deal with it on his own. He didn't even have anyone accompany him. He just climbed on his white horse and set off to confront Mr. Pederson. Unfortunately, according to him, Mr. Pederson was already dead by the time he got there. I don't think a person would run over there to intervene like that unless he cared deeply about the girl."

She paused, tilted her head, and said, "In fact, I'm beginning to wonder if Mr. Whitehead might care a little too much about Amanda." Mom shuddered and then kept going. "But even if I set that aside for the moment, we know for a fact that he took a sixteen-year-old away from a crime scene and hid her from the police." Her voice rose. "So why the heck hasn't he been charged as an accessory, or with kidnapping—or with something? Frank, why isn't that man locked up?"

Frank sighed. "I know in my gut Whitehead's lying about something. Believe me, if it were up to me he'd be in a cell until I got the truth out of him. Don't think I haven't considered it. But there are problems. For one, Amanda says she begged him to take her, so a kidnapping charge won't stick. For another, she corroborates his story that she pleaded with him to hide her and threatened to hurt herself if he contacted the police, so holding her against her will won't fly either. And finally, she confirms that he tried repeatedly to get her to turn herself in, and that he was the reason she didn't run away or hurt herself. To a jury it would look like he only helped Amanda, and he may even have saved her life. Yes, he harbored a fugitive and was an accessory, but the D.A. says a conviction would be an uphill battle at best. As long as Amanda sticks to her story, there's not much we can do to him."

Mom shook her head. "Okay, I get it. I can see how he would want to take her away from her father's dead body. But the average middle-aged man doesn't willingly hide a sixteen-year-old girl in his house, especially one who just killed her father. Not if that same man plans to keep working as a teacher. In fact, why is he still teaching, anyway?"

Frank shrugged again. "The principal told me that since no charges have been filed, Whitehead has every right to keep working."

Mom nodded. "I guess that's fair. But all I know is that something isn't right about his story, and I can't figure out why Amanda trusted him."

"I don't understand it either, but we've both seen young, decent teenage girls drawn to the wrong kind of guy, and I can never figure out why."

Mom shook her head. "It's never a simple answer, but I can tell you that most of those girls do have a common denominator."

"What's that?"

"Misplaced love."

"Huh?"

"When you're a teenager, everything revolves around who loves or likes you and who doesn't, and whether you feel accepted or rejected. Most teens are convinced their parents don't love or understand them. Rebellion and hormones are a terrible mix, and all too often a girl falls madly in love with the exact type of person her parents dislike most."

"But from what we know Amanda doesn't even have a boyfriend."

"I said 'they fall madly in love with the *person*.' It doesn't necessarily have to be a boy."

Frank furrowed his brow. "What? You mean Amanda fell in love with a girl?"

"No, Frank. I mean maybe she fell in love with the man who came and rescued her."

Whoa, I didn't see that one coming!

CHAPTER

After Mom and Frank talked some more, Frank concluded he needed to know a lot more about Mr. Whitehead. Good! Now maybe we could uncover some of those deep, dark secrets. I immediately sent word to Tito at the school and Hobo at Whitehead's house to be on alert.

The next day, about an hour after school ended, Ollie arrived to deliver a message from Goliath.

"Ollie what are you doing up and *(breath)* flying at this time of day?" Fearless asked.

"Goliath wanted you to know this ASAP, so he requested air mail service." Ollie replied and then continued. "He said to tell you Tito sent word that a detective had arrived when school let out and asked Mr. Whitehead a whole lot of questions. Tito said if you wanted the details, he would be available to meet."

I sent Ollie to let Tito know Fearless and I would meet him behind the school so that Goliath wouldn't have to send his cat guards.

When we arrived, I was surprised to find Goliath there waiting for us.

"Good to see you, Goliath, but you didn't have to come. There was no need for you to give up any sleep. You've got nine lives to support, I only have one."

"No problem, Spunk. When I'm awake, I always keep at least seven of my lives napping. That way my tank is never empty. Besides, I wanted to hear the new info."

The school seemed to be empty except for a herd of athletes running around outside and the band inside trying to play something loud and unidentifiable. Two cats were sitting beside Goliath. He explained that they were the basement cats, and since the custodian, Mr. Johnson, had just left for the hardware store, they thought it would be safe for both of them to be outside at the same time.

Mr. Bing and Mr. Bang were two handsome beige-colored boys with white socks and collars. They looked so much alike I asked, "Are you two twins?"

Bing answered, "I'm impressed. Very few are aware that cats can even have twins, but our mom did, and yes, we are."

"Why does it matter that Mr. Johnson is away?" I asked

Bang explained, "Mr. Johnson doesn't know we go outside, and we want to keep it that way. Being twins is a big advantage. When Mr. Johnson's on duty, one of us always stays inside. That way, if he comes down to the basement, one of us is always there to greet him. That one makes a big show of rubbing on him and asking for pets. Then he quickly runs off, vanishes, makes a quick dash along a hidden path behind the junk, and comes out on the other side of the room. Ta-da! Now Mr. Johnson thinks he's seen both of us. Meanwhile, Tito or some of his clan are usually in the basement too, so they run outside and alert the other brother. Before you know it, both of us are rubbing on Mr. Johnson, and any doubt he may have is quickly eliminated. So far we've managed to keep our secret safe."

I asked, "Why would he care if you go outside?"

Fearless explained it to me. "Spunk, if he knew they can get out *(breath)*, then he'd realize their friends can get in."

"Ah. I see."

Goliath started to giggle. "Tito that tickles!" We watched as Tito ran up Goliath's back. "Sorry, Goliath, but I need to give Spunky my report, and I'm in a hurry. Cook is in the kitchen doing her prep work for tomorrow, and I need to get over there and grab your cheese ration before she locks it in the fridge for the night."

"Then get on with it boy," said Goliath. "Times a-wasting!"

Once again Tito threw back his shoulders and stood proudly on Goliath's neck. When he clasped his wee hands over his belly, he brought to my mind Pastor John's Basset Hound, Charlie, who had given us a detailed description of his human standing in the pulpit looking down on his congregation.

Tito cleared his tiny throat. "Okay, the detective said his name was Frank. Goliath told me you know him, so I don't need to describe him, right?"

"Right."

"Okay then, here's what happened. The students had already left by the time the detective arrived. Mr. Whitehead was in his classroom finishing his paperwork. Detective Frank said he wanted to review Whitehead's previous statement, and if Whitehead wanted his lawyer present they

238

could go down to the station and wait for him. Thank goodness Whitehead said he'd talk to Frank without his attorney, or I'd have to ride the briefcase express again. Detective Frank read Mr. Whitehead's previous statement aloud and asked him if he wanted to make any changes. Whitehead said no. Detective Frank asked why Whitehead would keep a sixteen-year-old girl hidden in his house, but before Whitehead could answer that one, Detective Frank launched into a barrage of questions, asking Whitehead why did he do this, why did he do that. He seemed to be badgering him on purpose, but Whitehead stayed calm and repeated the same answers that he gave in his statement, word for word. Then the detective turned up the heat."

"How?" I asked.

"Well, he leaned in real close and asked Mr. Whitehead if there were any other sixteen-year-old girls he cared about in that same special way? Or maybe he liked them even younger? And how long had he had this special interest in young girls? At that point, I smelled Whitehead's anxiety skyrocket. The man started to stink! He kept muttering over and over that he was only trying to help Amanda.

"Then all at once things escalated. Whitehead's briefcase was sitting on top of the desk, and when Detective Frank leaned in even closer, he put his hand on top of it. Mr. Whitehead lunged forward and snatched that case right out from under his hand. Detective Frank was startled, and initially drew back, but then he leaned in again. This time, his face was just inches from Whitehead's. Detective Frank's voice became low and stern, and he asked, 'What have you got in there that's making you so nervous, Mr. Whitehead?

Why don't I just look for myself?" Detective Frank reached for the case, but Whitehead hugged it tightly to his chest and said, 'No sir, you may not. My papers are personal and private, and quite frankly none of your business.' Well, Detective Frank never did get near that case again, but he did say, 'A warrant will certainly make it my business, Mr. Whitehead.' Detective Frank left shortly after that. And that concludes my report, Ms. Spunky."

Tito was being so serious, I halfway expected him to throw in a salute.

"Thanks Tito. You are quite the proficient detective." I cocked my head. "I wonder if Frank really can get a warrant to look inside Whitehead's briefcase?" Another thought quickly followed. "Tito, is Mr. Whitehead still in his classroom?"

"He was before I ran down here to meet you guys."

"Then we need to act fast, because even if Frank gets that warrant, it may prove useless. I'm betting that as soon as Mr. Whitehead gets home, he'll move whatever is in his briefcase to a new hiding place."

I turned toward the tree where Ollie was perched and said, "It's a good thing you followed us here, Ollie. I need you to get word to Hobo and the raccoons pronto. Tell them what you just heard, and that we need them to resume full-time surveillance starting the moment Whitehead pulls into his driveway tonight. And ask them to post critters at every window. We need to have eyes on every room in that house if possible."

Goliath immediately interjected, "Yeah, we need to know where this rat hides his cheese."

CHAPTER  57

I t didn't take long. We hadn't even had dinner yet when Fancy-Pants told me Ollie was outside.

"Hey, Ollie! I hope you brought good news."

"Mission accomplished, Ms. Spunky. Right after White-head got home, Hobo saw him take a large brown envelope out of his briefcase. He looked around his office and then put the envelope on the top shelf of a bookcase. Hobo said all the sentries will stay in place until Whitehead leaves for school tomorrow morning, and that they'll return to their posts when he comes home tomorrow night, just in case he decides to move the envelope to another hiding place."

"Fantastic! Does Hobo have enough help?"

"Yeah, Einstein headed over there with a well-trained crew. Believe me, Whitehead's going to have eyes on him— but he'll never see the eyes."

"Great! Please let Hobo and everyone know how much we appreciate their help. We couldn't have tracked this rat without them."

Fearless leaned in close to me and whispered. "We have to get Frank *(breath)* into that house *(breath)*, right?"

"Right. And when he goes in, so do we. Ollie, we need to know if and when Frank heads toward Whitehead's house. Do you have any idea how we can track his whereabouts?"

"Yeah, you need GPS."

"GPS? That's a human gadget. We don't have one of those."

"Not the human kind, Spunk, I mean critter GPS—Good Pigeon Surveillance. All you need are pigeons posted on the telephone lines near the station and Frank's house. They're probably roosting there already, so no one will even notice them. Since they don't know which is Frank's car, I'll go put a marker on top of it."

"A marker?"

"Have you ever watched someone try to get dried bird poop off their car? Not so easy. Well, owl poop is three times as resilient, and the splatter pattern is sizeable and quite distinctive. It will even stay put if it rains! Besides, I bet Frank doesn't even look at the roof of his car, but in the event he does wash it off, I've got plenty more where that came from. Believe me, the pigeons know the look of owl poop well, and they won't have any problem knowing which car to track. Everyone knows pigeons are fantastic messengers, and when they're in GPS surveillance mode they fly in a flock, so if Frank heads toward Whitehead's house, one or two will veer off and come here to give you a heads-up. If you keep one of your family posted out here and they can tell the pigeons where you are, it should buy you enough lead time."

"Great idea, Ollie! But why would pigeons even talk to you? With all due respect, I'm guessing you've probably had an intimate dinner involving a few of their relatives."

"True indeed! That's why I plan to talk to the crows, who in turn will sound a call to arms for the pigeons. No one will be in harm's way. The pigeons wouldn't lift a beak to help me, but I'll make it clear it's a favor for you, Ms. Spunky. Creatures great and small for miles around know the good work you and the felines do, and most all consider it an honor to be able to assist you. I'm sure the pigeons will prove that to be true."

"I'm deeply touched, Ollie. Please relay my gratitude."

When Ollie flew off, Fearless nudged me with his head. "Hey, buddy *(breath)*, doesn't it feel good to know *(breath)* that our fellow citizens appreciate the work we've done?"

"It sure does, my friend! And I hope we never betray that trust."

"I know *(breath)* rule number five: Trust requires time to build *(breath)*, but only seconds to shatter."

CHAPTER  58

Later that evening we were lounging outside after a tasty repast when three pigeons got our attention by dive-bombing at our heads.

"Hey, watch it guys!"

The leader cooed, "Sorry, Ms. Spunky, but we've been cooing and cooing and you guys didn't notice."

"Then it's I who should apologize! I guess we're so used to you pigeons being around all the time we didn't notice anything unusual. Do you have news for us?"

"Yes, ma'am. We knew it was important, and that's why we had to get your attention. Our squad leader said to tell you Frank's car just turned onto the road headed to Gifford's farm, so he's close to Whitehead's!"

"Holy smokes! We've got to get a move on. Thanks for the alert. You guys did great!"

Fearless and I took off for Whitehead's house. We used every shortcut possible, but Frank was already inside the house when we arrived.

"Shoot, *(breath)* Spunky *(breath)*, now what?"

"First, my friend, let's rest a moment so we can both catch our breath." I plunked my rump down and waited. One good turn deserves another. I said "both," but Fearless was the one very short of breath after our long sprint.

"Thanks!" he said.

After a brief reprieve I said, "Okay, we need to get Whitehead to open the door. I think our tried-and-true bark-and-yowl method might do the trick. We already know the layout of the house, so once we're inside we should be good to go, right?"

"Yup."

After working out a few more details, we approached the house. On the count of three, I started barking as loud as I could, and Fearless let rip with his best and loudest yowls possible. It only took a few seconds before the door swung open, and Fearless and I stormed into the castle. We ran straight to Whitehead's office, with Whitehead and Frank both in pursuit and yelling, "Come back here!"

Fearless leaped onto the desk, and then in one graceful bounce made it to the top of the bookshelf. He extended one paw, reached down and seized the envelope, and yanked it forward. When he felt the balance shift, he retracted his claws and the envelope dropped.

Whitehead yelled, "No!" and lunged for the envelope, but I beat him to it. I snatched it up faster than a treat, and off I went. Both men were right on my tail as I ran into a bedroom, but they came to a screeching halt when I ducked under the bed. Luckily it was king size, so they couldn't reach me. Then I began working on the envelope. Fortunately there was only a flimsy clasp holding it shut.

By the time Whitehead had fetched a broom and aimed it at my head, I had completed my mission. I emerged with two pictures in my mouth and walked over to Frank.

Whitehead groaned, "Gimme those! You already said you don't have a search warrant. You have no right!"

Frank held his arm straight to fend off Whitehead. "What do we have here? Hold on, Mr. Whitehead. With all due respect sir, I don't need a search warrant for this, and I'm certainly not violating any laws. You invited me into your home. We were just talking when you—not I—opened the door and let these animals run in. From the moment I entered your house, I haven't opened a single drawer or closet. In fact, I haven't touched a thing. Then, without my knowing that they even existed, I was handed these pictures of teenage girls. Pictures of teenage girls found in the house of the same man who hid a teenage girl in his home. The same man who then kept that same teenage girl hidden from the police."

Frank bent over and scanned under the bed with his flashlight. "Well, looky there! More pictures of teenage girls! Mr. Whitehead, I think it's time you and I had a nice long chat. Get your coat, sir. You and I are going downtown."

Once we were all outside, Frank looked over at us and asked, "Are you guys okay to get back home, or do you want a lift?"

We answered by trotting off toward home. Frank called out, "Hey, you two!"

We turned and Frank gave us two thumbs up. I barked in reply. Our pleasure!

When Frank drove off, Fearless paused and looked upward, "I guess we should tell them *(breath)* the job's finished."

High above Frank's car, the GPS squad was obviously still on duty.

CHAPTER  59

Several hours later Frank phoned before stopping by for coffee and dessert.

"Are you sure you don't want some dinner first, Frank?" Mom said when he arrived.

"I'm fine. I grabbed a hot dog on my way over. Not great, but your pie will make up for it. Besides, I really came over to run something by you and get your opinion."

"I'm all ears."

We were too. Had Frank uncovered Whitehead's secrets?

Frank told Mom that he'd gone over to Whitehead's after a judge denied his request for search warrant because of insufficient grounds. He went there hoping to learn something more, however he could. As soon as Whitehead opened the door he asked if Frank had a search warrant. Frank said he had opted to play nice, and told Whitehead that he didn't have a warrant and that he simply wanted to apologize for being so hard on him at the school. Whitehead let him in, and they began talking. About ten minutes later, he said, the most horrific critter noises erupted on the front porch, and he went on to describe to Mom what had happened after Whitehead opened the door.

Mom's jaw dropped in astonishment. She repeatedly looked down at us and then back at Frank, all the while shaking her head, and muttering, "Amazing! How in the world…?"

"Don't ask me, Hannah. I have no idea how those two knew I was there, let alone how they knew about that envelope. It defies all logic."

I snorted. Maybe human logic.

Frank continued, "When I got Whitehead downtown, I knew I didn't have much to go on. There was nothing pornographic about those pictures. They were just regular pictures of teenage girls. He also had a lot of information about finding runaways and lost kids, but none of it seemed particularly sinister. My instincts said he wanted to talk, and since he said he didn't want a lawyer present, I tried befriending him. After coffee, a few donuts, and some coaxing, he opened up."

Mom leaned in and said, "Terrific! What did you learn?"

"Not at all what I expected. He told me he grew up in Chicago, and at nineteen he was in a relationship with a girl and got her pregnant. Her name was Alicia Dunstan, and she was sixteen at the time. He proposed to her, but her mother sent her away and wouldn't tell him where. The mom filed charges against him for statutory rape, but less than an hour later she withdrew the complaint. From what Alicia had told him about her mother, he thought she dropped the charges because she didn't want people knowing what her daughter had done. He was never arrested, but the mother threatened to go back to the police if he ever tried to contact Alicia again. He was terrified, so he left it alone.

"About seven months later the family moved away, and he never saw or heard from Alicia again. But about five years ago, he said, he felt compelled to see if he had a child out there, so he started his own investigation. He learned that there used to be a home for unwed mothers about fifty miles south of here in Lakeland. It closed about ten years ago, but Whitehead hired a private detective who located a woman who'd been a clerk there. Of course she insisted that the information she had was confidential, but apparently her ethical commitment dropped significantly when she saw some money.

"She said she did remember a sixteen-year-old girl named Alicia. The reason she remembered her was that Alicia looked a lot like her own daughter, so she felt drawn to her. Without any further prompting, she correctly recalled Alicia's last name and the year she arrived at the home, so Whitehead was confident that the information was correct. The clerk said Alicia gave birth to a baby girl that summer, and named her April. A few months later, a couple who lived in the area adopted the baby. The woman said their name might have been Johnson or Jansen, but she wasn't certain.

"Alicia left Lakeland shortly after the child was adopted, but the clerk didn't know where she went. Whitehead said he couldn't afford to continue using private investigators, so he began his own investigation. Knowing that the adoptive parents had lived in or near Lakeland gave him a place to start. He applied for jobs around the area, and three years ago he was hired by our high school.

"All he knew was that his daughter was born at the home in Lakeland in the summer of that year, that her name was April, and that a couple, possibly named Johnson or Jansen, had adopted her. He began trying to track her by talking to people in the area and using online tracking services. He admitted that finding her became an obsession. Since she would now be close to eighteen, he said, he felt a sincere affection for the teenage girls in his class, especially girls like Amanda who were hard-working, polite, considerate, and reminded him of the girl he hoped his daughter had become. He admitted that he gave Amanda preferential treatment and tried to show her special kindness. He thinks that's why she decided to confide in him. When she told him about her father abusing her, all he could think of was what if it had been his daughter. He gave Amanda his cell phone number and told her to call him any time, day or night, and he would come get her.

"He said he was up half the night thinking about it, and the next morning he couldn't contain himself. So yes, he said, he foolishly headed off alone to her house to right all wrongs.

"But when Pederson was murdered, everything spiraled out of control. He refused to abandon Amanda, but he was terrified that if the police investigated him they might uncover his past sexual relationship with a minor, and his life and career would be destroyed. That's why he hid everything related to his past in that briefcase and guarded it with his life. He claims he told us exactly what Amanda wanted him to say, and that most of his story was true, except for two vital points.

"First, Mr. Pederson wasn't dead when Whitehead arrived. He was very much alive."

Bobby head-butted me in the side. "Hey, Spunk, he just validated your nose."

I snorted, "My nose didn't need validating. Whitehead needed to tell the truth."

Mom asked, "So if Pederson was alive when Whitehead got there, did Whitehead kill him?"

"He admitted to getting angry when Pederson turned and walked out of the living room after he confronted him with the abuse allegation. He admitted that he grabbed Pederson, and they had a minor scuffle in the kitchen. But he swore that when he left the house Pederson was still alive and well."

Mom's brow furrowed. "Well then, I'm confused. Didn't he originally say that he was the one who told Amanda to go to school and act as if nothing had happened, and that he would then pick her up? Why would he tell her that if Pederson was alive and well?"

Frank nodded. "Because he lied about the timing as to when he gave her those instructions. He says when he left, Amanda and her father were alone in the house and both were fine. It wasn't until at least an hour later that Amanda called and told him she had murdered her father.

"I will say this, he certainly is being very cooperative. In fact he has even agreed to take a polygraph and he has voluntarily turned his laptop over to me."

Mom shrugged and said, "Frank, given his apparent openness and all the details he has told you, my impression is either he has rehearsed this story a lot or else he might just be telling you the truth."

"And if he's telling the truth, he isn't the murderer." Frank sighed. "Far worse, the prosecution now has a great witness against Amanda."

After Mom and Frank finished talking, Frank left and I followed the boys outside. We needed a break.

"Geez Louise, Spunk, *(breath)*, whaddya think?"

"Rule number eight, my friend," I said. "You can't put marrow back into a bone."

Fearless nodded. "I agree. Wishing can't change the facts."

Bobby asked, "Do you believe the dude's story, Spunk?"

"I don't have any evidence to the contrary, Bobby. My nose said he entered the house alone and went first to the living room and then into the kitchen. His scent was on Pederson's body in several places, but not on the knife. I also know he left the house alone, and that the high-heeled woman and sneaker lady stepped on top of his prints, so he was there before them. That makes sense, since they found the body. But there were so many of Amanda's footprints everywhere I couldn't tell if hers were on top of his too or not."

Sweetie chimed in, "Frank seems to think Whitehead's telling the truth, especially since he agreed to be hooked up to one of those human truth machines and gave up his laptop for investigation."

Fancy-Pants added, "Don't forget, Mom said his story may well be true."

Bobby began grooming as he muttered, "Now what, ole' wise one? Are we done?"

I gave myself a full body shake and then said, "Heck no. It's time to start digging another hole."

CHAPTER  60

After several lengthy discussions, we concluded it was time to investigate Amanda's mother. We chose her as our next target mainly because we knew so little about her. But none of us would deny the fact that the way she was treating her daughter helped push her to the top of the list.

Early the next morning Sweetie, Fearless, and I headed to the Pederson house. Fancy-Pants and Bobby set off to locate Ollie, because we needed to get word to the pigeons that the GPS squad could stand down.

When we arrived, Sweetie positioned himself so that he could watch the front door and the garage, while Fearless and I began an inspection of the perimeter. Fearless scampered up a tree in the backyard and found several limbs with unobstructed views into the upstairs rooms. Meanwhile I examined the ground floor windows, many of which were hidden behind bushes or hedges. The windows were held shut with hooks and when I nudged one of them with my head, I found there was some wiggle room. This meant the windows hadn't been painted shut, and the hooks had some play in them. I also observed that the big hydrangea bushes around the house could easily conceal spies for the kitchen and living room.

When we had completed our reconnaissance, we chose our own surveillance posts and waited to see what we might learn.

Thirty minutes later the garage door opened and Mrs. Pederson backed her car out of the driveway and drove off down the street. Like many people, she left the garage door wide open. We made the most of the opportunity and scoped out the garage, then returned to our posts. To our delight, only twenty minutes passed before Mrs. Pederson returned. Once the garage door shut, we scampered behind the hydrangeas and watched her go into the kitchen and set down a newspaper and a bag from a local fast-food joint. From the bag she withdrew a large coffee and two sausage biscuits, giving us hope that if this was her morning routine, we could use it to our advantage.

Since I already knew the interior layout, I concluded that we had sufficient data for now. Sweetie volunteered to stay behind and watch Mrs. Pederson while Fearless and I headed to the campus to see Goliath for a planning session.

No cats were visible when we arrived at the college library. They were probably sound asleep at this hour, but Fearless knew the hidden entrance to Goliath and Einstein's basement abode. I waited outside while he undertook the dangerous mission of sneaking in to wake up Goliath. Fearless said he sincerely hoped Einstein wasn't also sound asleep in there. If Fearless was mistaken for an intruder, it might prove harmful to his well-being. But when I heard no yowling, I took it as a good sign. Fearless emerged unscathed, and Goliath was right behind him, kind and gracious as always.

"Morning, Ms. Spunky. You timed your visit well. I was just settling in after a delightful but unusually long and escapade-filled night. Normally I'd be fast asleep at this time."

Fearless added, "Einstein is still out and about *(breath)*, so I didn't have to poke and run."

"Thanks for being cordial," I said, "despite our early arrival. If you'd be so kind, we need a consultation."

We brought Goliath up to speed about Mr. Whitehead and our next investigative prey, Pederson's estranged wife. After considering a moment, Goliath offered a plan.

"I can post sentries over there full time. If she leaves the garage door open again, Tito can go in and wait in the garage until she returns. Then when she goes into the house he can sneak in right beside her."

I expressed a concern. "Tito has proven himself a great and courageous spy, but what if she sees him and there's no way out? He'd be stuck in there, and she could hurt him. I'm not comfortable with that. He needs a backup plan."

"Is there an inside door leading to the basement area where you saw those windows with the hooks?" Goliath asked.

"No, just stairs."

Goliath nodded. "Okay. How long do you think Tito needs to be in there?"

"Hard to tell. Depends how long it takes to see or hear something we can use."

Goliath paused and then said, "Okay, what about this? Einstein can hide in the garage with Tito and streak in when

Mrs. Pederson opens the door to the house. In all likelihood she'll freak out when she sees Einstein, and that should be enough distraction for Tito to make his move unnoticed. Given what you said about those windows, Einstein could race downstairs, pop one of the hooks, and be out the window before Mrs. Pederson even gets down the stairs. That would leave Tito an open window as an escape route."

I nodded. "Yeah, those hooks seemed loose enough for Einstein to pop one free, and the hinges are on the outside, so he could push it open and escape. But the window will fall back down, and it's too heavy for Tito to push up, so what good would that do?"

"Easy to solve," said Goliath. "Einstein goes in armed with a rag. All he has to do is drop that rag onto the window-sill on his way out to prevent the window from shutting completely. Tito only needs a tiny slit to get through, and if it's only open a crack Mrs. Pederson may never notice it."

"Sounds good," I said. "But for my peace of mind, would you keep a sentry posted outside that window so I know for certain it stays open?"

Goliath smiled. "Spunk, Tito will be touched that you care so much about his safety. I'll make sure sentries are in place twenty-four–seven. In fact, I'll go one better. I'll arrange an SOS signal with Tito. If he's in trouble, he can issue the SOS, and we'll start hurling ourselves against the back door and he can escape that way."

Now I smiled. "Fantastic! You've covered all my concerns. If Tito's agreeable, you or I can be outside the window every night to get his report. And we'll bring food so the little fellow will be well fed."

Goliath cleared his throat and said, "You do know never to let Tito hear you call him little, right?"

Fearless answered, "Yeah we know *(breath)*, but it's so darn hard not to crack a smile *(breath)* when that little cutie puffs himself up to deliver his reports."

Goliath chuckled. "Why do you think I let the boy stand on the back of my neck? It's the only way I know he won't see my big Cheshire grin!"

CHAPTER  61

Before we headed home, we stopped at the Pederson house and picked up Sweetie. He had nothing new to report, and like us, was getting hungry. When we got home just before noon and walked in the back door, we learned that Mom had our afternoon already planned.

"Well, where have you all been? Out having an adventure?"

I tilted my head and gave her my well-practiced look that said, "Me? I don't have the slightest idea what you're talking about." Fearless and Sweetie opted to play innocent and began grooming themselves. I do admire this feline avoidance technique. Cleaning their whiskers is a behavior that humans find charming, and they never realize cats use it to avoid looking at them. Dogs, on the other hand, are known for cleaning their butts, which to humans is anything but endearing.

Then Mom announced her news. "Well, while you were out there doing whatever, Nancy called. She was between classes. She said Principal Ames had given her permission to leave school during lunch and her study hall so that she could go see Amanda again, and she asked if I could drive her. She also asked me to bring you and Sweetie along—which of course I was going to do anyway, but I am delighted that she personally invited both of you. I've cleared everything with Captain Swenson, and we'll pick Nancy up in half an hour."

I nudged Sweetie. "Looks like you changed Nancy's attitude about cats!"

Sweetie purred, "Was there ever any doubt?"

"So, my friends," Mom said, "eat your late breakfast while I change my clothes, because we've got to get a move on."

Before we headed out I made sure Bobby and Fancy-Pants knew about our plan for the Pederson house. They agreed one of them would stay outside and notify Fearless of any incoming messages. Meanwhile Fearless settled onto the couch for a nap, of which I was more than a little envious.

When we arrived at the school Nancy was waiting on the front steps. After warm greetings all around, Mom said, "I'm so pleased you're doing this, though I'm a little surprised you had me pick you up here. Aren't you worried 'the girls' might see you?"

Nancy raised her chin, straightened shoulders, and said, "Amanda is far more important to me than those dimwits. If they have a problem with this, they can—"

Mom quickly interjected, "Fly a kite? Take a long walk on a short pier? Suck an egg?"

Nancy laughed. "Yeah, something like that."

Capt. Swenson welcomed us and took us into the same visiting room as before. It was good to see that Nancy was much more comfortable than the last time we were there. I hoped the same would be true of Amanda.

I was not disappointed. Amanda came in smiling and immediately hugged Nancy. Definitely an improvement! And of course Amanda didn't neglect Sweetie or me.

"I'm so glad Nancy brought you two along! Now I have my three best friends all in the same room at the same time."

Sweetie went over to Amanda and gave her a loving face rub, while I raised my front paw for a wave. But I didn't abandon my post in Nancy's lap. Sweetie and I had agreed that I would stay with Nancy while she connected with Amanda. Hey, it had worked last time!

This time both girls seemed oblivious of their surroundings. They scooted their chairs close together and acted like two teenagers chatting over burgers and fries. Nancy filled Amanda in on what was happening at school and all of Pamela's nonsense. They giggled and squealed in all the delightful ways only teenage girls can. Then, all too soon, the bubble burst and silence filled the room.

Finally Nancy spoke. "It must be so terrible to be in here. Why in heaven's name are you doing this? You didn't kill him. Why, why do you keep saying you did?"

Amanda dropped her head, sighed, and quietly said, "I have no choice."

"Why not?" said Nancy, calmly but deliberately.

Amanda raised her head, looked Nancy in the eye, and with quiet resolve said, "I just don't have a choice, that's why."

Nancy pulled back and studied Amanda. She tilted her head and said, "You're protecting someone. Who?"

Amanda sighed again. "It doesn't matter, Nance. My confession stands. The less you know, the better."

Nancy's voice grew louder as it filled with anger. "Why are you doing this? Who could possibly be worth your life? Who, Amanda, who?"

Amanda lowered her voice. "Hush, or they'll hear you right through the walls."

Nancy dropped her voice. "Amanda, we've been friends forever. I swear, I won't tell a soul, even if the police threaten to lock me up too. But I have to know why you're taking the blame for murder. Please tell me, I'm begging you, please, please tell me!"

Amanda paused, scrutinized her friend's face, and then nodded. She leaned over and put her lips close to Nancy's ear and whispered.

Nancy's eyes sprang wide open. She jerked her head away and stared at Amanda.

Amanda gently pulled Nancy back, leaned in to her ear again, and continued. Nancy's brow furrowed as she whispered, "But, you don't…"

Amanda cupped her hand around Nancy's ear and began telling her the entire story.

Nancy's eyes got even wider, and her jaw dropped open.

Thank goodness animals not only have keen ears, but are good at keeping poker faces. Because we, too, heard every word.

Now the three of us knew a whole lot more than we knew before.

Nancy shook her head in disbelief. "But why can't you tell the police? Why do *you* have to do that? You don't even—"

Amanda cut her short. "Hush. I told you I trust the captain, but you can't let a name slip out. The only way I can trust that you won't slip up out there is if you never slip up in here. Nance, it means so much that I finally have someone I can really talk to, but you have to swear to me you'll never repeat what I told you."

Amanda's voice deepened and became stern and demanding. "Swear it, Nance, or you can't come back. If you tell anyone, I'll call you a liar. I'll deny all of it, and I'll never ever speak to you again. I mean it Nance. I have no choice."

Sweetie leaned in and tried to calm Amanda. I shifted my weight on Nancy's lap, hoping to increase her awareness of me and defuse her reaction to Amanda's anger.

The sigh Nancy released came from deep within her soul. "Okay. I hate what you're doing. It's wrong, terribly wrong, but I'll do what you ask. I swear, no one will learn about this from me. I swear it, I really do."

"I believe you. You've never betrayed me. But you have to understand that if you betray me now, my whole world will fall apart. I'll have nothing left. You understand that, right?"

"I still don't agree, but that's not the point, is it? We've kept each other's secrets since we were kids, and I swear I'll keep this one as well."

Nancy's voice then became even quieter, "Are we allowed to talk about—"

Amanda wrapped her arms around Nancy and pulled her close, but her eyes were fixed on the mirrored wall. "How about we agree to never mention a name, but only use 'you-know-who' and to only speak about it in whispers, never saying anything loud enough for anyone to hear."

Thank goodness, Sweetie and I weren't just "anyone."

Nancy nodded and whispered, "I can do that. But—"

Amanda cut her off. "No buts, otherwise I can't trust you to do what I need you to do."

Nancy paused, furrowed her brow, and then hesitantly asked, "And...what might that be?"

Amanda again stared into the two-way mirror. She whispered, "Do you have a paper and pencil in your purse?"

"I think so." After rummaging around, Nancy pulled out a folded blue flyer and a pen. "Will this do? It's a stupid bake sale flyer, but the back's blank."

Amanda nodded, and in a hushed voice said, "Perfect. Okay, I need you to call 'you-know-who' and assure them that I'm sticking to our agreement."

Nancy sat back in her chair.

"Obviously," Amanda continued, "*I* can't call 'you-know-who' from here, my calls are probably monitored, and my—" Amanda hesitated and then said, "and *they* can't come here. I know you don't agree with me, but it's driving me crazy that they might think I'll betray them. Please, Nance, it would be such a relief to know that they've been told I'm sticking to the deal. Will you call?"

Nancy's fingers dug into my fur, reflecting her conflicted reaction. As her anxiety rose, I worked at emitting a greater wave of calm. Gradually I felt a balance forming between the two. Nancy then slowly said, "Okay, I'll call. Tell me exactly what you want me to say."

Amanda wrote numbers on the back of the flyer and handed it to Nancy. Then she cupped her hand over Nancy's ear and whispered exactly what she was to say.

Her voice was barely audible, but we heard every word.

Sometimes maybe it's better not to have critter ears.

CHAPTER  62

When we were all back in the car it was obvious to Mom that something important had happened. Nancy was silent, except for a minimum of polite responses to Mom's inquiries. Mom quickly accepted the futility of probing any deeper and wisely remained silent.

After dropping Nancy back at school, Mom shook her head and said, "I wish I knew what happened in there. Whatever it was, it was serious."

You have no idea, Mom. No idea at all.

By the time we got home Fearless was fully rested. Which was a good thing, because once he learned what we'd heard he immediately set out to fetch Goliath ASAP. Bobby volunteered to find Lion King and bring him here. Apparently, after their last rendezvous Bobby and Lion King had become buddies. For a young rascal like Bobby to have Lion King as a mentor was not only an honor, it was also a great benefit to us all.

Before he set out, Fearless told us the good news that had arrived while we were at the jail. Mrs. Pederson's trip to the grocery store had resulted in Tito and Einstein successfully breaching the Pederson house. Einstein reported that as he ran through the door he purposely brushed against Mrs. Pederson's leg, causing her to scream and to drop her bags, spilling the contents of her purse on the floor and providing the perfect distraction for Tito's entrance. The diversion also gave Einstein ample time to get down the stairs unnoticed. He was able to unlatch not just one, but three windows. By the time Mrs. Pederson came stomping down the stairs he was already outside under a hydrangea bush. He waited to make his next move until he heard her pounding back up the stairs muttering that she needed a drink. Once the coast was clear, he sank a full set of claws into the wooden window frame and pulled it open, then held it open with his body and inserted a rag to keep it from shutting.

Sentries had been posted beneath every window and they'd be relieved at various intervals so the neighbors wouldn't notice the large influx of cats. Each sentry knew what to do in case he heard a high-pitched SOS squeal and Tito would meet us outside at midnight to give us a report. I was pleased that all had gone well, with no injuries reported.

Little did we know how vital our tiny listening device would turn out to be.

CHAPTER 63

Fearless returned with Goliath and Einstein, and shortly thereafter Bobby and Lion King arrived. Sweetie and I told them what we had heard at the jail. We now needed ears in Nancy's house too, and we only had a short time before she went home after school. Since Fancy-Pants had been her original tracker, he was dispatched to the school to send us word when he saw her leaving and to follow her home. Sweetie went along as messenger.

Goliath said he thought Tito's cousin Belvidere could be the ears we needed. In fact, it was only yesterday that Belvidere had asked Goliath where he could sign up to see some action.

Goliath snickered slightly as he said, "Now, I want to warn you, Belvidere is a little more flamboyant than Tito."

Fearless cocked his crooked head even further and said, "More flamboyant?"

"Yeah," Goliath said with a chuckle. "I'd say he's definitely more colorful than Tito. You'll see for yourself, but I can personally vouch for his credibility and bravery."

"If you trust him, that's all we need to know," I said. "Can you manage to get him to Nancy's before she gets home from school?"

"Shouldn't be a problem," said Einstein. "I can head over to the school right now and talk to Bing and Bang. They should be able to locate Belvidere easy-peasy."

"But Bing and Bang don't come outside. Oh, I forgot—they do, but one at a time. And besides if they can get out, you can get in."

Einstein nodded, "Exactamundo! Once I find Belvidere, I'll fill him in on the plan and then I'll personally carry the boy over to Nancy's house. I can get directions from Fancy. Hey, Spunk, you've been in Nancy's house. If we use the same entry technique we used at Pederson's, how do I get out?"

I paused, visualized the layout of Nancy's house, and said, "I don't think I saw an escape route. Maybe it would be better if I intercept Nancy. I think she'll let me in, and Belvidere can ride hidden in my scruff. Once I'm inside I'll look for escape routes, but you should make sure Belvidere knows the SOS signal, okay?"

"Got it." Einstein then headed off to find Belvidere, while Goliath stayed to finalize our plan.

We opted to use four-legged trackers whenever Nancy left home or school. But since we had already assigned all our feline sentries to the Pederson house, we would need more help. So Lion King set off to speak to Nosey. A bloodhound's howl can be as effective as a town's emergency alert siren. His call for canine volunteers would be heard for miles and miles. Lion King said he'd meet the recruits in the woods south of Nosey's and personally conduct their orientation meeting.

I sent Bobby to Ollie's favorite daytime perch to alert him that we would need the GPS squad to follow Nancy if she were to get in a car. I also suggested to Bobby that after he found Ollie, he should join Lion King at the dogs' orientation. Observing Lion King's superb feline-to-canine diplomatic skills would serve young Bobby well. Even the local canines respected the King, and that was not only highly unusual, but also admirable.

After we had finished mapping out a plan, I headed to Nancy's house. When I arrived, Einstein and Belvidere were on the porch waiting for me. Einstein was catnapping in a chair, and Belvidere was standing guard on the windowsill. As soon as I spotted Belvidere, I stopped and pretended to water a bush. I needed that moment to get my face back to a neutral expression. Goliath wasn't exaggerating when he said "flamboyant." I never thought clothes could be so tiny, but sure enough, Belvidere had on a paisley vest, a red cravat, a herringbone tweed racing cap, and carried an umbrella smaller than a toothpick.

As I went up the walkway, he threw back his shoulders, stood tall and exclaimed, "Blimey, Ms. Spunk, how do? Jolly good to make your acquaintance!"

The British accent was adorable!

I nodded and said, "The honor is all mine, Belvidere. How are you?"

"Everything's tickety-boo," said the dapper little mouse.

"Is that the same as hunky-dory?"

"Yes, ma'am."

"Goliath told me you're Tito's cousin. Would I be correct to say you two are distant cousins?"

"Spot on, missy! Years ago me mum came across the pond, and she met me dad. He was a Yank born south of here in a land called Illinois. A flatlander, he was. He was also a tad dodgy, but a good-hearted bloke. The poor chap never could master the queen's English, but I like to keep the old ways alive for me mum. But I do admit I would have been royally duffed if Tito hadn't taught me how to talk like a cheesehead."

"Duffed?"

"Sorry, you'd say I would have had my ass whupped. Tito said if I wanted to survive around here I had a choice: lose the paisley, or talk like a cheesehead. Personally, I'd feel wonky if I wasn't dapper, so I opted to learn the language.

"Now, Miss Spunk, enough of all this chin-wagging. I'm right chuffed that you chose me for this important mission, and I want no cock-ups; so I think I'd best be speaking cheesehead."

"That might be a good idea, so that there are no misunderstandings. But I'd love to hear more of your native tongue at another time."

We talked through my plan to get us into Nancy's house, and as we talked it became obvious that Tito had taught Belvidere well. He sounded like a real homegrown Wisconsinite, although in my opinion to pass as a true cheesehead, he should lose the vest and don a Packers' cap.

Before long Nancy arrived from school and I wasn't surprised to see her alone. Her time with Amanda had been extremely stressful. She looked exhausted, but she lit up when she saw me sitting on her stoop. I ran down the sidewalk to greet her.

"Spunky! What a wonderful surprise!" She looked around and said, "Are you here all by yourself, or is Dr. Richards waiting in the car?"

I jumped against her leg and gave her the deluxe wag-and-wiggle package.

"Looks like you're here by all by yourself. How nice of you to come see me! You're the perfect pick-me-up. Want to come inside?"

I ran back to the porch, then turned and waited beside the pot of geraniums. We had already determined that the rim of the pot was the perfect height for Belvidere to climb onto my back. Once he was on board and hidden in my scraggly scruff, he latched his umbrella handle onto my collar and whispered, "Ah, like being inside a cozy. Good to go, boss."

I sat down and offered my paw to Nancy. She laughed. "My, my! Aren't you a good girl! You remembered the rule about dirty paws. I appreciate the thought, but in all honesty I'm too tired to care. Come on, girl, let's go in."

The moment I started forward, Belvidere grabbed a hunk of fur. As I ran into the house I heard a tiny but delightful "Tally-ho!" I headed straight to the living room, where Belvidere quickly dismounted. He was safely tucked away under the couch before Nancy had even shut the front door.

"Spot on, Spunk," Belvidere whispered. "I'm good to go!"

Nancy came into the living room and said, "You sure are quick! How about we go into the kitchen and see if I can find us a snack? But first I need to use the bathroom. You wait here, girl."

I sat my rump down to indicate that I was obeying, but I lied. As soon as the bathroom door closed, I scampered around the house looking for an escape route. I couldn't find anything workable. I skidded back in front of the couch with enough time to relay my findings to Belvidere.

"Sorry, my friend, but I see no way out of here except by the doors."

"No problem," Belvidere replied. "I'll have a look-see after everyone nods off. I'm sure I can find a hole some-where—and some tidbits to eat."

Nancy returned before I was able to tell the boy about her mother being a clean freak. I was afraid tidbits were going to be few and far between.

When we got to the kitchen Nancy took a chicken leg out of the refrigerator, and said, "This should do us just fine."

I sat down beside her chair. She tore off a piece of chicken, handed it to me, and said, "Here you go—some for you and then some for me."

When we finished off the chicken, Nancy got up and washed her hands, then sat back down and patted her lap. I jumped up, put my paws on her shoulders, and laid my head under her chin.

"Ah, aren't you sweet! Is that a doggie hug?"

I'm a great hugger!

When Nancy sighed, I looked her in the eyes and cocked my head. She said, "Spunky, what am I going to do? My very best friend in the whole world is stuck in jail because she won't tell the police what's really going on, and now she wants me to talk to… 'you-know-who.' Sorry, Spunky, but I promised, and a promise is a promise. Besides, you were there, so you already know. Dang it, Spunky, I don't want to do it, but I promised Amanda I'd call, and I will. But for right now all I want to do is sit here quietly with you and pretend none of this is happening."

That could be arranged. I turned and eased myself down onto her lap. There we sat for the longest time. The stress from Nancy's body drained like sand through an hourglass. Unfortunately, time itself did not stand still.

Nancy let out a deep breath before saying, "Thanks Spunky. I wish I could sit here forever, but I need to get dinner started before my mom gets home, and it wouldn't be a good thing if she found you here. Time to go, my friend, but I do thank you for making my day better. I love you girl." She kissed the top of my head and gently set me down. When she rose and turned to push her chair in, I quickly scampered into to the living room before I headed to the front door. As I left I heard a tiny voice from under the couch say, "Looky there! Chicken delivery! Great room service. Thanks, Spunk!"

Hey, dog cheeks can hold a lot of chicken.

CHAPTER 64

By the time I got home, all I wanted was a drink of water and a soft bed. But Mom had other plans.

"There you are! Jacob called and said Quincy was acting restless and seemed determined to go to the park, and he invited us to join them. So come on, girl! It sounds like your friend needs a good romp."

Holy moly, I'm getting too old for all this nonstop gadabouting! But my friend needed me, so it was worth the effort. Besides, Quincy always refreshes my soul. After a satisfying drink, I followed Mom to the gate and off we went.

Quincy was definitely more wiggly than usual. "What's up boy?" I said. "You seem a little edgy."

"I heard Nosey's shout-out for volunteers, but you know I can't leave whenever I want. So I begged and begged until Jacob finally relented and we set off for the park. I knew the odds were in my favor that he'd invite you two, and I figured that would be my best chance to find out what's going on direct from the horse's mouth. I want to help, but being a town dog I can't just come and go like you countryfolk."

"Thanks, Quincy. I know you'd help if you could, but your safety is more important. Town traffic can be deadly, and I think there are a lot more weirdoes in town. I know you'd love to help , but I'm glad Jacob keeps you safe."

"I've been a townie all my life and believe me I don't mind a couch and a heating vent one iota." Quincy said. "Jacob's a great dad and a patient, dedicated ball-thrower, but I don't like not being able to help you."

"Tell you what," I said. "If you really want to help me right now, you can run yourself ragged around that big tree over there while I lay this weary body down and take a short rest. If you stop and lie down in front of me every once in a while, I'll fill you in on all the current happenings. How's that sound?"

"My friend, if that's what you want, then that's what you'll get."

I chuckled. "Just watching you run will probably be all the exercise I can handle right now."

A true friend puts forth the effort to help you the way you need it, even if it's not the way they want to do it.

CHAPTER  65

Little did I know that my rest time in the park would have to sustain me for quite a while. I had hoped for an uninterrupted night's sleep, but about ten o'clock Ollie arrived. He reported that Tito had snuck out of the Pederson house early and sent word to Goliath that he needed to see us right away. Fearless and I headed over there, while Ollie flew on ahead to tell them we were on our way.

We found Tito perched on Goliath's neck and ready to report. "Good, you're here. I heard stuff that could be important. I didn't think it should wait until our scheduled midnight report time."

I nodded. "That was smart of you, Tito. What's going on?"

Tito took a deep (albeit little) breath and began his report. "About twenty minutes ago Mrs. Pederson received a phone call. She didn't address the caller by name, and of course all I could hear was her side of the conversation, but this is what I heard. After a bunch of uh-huhs she said, 'When did she tell you that? Did she say anything else? Okay, then we must meet tonight. Just do as I say! I have the money. I want this finished! Can you get to the mall?

What about the school parking lot? All right, be there in an hour.' Then she really got agitated and yelled, 'Just be there!' and slammed the phone down.

"I thought you should know right away, in case it's important."

I concurred. "Good reporting, Tito! You've got an excellent memory—and you're right, it does sound important."

I turned to Ollie and asked, "Will you follow Mrs. Pederson's car when she leaves?"

A hoot confirmed that he would.

"But Spunk," Tito objected, "we have to hear what happens at that meeting. It's imperative that I be in the car!"

I shook my head. "No way, Tito. I don't trust that woman, and we can't be sure where she's going or what will happen. You could get trapped in a bad situation."

"I'll be hiding in the car, so I'll be safe. Besides, Ollie will be nearby. He'll swoop in to defend me, right Ollie?"

Ollie said, "Sure thing. Every critter runs from these talons, even humans. I'll get her on the run if I have to, and you'll have time to escape. Then, if need be, I'll fly back and pick you up."

I shook my head and marveled. First, owls and cats, now owls and mice, all working together! It was beyond even my imagination.

"All right," I said, "if Ollie's willing to look out for you, fine. But it's possible that even the magnificent Ollie could lose sight of her, so I think we should use the GPS team as your backup. They can also carry messages. Tell them we're setting up our command headquarters at the library, and ask them to send regular updates. That way we can send assistance if needed. Is that okay with you, Ollie? Do we have time to meet with the GPS commander?"

"That's fine, Spunk," Ollie said. "Backup is good. The GPS already has two squads on standby at Nancy's house, and I'm sure General Homer will let us use one of them to follow Mrs. Pederson."

I nodded. "Sounds like a plan. Tito, how are you going to get into the car?"

Tito leaned forward and said, "Spunk, have you seen that woman's purse? Egad, it's bigger than Whitehead's briefcase, with twice as many folds. Riding that taxi will be a piece of cheese."

"Okay, Tito, you'd best go back in and keep an eye on things. We'll keep a sentry posted out here so if anything changes let him know and he'll update Goliath. Thanks again for alerting us."

As Tito turned and walked away, I called to him, "Tito, you did real good. Promise me you'll be extra careful, okay?"

He turned back and faced me. His tiny chest swelled. He saluted and said, "Yes, ma'am, I promise."

CHAPTER  66

Just as Tito's tiny tail slipped through the window, the second wave hit.

Einstein was out of breath when he skidded to a stop beside Goliath.

"Good, you're still here. I ran to Spunky's house first looking for you, but her sentries told me that she headed over here. I'm glad I can finally stop running."

"What's up, buddy?" Goliath asked.

"I got to Nancy's house at just the right time. You'll be pleased to know, Spunk, Belvidere has already found several escape routes, and he's not alone."

"What? How can that be? I was there, Nancy doesn't have any pets."

"Not that she knows of!"

"Huh?"

Einstein smiled. "Yeah, Belvidere found Sophie or I should say Sophie found Belvidere. Apparently, she smelled an intruder and set out to see who dared to trespass in her house. I got to meet the gal and she's one good-looking 'mousette.' She's been living at Nancy's for quite a while.

She showed Belvidere at least five different ways in and out of that place. He said he'd tell us the whole story later—but that's not why I came to find you. He also said Nancy phoned someone, and she's going to meet them in about an hour. Mrs. Evans left after dinner to work an extra shift, so no one but us will know she's gone."

My brow furrowed and I asked, "Did Belvidere hear Nancy say she had the money?"

Einstein shook his head. "I told you everything he told me, but he was rushing me to get going to get you. We've only got a short time left before he said he was going back inside in case something changes, so we'd better hurry."

I was confused but now wasn't the time to figure it all out. "Goliath, Fearless and I will go to Nancy's. Why don't you head back and set up our headquarters. You should be there so you can act on any incoming alerts. Come on, Fearless, let's go."

This time Fearless knew not to wait for an elder, and ran ahead lickety-split. Good thing, too, because by the time I got there Belvidere was already inside.

Fearless was quick to reassure me. "Fear not, Spunk, I got a full report, and I filled Belvidere in *(breath)* on Tito and Mrs. Pederson. Belvidere is determined to go with Nancy *(breath)*, same as Tito is with Mrs. Pederson. He already found a way to do it. *(Breath.)* She put a gray hoody next to her house keys *(breath)*, so he'll hide in the hood. *(Breath.)* I told him the team would be tracking them. *(Breath.)* He said as long as he can stay on her clothing or in her purse *(breath)* he should be fine, and he'll come back when she does."

"What did he hear her say?"

"Belvidere heard *(breath)* 'Hello, this is Amanda's friend, Nancy.' *(Breath)* 'Amanda told me to call you, and to tell you that she is sticking to your deal.' *(Breath.)* 'Today, when I was at the jail.' *(Breath.)* 'Yeah, she told me everything.' *(Breath.)* 'That's right, everything. *(Breath.)* 'Why do you need to see me?' *(Breath.)* 'No, she didn't say anything about any money.' *(Breath.)* 'No, I don't drive.' *(Breath.)* 'I guess I could meet you there, but...' *(Breath.)* 'All right, already! Goodbye to you too.'"

"You're sure that was all he reported?" I asked.

"Yup."

I shook my head. "Criminy! Everything is moving too fast. Do you know if the tracking teams are ready to follow her?"

"One canine-cat team is all set to go *(breath)*, and a GPS squad is already perched in place."

"I think you should go find Lion King and fill him in. We need sentries at both houses, plus trackers on the move, and even with the additional canines he's recruited we might need more help. Lion King is the one to get us what we need. I'm heading over to the command center now. Join me there later."

As I trotted toward the campus, I tried to figure out why Nancy was asked about money and why did Mrs. Pederson say she had the money. What money? I had a premonition and it was unsettling. Nancy could be headed for trouble.

I abruptly changed course and headed for the Pederson house. Tito could be assigned a different bodyguard, but Ollie's scary talons had to follow Nancy.

When I got there, the garage was empty. Ollie was already airborne.

I was too late.

CHAPTER 67

I turned and ran full-out to command central. When I arrived, unfortunately, my premonition had become a reality.

Nancy's life was in peril!

Goliath quickly updated me on the alerts he'd received. Both teams of trackers had followed Nancy as she walked to the school parking lot, one team on the ground and one team in the air. They said she appeared startled when Mrs. Pederson suddenly got out of her car and loudly asked, "What are you doing here?"

Nancy replied, "What are *you* doing here?"

Before she could answer, a black SUV came speeding across the lot toward them. The headlights were blinding. The car screeched to a halt, the door flew open and a short, stocky man with long, dark greasy hair stepped out. When he raised his arm, they saw the gun.

"Okay, you two," he said. "Time to take a ride."

"You!" exclaimed Mrs. Peterson, "What in God's name are you doing? I brought the money. It's in the car. Now, put that thing away."

The man's face grew dark and revealed his rage as he snarled, "Bitch, you don't get to tell me what to do anymore. Now, both of you move real slow over to her car and get the money." He raised the gun higher and demanded, "Now!"

Mrs. Pederson, obviously shaken, began moving slowly toward the car. Nancy followed her as close as a shadow. Mrs. Pederson reached in through the window and retrieved a large cloth bag.

"Okay," the man said. "Both of you, over here. Put the bag in the back seat of my car." They obeyed.

The man then forced them both into the front seat, with Mrs. Pederson behind the wheel. He got in the back with the gun pointed toward their heads. The ground trackers reported seeing Belvidere's head sticking out from under Nancy's hoody, but no one had seen Tito. They confirmed he hadn't been clinging to Mrs. Pederson's purse, and when they went back to check her car he wasn't there.

Tito was MIA.

The car drove off. It quickly picked up speed, and the ground trackers couldn't keep up. They had to drop back. Ollie and the GPS were now on their own.

All we could do was wait.

CHAPTER 68

I't's true, critters live in the moment. But when someone you care about is in danger, that moment can be far too long.

I hoped one of the pigeons would bring us an update soon. Meanwhile, the ground crew returned to home base and waited for their next assignment. But first we needed to know where to send them.

All eyes stayed fixed upward. Finally Goliath shouted, "Incoming! To the northwest!"

The courier landed on a tree limb and then gracefully fluttered to the ground. Despite being surrounded by cats, he wasn't afraid. He knew he was in the neutral zone.

With his head bobbing, he marched over and said to me. "Private Coo reporting in, ma'am. We followed the suspect's car, which now contains both female targets. The car entered the parking lot of the abandoned warehouse just south of the old Piggly Wiggly. My squadron and Ollie are standing by at the site. Ollie's trying to find a way to get inside, but as of when I left he hadn't found one."

This time we left half of our brigade behind with Goliath. If the man moved to a new location, I knew we might find ourselves at an empty battlefield.

Rule number ten: Never deploy all your weapons at once. Maintain a reserve.

Fearless and I led the first assault team. We were ready to rumble.

CHAPTER 69

If not for the empty streets and the cover of darkness, it would have taken more time and far greater covert maneuvering to move our army of cats and dogs through town. It was already close to midnight, and the only person we saw was a man coming out of a bar. He did a double take, but from his unpleasant alcoholic smell and wobbly stance, I reckoned he wouldn't be calling the authorities.

Security lights illuminated the front of the old warehouse and its parking lot. I checked out the black SUV, and my nose told me that Nancy and Mrs. Pederson had gotten out and walked into the building. A man had walked behind them. I repeated my scan. My nose recognized this man, but I had no mental image to match his scent.

There was no time to ponder that now. Ollie landed beside me. "I flew around the building, and several of the GPS squad walked the perimeter. We can't find any way in except those two doors in front, one for freight and the other for people. There are two ground-level windows in the rear, but they're covered with wire mesh. The roof has two big skylights, but they're secured under metal cages. Otherwise, it appears to be one big concrete box. There are water pipes and other lines going in at the back, but we couldn't find any holes big enough for even skinny Einstein to get through. Sorry, Spunk. What do you want to do?"

"There's only one thing to do: get the man to open that door."

Ollie countered, "Okay, so we make enough noise and he opens the door. But once he sees this horde of critters coming at him, he'll slam that door shut faster than I can dive-bomb."

"Then let's lose the horde."

Ollie shook his head. "Even if you and Fearless do manage to get inside, once the door shuts you'll be locked in there with him *and* his gun."

"Yeah, but at least then we'll be on the right side of the door."

Ollie said, "I don't like it."

"Me either, but Nancy's inside, and we can't help her out here. We're going in. What I need you to do is fly as fast as you can back to command central. Tell Goliath to take a crew and go raise a ruckus at my house, and don't stop until Mom comes out and is ready to follow them. She knows we're out here somewhere, and she knows Goliath. If he shows up all agitated, she'll follow him, no doubt about it. Tell Goliath to walk around the car until she realizes we're not within walking distance. She'll need directions, but I'd never ask Goliath to get in a car, so Ollie, would you please go with him. You can fly low and show Mom where to go. I'm betting she's smart enough to call Frank before she heads out the door. It's our best bet to get the humans over here fast."

Ollie took off, and Fearless and I began concocting a plan. We needed to make enough noise so that the man would open the door, but the trick would be to prevent him from slamming it shut so fast that we would also get slammed as we slipped in. I handpicked one of our best canine howlers, and Fearless chose two outstanding feline yowlers. I moved the rest of the crew way back in the parking lot, far enough away that they wouldn't be seen as a threat, but close enough that they'd definitely be noticed. I separated them into lines of ten critters each, forty feet apart. We outlined our plan to them. The stage was now set, and it was show time.

The team assigned to the door began howling and yowling.

Inside, I heard heavy footsteps approaching. Then a shout. "Hey! What's going on out there?"

The moment the man spoke, silence fell. As we expected, his interest vanished.

Although feline curiosity is legendary, it's usually tempered with caution. Humans, on the other hand, can't stand not knowing what is going on. I was betting this guy would prove this to be correct.

The footsteps moved away, and when they did, we began the ruckus again. The footsteps returned, and when they reached the door we stopped. The footsteps moved away, and we started up again. It took three full cycles before we heard the door lock click.

As the door handle turned, I nodded. The yowlers and howlers ran off. Fearless and I flattened ourselves against the building so we would be hidden behind the door.

The door opened a crack and then slowly swung wider. As planned, once the door was wide enough so our team coordinator could see the man's eyes, the first line of our ensemble turned around three times in unison, gave a bow, and ran off. Then line two performed the same routine. Then line three. Then line four. Then…

Our amazing feline–canine dance troupe succeeded in mesmerizing the man. He never saw the two four-legged ninjas slipping around the door and entering his den.

CHAPTER 70

Inside the warehouse, the only light came from the security lamps in the parking lot shining through the skylights and back windows. The illumination in the middle of the room was dim and melted outward into complete darkness on three sides. Nancy and Mrs. Pederson were to the left of the door in the middle of the room, tied to chairs with clothesline, their arms behind them. When Nancy spotted us her face lit up. But when her mouth began to open we raced to her side. I quickly rose and put my paws on her thigh, gave her a hard stare, and firmly jerked my head sideways toward the door in the hope she'd understand she needed to keep quiet. Nancy was a clever girl, and when Mrs. Pederson started to speak, Nancy whispered, "Hush. We don't want him to know they're here."

As soon as the man slammed the door shut, Fearless and I ducked under Nancy's and Mrs. Pederson's chairs and hid behind their legs. The man came stomping across the room.

"Darnedest thing you ever saw—dancing dogs and cats! No one will believe me, so I taped it with my phone. I'm putting this sucker on YouTube! I'll bet it goes viral!"

292

Then he abruptly stopped smiling and growled, "Okay, the fun's over."

The man shoved the gun under his belt and moved across the room to an overturned box. On the floor next to the box was a blue cloth bag. He sat on the floor, took a handful of money out of the bag, and began counting aloud. "Ten, twenty, thirty, forty, fifty..." He kept going until he got to one hundred, then he set the stack aside and began counting out another hundred. When he finished that one, he reached into the bag for more.

Mrs. Pederson spoke up. "It's all there, just like you asked, all in tens. If you let me go, I can get you more. The people at the bank know me; they'll cash a big check for me, no questions asked. I promise."

The man stopped counting and asked, "How much?"

"At least another five grand. You could go a long way on ten grand. Think about it. I swear we won't breathe a word to anyone. Will we, Nancy?"

Nancy slowly said, "Not a single word."

Mrs. Pederson kept going. "Amanda is sticking to the deal, so you know she's not talking. I can get the money tomorrow morning, and you can be on your way. You said you always wanted to see the Pacific Ocean, and now you can. Wouldn't that be wonderful?"

The man stopped counting. He turned and snarled, "How the hell would you know what I want?"

Mrs. Pederson paused, then hesitantly said, "You told me about it in the letter you wrote me, remember?"

"What? You got that letter? I mailed it to Wisconsin. How did you get it in New York?"

"It was forwarded."

"Woman, your mouth is your worst enemy!" the man said. Until this moment I thought you never got it. But now I know you got it, read it, *and* you never answered it."

Mrs. Pederson's voice turned syrupy sweet. "Now, you know I didn't know where you were."

"The envelope had a return address on it, bitch."

Mrs. Pederson didn't have a comeback for that one. Her voice softened and sounded sincere. "I know I let you down. That's why I want to give you more money, to try and make it up to you, and to give you another chance."

The man looked over and snickered. "You're lying!

"Anthony, please just let us go."

The moment Nancy heard the name 'Anthony' her body tensed. She knew that name!

"You've never cared about anyone but yourself." Anthony's voice got louder. "You're a lying bitch. I know one thing's for sure: If I let you go I won't see another penny, but I sure as hell will have cops all over my ass. You're forgetting one very important thing. The cops don't even know I exist, so they're not looking for me. Amanda's not talking, and I'm gonna make damn sure you and Miss Nancy won't be saying a word to a soul. In fact, you won't be flapping your gums to anyone ever again." His cold, sinister laugh gave me shivers.

Mrs. Pederson tried again. "Anthony, I swear to you—"

Anthony stood up and stormed over to Mrs. Pederson. The smack of his hand against her face made us all cringe. He bellowed, "Shut up! Shut your pie hole! I'm sick of listening to your lies!"

He turned angrily to Nancy, and with his face inches from hers he demanded, "You got anything you want to say, Missy?"

Nancy shook her head slowly and silently.

I so wanted a piece of that ankle! But his gun was pointed at Nancy's head. I might not have been able to hurt him, but I did get a good snootful of this man called Anthony. Now I had a face to go with the scent that I already knew—and a name.

He returned to his box, laid the gun on the floor, and resumed, "Ten, twenty, thirty…"

CHAPTER  71

I leaned against Nancy's leg to reassure her we were still there. All was silent except for Anthony's counting. I hoped he'd would lose track and have to start all over again. Time was running out, we needed the humans now!

Dang, Mrs. Pederson, that woman could not keep her mouth shut. "Anthony, please, just tell me what you want and I will make it happen for you."

Anthony reached into the bag for another handful of money. He shook his head and said, "Woman, you have got to be the stupidest broad I've ever known. Tell you what. It looks like this is the last of the money, so once I finish counting it I'll give myself a treat and smack you around some more, just for the fun of it. Then I'll blow your friggin' head off."

Fearless and I hunkered down; ready to launch.

The next instant changed everything. The room filled with a piercing cry of pain as Anthony yanked his hand out of the bag. Lo and behold, clamped onto Anthony's little finger were Tito *and* Belvidere! Anthony flung his arm every which way trying to dislodge them, but their teeth were clamped deep into his flesh, and they weren't about to let go.

The moment Anthony turned his back, Fearless and I shot forward.

I hit low, my teeth sinking deep into his ankle. Fearless hit high, sinking his claws into the middle of his back. Anthony's cry turned to an agonized howl.

Then his free hand reached for the gun. I knew Fearless was safely embedded in his back; Anthony would have to shoot himself in order to get Fearless. I, on the other hand, was a sitting duck. There was no choice. I was not letting go!

The next sound I heard was sweet music to my ears. No, not a siren. No, not the humans. It was the rhythmic cadence of hooves pounding across the pavement toward the rear of the building. I glanced up just in time to see Ms. Massey's beautiful back legs smash through one of windows. Her bray shattered the air. Her powerful legs shot out again. This time she shattered mesh, glass, and the wooden frame all in one punch.

Lion King leaped through the opening, leading the charge. His wingman was none other than my brother Bobby! Behind them streamed a passel of dogs and cats, and even Ollie!

Anthony hobbled backwards as fast as he could. "No! No! Stop! Help!"

Lion King's guttural yowl was fierce and terrifying. He launched upward with a bold and powerful leap aimed at Anthony's throat. Anthony's hands flew up and caught him in mid-air as Lion King's savage hiss sprayed Anthony's face with spittle. Blood erupted as the feline's claws shredded the skin on both cheeks. Anthony screamed and viciously threw him to the floor. Lion King landed on all fours, turned and readied himself for a second attack. Bobby beat him to the punch. He hurled himself upward following Lion King's trajectory. Anthony twisted to the left and Bobby's claws sank deep into his upper right arm. Anthony bucked and wailed but failed to dislodge two mice, two cats, and a dog.

The floor trembled. I glanced backwards and saw Samson, a huge beautiful Saint Bernard running full-out right at us. His eyes were locked on Anthony's backside. When he was within a few feet, he lowered his head and I leaped away. The magnificent beast executed a no-holds-bar, full-force slam into Anthony's knees.

Anthony never had a chance.

Mom, Frank, and Tony arrived shortly thereafter. Fearless and I opted to wait for them outside. We wanted them to see that we were unharmed and that things were under control. With all those critters inside, it was best that everyone remain calm. As expected, when the humans walked through the door, they halted. I knew the scene that lay before them would take a moment or two to comprehend. There was blood-splattered money strewn all over the floor, and a man they didn't know lying on the floor in the fetal position. He was confined within a unique but obviously secure jail. On the outer perimeter, a massive German shepherd was on the right, and an equally impressive rottweiler was on the left. Then came the middle circle of defense, two Chihuahuas, two Pekingese, and two Shih Tzus. Lastly, we had the upclose-and-personal detail—five cats, one guarding his head, one his back, one his arms, one his legs, and the last one guarding his rump. The cats sat perfectly still except for their tails swishing back and forth. All eyes were fixed on their prey.

Actually, Anthony had learned the "stay" command quickly, for a human. Our training technique was simple. If Anthony budged even a smidgen, the big dogs gave deep and menacing growls, the little guys began yapping fiercely, and a well-honed set of claws strongly suggested it would be better if he stayed perfectly still. The cherry on the cake, so to speak, we had added just for fun. Ollie was perched on Anthony's thigh, and as the humans walked in, he let loose a glorious victory screech and spread his huge wings. Definitely impressive!

When Frank moved in to handcuff Anthony, the animal jailers backed off and quickly departed. Mom and Tony untied Nancy and Mrs. Pederson. Then Mom wrapped a shaking, crying Nancy in a different restraint—her loving arms.

Mrs. Pederson began flapping her gums. "Thank God you got here in time! That maniac was going to kill me. He's crazy! Thank God you saved me." The moment she was untied she stood with one hand fluttering dramatically to her brow. Then in an exaggerated girly voice she said, "I need fresh air. I feel faint." To my eye, however, her gait seemed strong and perfectly steady as she made a beeline for the door.

Tony quickly nabbed her and sat her right back down. "No, ma'am, you're not going anywhere until we know what's going on here."

With scared and questioning eyes, Nancy peeked over at Mrs. Pederson.

Mrs. Pederson shot back a cold and threatening glare. Her message was clear: "Keep your mouth shut."

CHAPTER 72

Even though Frank didn't have the slightest idea who this man was or what he had done, he hadn't hesitated to handcuff him. Frank knew we would never employ critter jail without a good reason. He had no idea what had caused the tiny puncture marks on the man's bloody finger, as Tito and Belvidere had long since departed. On the other hand, based on his previous experience he had no trouble identifying the weapons used on the man's ankle, back, arm, and face. He looked at me and asked, "Am I correct, Spunk, you're the ankle and Fearless is at least one or more of these claw marks?" A single bark told him his assumption was correct.

Frank now demanded a name from the unknown man. Anthony's only answer was silence.

Frank looked at Nancy and Mrs. Pederson. "Who is this guy?"

Unbeknownst to the humans, Mrs. Pederson lied. "I don't know. He said his name is Pete. I was at the school to meet Nancy to talk about Amanda. Then this guy showed up and said he had been out walking and lost his dog. He asked if we'd come help look for him." When Frank raised his eyebrows in disbelief, she quickly added. "I know, it was odd, especially so late at night. But I couldn't stand the thought some little dog alone and scared so we went with him. But when we got here, he tied us up. I don't know why, maybe we scared the poor man. The whole time, though, he was a perfect gentleman and didn't hurt us one little bit. We just want to go home and get some sleep. Isn't that right, Nancy?"

The whole time she spoke, her eyes stayed locked on Nancy's face. Nancy slowly nodded once, but stayed silent.

Fortunately, I wasn't the only one who noticed how lame Mrs. Peterson's story was. Frank shook his head and said, "Mrs. Pederson, do you really expect us to believe that cock-and- bull-story? You're telling me that you willingly got into a car with a strange man and then freely followed him into an abandoned warehouse in the middle of the night? Maybe you were born yesterday, but I wasn't. When we came in here you were screaming that this 'maniac' had tried to kill you. Now you're praising his politeness?"

Mrs. Pederson's hand flitted about her neck as she said, 'Oh, when you came through that door, I didn't recognize you, so I lied on purpose. I wasn't sure who you were, so I thought it best to tell you that Pete was dangerous. In truth he's been very nice. So let's forget the whole thing and we can all go home."

Frank gave Tony a knowing look and then said, "Before we discuss any of that, we'll take both of you to the hospital to get checked out."

Mrs. Pederson protested loudly. "No! No hospital! I'm going home. I'm not going to the hospital. I told you, he didn't hurt us. We're fine."

Tony leaned into Mrs. Pederson's face and smirked. "Then what's this big red mark on the side of your face? It looks quite puffy."

Mrs. Pederson's hand flew to her cheek as she spouted, "Oh, that! Clumsy me, I smacked myself in the face earlier with the cupboard door. I'll put ice on it as soon as I get home."

Tony rolled his eyes, shook his head in disbelief, and then calmly asked Nancy, "Are you hurt anywhere?"

Nancy quietly said, "No, I'm fine. He didn't hurt me. I don't need a doctor. Please, can we just go home?"

Frank looked directly at Nancy and said, "Sorry, sweetie, we can't do that just yet. Since you both say you're fine and are refusing to go to the hospital, we'll go right to the station and take your statements. After that, I promise, we'll take you home."

Mrs. Pederson was having none of that. "No, no way, not tonight. We're going home. We can do all that statement stuff tomorrow. Just let the man go, and let us go on our way. Don't you understand, Nancy and I are exhausted? We need sleep!"

Frank made eye contact with Tony and jerked his head toward the door. Tony took Mrs. Pederson's arm and led her out, saying gently but firmly, "We're going to the station, ma'am. You can go the easy way or the hard way, but you're going." It looked like he was trying to rein in a smile as he said, "Besides, we have some nice cold ice packs at the station, so maybe we can tone down all your puffiness."

Even as Tony drove her away we could still hear Mrs. Pederson's unceasing declarations that she wasn't going to press charges because "Pete" had done nothing wrong! Clearly, she wanted to make sure "Pete" knew she was keeping her end of the deal.

Meanwhile Frank informed the man he knew as "Pete" that he was under arrest for kidnapping, illegally detaining a minor, and carrying a handgun without a license. He then handed him over to two patrol officers, with instructions to go first to the hospital and have the man's wounds treated. Frank pulled a business card out of his pocket and wrote something on the back. He instructed the officers to tell the doctor that the source of the bite marks on the man's finger was unknown, but certified police animals had inflicted the wounds on his ankle and parts of his body, and their immunizations were current. The other claw marks had in all probability been inflicted by feral cats whose whereabouts were unknown. He handed the card to one of the police officers and said, "Here are the certified animals' names. The hospital can verify their status with headquarters. They can call me if they need more information."

In Wisconsin, if a certified police animal bites someone, it can stay on duty while being observed for any changes in their health. Quarantine is no longer required. Since the police department makes sure that immunizations are current, the risk of rabies and other diseases is virtually nil. The law originally applied to K9s, but two years ago, Capt. Swenson got the town board to expand it to include certified felines. After this adventure, I wondered if we might get mice added to that list.

Now that Mrs. Pederson was no longer there to interrupt, Frank approached Nancy and said in a kind voice, "I don't know you, but Dr. Richards has told me a lot of good things about you. I'm Detective Frank Taylor. Is there anything you want to tell me?"

Nancy hesitated, but then slowly shook her head side to side.

Frank had no way of knowing about Nancy's promise to Amanda. He said gently, "Okay, but we need to call your mother and let her know you're all right. Do you want to call Mrs. Evans, or should I?"

Nancy's lip trembled as new tears filled her eyes. Her words quickly tumbled out between sobs. "She'll freak out if you call. She's working the night shift. She's doesn't even know I left the house. I'm fine. Why do we have to tell her anything?"

Frank looked at Mom, who apparently anticipated his next move and nodded her assent. "Okay," said Frank. "For now let's just get you to the station. Dr. Richards will stay with you, and we can decide the best way to proceed after that. But I'll make you this promise: I won't let Mrs. Pederson anywhere near you, okay?"

Nancy rapidly nodded her head as she exhaled in relief.

CHAPTER  73

Since we were there, Fearless and I got to ride along in the squad car. We knew Mom wasn't about to exclude us, and besides we're certified police critters, so we also went into the station house.

Frank again broached the subject of calling Nancy's mother and again Nancy begged him not to. Nancy explained to Frank that her mother suffered from germaphobia and even hearing that she had to walk into this station would really upset her. She said her mother would do it, but it would be very difficult. Telling her at home would be kinder and much easier for Nancy as well. Frank wanted to make sure he acted responsibly so he offered a compromise. He would request that the on-call social worker from Children Services be present when they talked. Nancy agreed. He then asked Nancy to wait with Mom while he made that call and initiated the paperwork on "Pete." Frank's wink to Mom told me there was another reason for leaving them alone. After bringing in an array of comfort foods, including hot chocolate, soda, granola bars, doughnuts, and the blanket Mom asked for, Frank left the four of us alone in the interrogation room.

Mom wrapped the blanket around Nancy's shoulders and then sat down next to her. Mom's voice was soft and kind. "I'm so sorry all this happened to you. It must have been really scary." Nancy sipped her hot chocolate and nodded.

Mom then gently asked, "Can you tell me what happened?" Nancy said nothing.

Fearless was already up on the table, but he waited to make his move. Mom looked down at me and nodded. I walked around to Nancy's side, and I rose up and put my paws against her thigh. Nancy looked down, smiled, patted her lap, and I jumped up. As before, I put my paws on her shoulders and looked into her eyes. Then I laid my head on her shoulder and gave her a warm doggie hug. She put down her hot chocolate, hugged me back, and whispered. "You were so brave. You're my hero!"

Then she began to cry softly. She and I stayed like that for a while before I moved and surprised her with several quick kisses to her nose. As I hoped, she giggled, and I felt a door to her soul open. Now maybe Mom could get in.

I turned and lay down. Nancy knew exactly what to do and began stroking my back. Then Fearless made his move and walked over and lay down in front of her. We knew that Sweetie had permanently changed Nancy's mind about cats, and now that she had seen Fearless attack her attacker, she didn't hesitate to reach out and stroke his head. She leaned toward him and whispered, "You were very brave, too. Thank you, whoever you are."

Mom smiled. "His name is Fearless."

Nancy smiled too. "Well, he certainly lived up to his name tonight."

"Nancy, I think you also were very courageous" Mom said.

Nancy quickly said, "I didn't do anything."

At the warehouse, when Mom was holding Nancy she would have felt if Nancy's body reacted to what was said. She also heard the hesitation in Nancy's voice as she answered Frank's questions. Given all that and her previous observations of Nancy after visiting Amanda, I suspected Mom knew Nancy was holding something back. She just didn't have a clue what that might be.

Mom then took a risk, but one that was based on her ability to see what others often fail to notice.

"Nancy," she began, "I think you're trying very hard to do what you think is right. But the problem is you're no longer sure what the right thing is."

New tears fell upon my back.

Mom continued, "Sometimes there are no good choices, only hard ones. But I think you already know in your heart what you should do. I want you to know you don't have to do this alone. If you'll let me, I'll try to help you."

As Nancy's tears fell faster, sobs shook her body. Mom stayed silent but wrapped both arms around Nancy and held her tight.

Nancy leaned into Mom's chest and sobbed, "But, I promised. I promised."

CHAPTER  74

M om stayed quiet and hoped Nancy would emerge from her hiding place.

Nancy was silent and kept her head down. Then, as she gently stroked my back, she began muttering. She wasn't really talking to us, not yet anyway. She was trying to put words to perhaps the hardest decision of her young life. Then she began telling Mom her thoughts.

"I promised Amanda I'd never tell. I've never broken a promise to her, not once in my entire life. But if I keep the promise my friend will be in jail forever. But that's exactly what she wants me to do. She told me why, and I understand her fear, but until last night I only knew what Amanda told me about—." Nancy hesitated. Maybe she remembered that Mom didn't know anything about Anthony. She continued, "I can tell you this, Pete is a really, really bad man. He's the one who should be locked up, not Amanda. But, if I break my promise, Amanda will never forgive me. She's already told me that if I tell anyone she'll never let me see her again, and our friendship will be over. So if I break my promise, my best friend hates me *and* she could be in jail forever, *and* she'd never let me see her again. That means if I break my promise, we'll both end up alone." She dropped her head and sighed. "I don't want her to be alone."

As Mom gently stroked the back of Nancy's head, she said softly, "I know you love Amanda. She's like a sister to you. But when we love someone, are we obligated to help them ruin their life? Like it or not, you can't stop Amanda from destroying her own life. Only she can do that. You made it sound like your promise to Amanda and what you do about Pete are somehow connected. If that's true, then maybe it's time to weigh all the costs of keeping that promise—not just the cost to you and Amanda, but also the cost to those who could be harmed if Pete goes free. You just said he's a really bad man. Is that a cost you can live with?"

Nancy quietly asked, "But how do you know who you should protect?"

"Maybe you need to ask yourself an even harder question. Whom are you really trying to protect? You said keeping this promise could harm Amanda; but doesn't it also end up protecting you by assuring your friendship won't end?"

Nancy sighed. "Both are true."

Mom smiled lovingly at the young girl's honesty. "As hard as it may be, I believe you'll make the right choice. Over the past few weeks, I've had the opportunity of getting to know you, and no matter which choice you make, it won't change the fact that you're a good person."

Nancy shook her head slowly and said softly, "I know what I should do; I just don't want to do it."

"From what I've seen, you're much braver than you realize. But you don't have to carry this burden alone. Tell us what you know, so we can help you."

Maybe it was her lack of sleep or maybe she was tired of not knowing what to do. Maybe Mom's caring words made a difference, or maybe that last strong wave of love I sent up through her hands pushed her over the edge. What I do know is that the deep sigh we all heard drained Nancy's remaining resistance.

"Could you ask Detective Taylor to come back in, please?" she said.

CHAPTER 75

When Frank came in, a social worker from Children Services, Ms. Graves was with him. She introduced herself and told Nancy that Detective Taylor had already filled her in on the details of kidnapping as well as her connection to Amanda Pederson. After asking Nancy several questions to confirm her well-being, she indicated that the interview could proceed.

Nancy began telling the humans what we critters already knew. She took them back to the day Amanda's behavior had changed so radically. She said she now knew that was the day Amanda first met Anthony.

It was also the day Amanda learned that she had a brother.

And his name was Anthony—Anthony *Nelson*.

Amanda and Anthony met multiple times and shared the stories of their lives. Nancy then began telling the story that Amanda had told her.

The first time Amanda saw her mother as a sloppy drunk was the second summer she went to New York. After the second night of Mrs. Pederson drinking to excess, Amanda called her father and told him she wanted to come home. When she got back, her father sat her down and they had a long talk about her mother being an alcoholic. He told her that her mother had started drinking after they were married, and it only got worse and worse. The only time he remembered her not drinking was when she was pregnant with Amanda and for about three years after she was born. He told her about their frequent arguments and her pattern of storming out and staying away for long periods. But she had always come back—until twelve years ago, when she didn't. He thought the reason she left for good was because she had received an inheritance and no longer needed his paycheck.

Anthony was born almost five years before Amanda. He was raised in New York by a woman named Anna Reynolds, who Anthony said was a good and loving mother. He knew that she and Mrs. Pederson were high school friends who had stayed in touch over the years via email. When Mrs. Pederson was pregnant with Anthony, she called Ms. Reynolds and told her that Mr. Pederson was abusing her and that she feared for the baby. Ms. Reynolds had never married; she had a well-paying job at a publishing company, and a large guest bedroom. Mrs. Pederson begged her to let her stay with her until the baby was born. Ms. Reynolds agreed.

Years later Ms. Reynolds told Anthony that Mrs. Pederson had admitted to having an extramarital fling that had resulted in her pregnancy. As soon as Mrs. Pederson knew she was pregnant she did the math, and she knew it wasn't Mr. Pederson's child. But she didn't say a word to anyone. Instead, she orchestrated enough romantic evenings with Mr. Pederson that he never questioned her fidelity, and when she told him "they" were expecting a baby, he was delighted.

But when she was almost six months pregnant, she and Mr. Pederson had a big fight. She bragged to Ms. Reynolds how good it felt when she cut Henry off at the knees by telling him that the baby wasn't his. The next day, while Mr. Pederson was at work, she packed her bags and left. She was quite proud that she left no clues to where she'd gone.

No one knew exactly what Mrs. Pederson told the hospital, but Anthony's birth certificate showed that his father's last name was Nelson and that he lived in Hoover, about one-hundred miles north of Clearwater. Ms. Reynolds and Anthony came to believe she had made a copy of her marriage certificate and altered the name of her husband and the town they lived in.

Ms. Reynolds told Anthony that within days of his birth Mrs. Pederson started drinking heavily, picking fights with her, and refusing to take care of the baby. Then one night, while everyone slept, Mrs. Pederson packed her bags and left. Ms. Reynolds didn't know how to find her, since she had never known her real address. She feared that if she filed a missing person report the police would find out about the baby, and she couldn't bear the thought of losing him. So she made her decision. She hid his birth certificate, told people he was adopted, and let Anthony grow up believing that she was his mother.

Anthony told Amanda that he always had trouble in school. He couldn't pay attention, and he even had a hard time sitting still. Ever since he was young he had been labeled a "problem child," and the older he got the more trouble he got into. By the time he was thirteen he was drinking and doing drugs. By sixteen he was in a jail cell. When the judge offered rehab as an alternative, Ms. Reynolds was grateful. Wanting to do the right thing by her son, she told the social worker the truth about his birth mother, but not before she told Anthony.

Sadly, the rigid restraints of the law had no heart. Since Ms. Reynolds was not legally his mother, Anthony became a ward of the state. Things went downhill even faster after that.

By eighteen Anthony was back in jail. He told Amanda that as he sat in the cell he obsessed about finding the woman who had abandoned him. Over the next three years his obsession simmered and his anger grew.

Upon his release, armed only with his birth mother's name and that she lived in Wisconsin, he began his search. He located an address for Mr. Henry Pederson in Clearwater and sent a letter to Mrs. Pederson at that address. He told her who he was and all the things he dreamed of doing, though he failed to mention his criminal record. He never got a reply.

He intensified his hunt. Several months later, using public records, social media, and Internet searches, he found the right Ruth Pederson. She was actually living in New York. He went to her apartment.

Mrs. Pederson was the one who told Anthony that he had a sister, living in Wisconsin, and her name was Amanda.

That was where Nancy cut off the story of Amanda's and Anthony's backgrounds. She changed course, and began telling Mom and Frank what had really happened during the kidnapping at the warehouse that night. She said Amanda asked her to call Anthony, which she did. She agreed to meet him in the parking lot, but when she got there, he wasn't there—Mrs. Pederson was. She had no idea why. Nancy reminded them that she had never set eyes on Anthony, so she had no idea that he was the man with the gun until much later when Mrs. Pederson called him by name.

She related how he forced them into the warehouse and tied them up. Tears flowed down her cheeks as she described Anthony smashing Ruth in the face and saying he intended to kill both of them.

Then, in an instant, Nancy's mood dramatically lightened. She raised her head, sat straight up, and beamed as she said, "Then Miss Spunky and Fearless sprang into action and attacked him. They sure showed that asshole who was boss! You should have seen what happened next. Like magic, the back window smashed open and the most magnificent army of critters came pouring in. There was even a huge owl! It was incredible! In no time at all they turned that SOB into a quivering blob, lying on the floor and sniveling like a baby. It was the greatest thing I've ever seen! These two are my heroes."

Then she stopped. That was as far as she would go.

Apparently, Nancy had made a decision. "I've given you enough of the story to send you in the right direction, but I won't betray my friend any further. The rest of the story is Amanda's to tell. Whether or not she does is up to her. And if she asks me to, I'll refuse to testify against her brother. That too will be up to her. "

She turned to Mom and said, "This I can live with."

Mom smiled, kissed Nancy's forehead, and said, "You did fine, and I'm proud of you. Frank, I think it's time we let Nancy go home. She's earned herself a good rest."

CHAPTER 76

Mom, Fearless, and I went with Frank to Nancy's house. Ms. Graves followed in her own car. The plan was if Mrs. Evans was home they would tell her what had happened, but if she was still at work and blissfully unaware, then Mom could return tomorrow so she and Nancy could tell her mother together. As it turned out, Mrs. Evans was still at work, so we made a plan to come back later in the day after Nancy got some sleep. Nancy requested that I, too, be present.

On the way back to the station Mom and Frank discussed their options. The good part was that Mom called Professor Hoffman, who said he wanted to be present when they spoke to Amanda, and he promised to hurry right over. Frank called Mrs. Jackson, Amanda's appointed guardian. She had given him her cell phone number and told him to call any time if he needed her. After Frank apologized for waking her so early in the morning, she said she would jump in the shower and be there as soon as possible.

The next part wasn't so good. Frank said that as soon as we got back he would confront Mrs. Pederson. After everything he'd heard, he was more than ready to do battle with her. But Fearless and I knew that talking to her first was ass-backwards. She was a creative and proficient liar, and if the Frank didn't know more of the truth first, she could easily lead him down another false trail.

When we arrived at the station Frank said with a slightly wicked smile, "Okay, I'm off to talk to our mother of the year."

He turned and headed toward another interrogation room, where Mrs. Pederson was still waiting. Fearless adeptly ran across his path, causing Frank to stumble. "Hey, watch out Fearless! I almost stepped on you." That brief pause gave me ample time to grab the leg of his pants. His head jerked downward. "What the heck?"

I began pulling him in the opposite direction.

"Spunky, stop this nonsense. Let go!"

I pulled even harder. Mom chuckled, "Frank, I think Spunky's being quite clear. She thinks you're headed in the wrong direction."

Frank stopped and said, "Oh, okay. She won't give up until I do it her way." He leaned down and said with great respect, "Alright, madam, where would you like me to go?"

I let go of his pants and walked toward the cells. First, he needed to talk to Anthony, and then Amanda. After that, he'd be better prepared to handle Mrs. Pederson's lies.

In exchange for two cans of Coke, three doughnuts, and the promise that Fearless and I sit as far away from him as possible, Anthony cautiously agreed to answer some questions. Frank told him selected parts of what Nancy had revealed, and Anthony confirmed that he had located his mother about two months ago. When he learned that she was actually living quite close to him in New York, he was deeply hurt that she had never attempted to contact Anna Reynolds or him. He said that when he confronted Mrs. Pederson, she vehemently denied that she was his mother, but when he showed her his birth certificate, she shrugged her shoulders and offered to buy him a drink. He laughed as he bragged that not every mother could drink her own son under the table, but she could and she did. He said he disliked her immediately, but when she invited him to stay with her he figured it meant a roof over his head and free booze. A week later, he figured she got tired of sharing, because that was when she sprung the news on him that he had a sister, and that her father was a wealthy banker. She gave him a wad of cash and said, "Get out. Go mooch off of them."

The session ended when Frank started asking a bunch of questions and Anthony said, "That's it. No more. I'm done talking."

We went back to Frank's desk and waited. Soon Professor Hoffman and Mrs. Jackson arrived, and after some discussion they agreed that Amanda wouldn't talk if all of them were staring at her, so first Professor Hoffman should talk to her by himself. Since the state recognized him as Amanda's therapist, Mrs. Jackson said she did not have to be present during their discussion.

So it was that Professor Hoffman alone accompanied Fearless and me to an interview room, and after a minute or two a bailiff led Amanda in.

Our session had a good beginning. Amanda was so delighted to see Fearless and me that she clapped her hands like a three-year-old seeing a new puppy. When she sat down we took our therapeutic positions. Professor Hoffman sat on her right, I sat on her lap, and Fearless stretched out on the table in front of her. Now Amanda was well insulated.

Professor Hoffman began, "A lot has happened since we last met. First, I want you to know that we know about your brother Anthony."

Amanda quickly looked down and said, "I don't have a brother."

"We can talk about all that in a minute. But it is important that you know Nancy and your mother are safe, but early this morning your brother, Anthony, kidnapped them. Fortunately, he didn't harm them."

Amanda's head jerked upward and her face flushed with anger. "He did *what*?"

Fearless reached out a paw, and I snuggled closer. Professor Hoffman gently laid his hand on her arm. "They're okay, Amanda. I swear to you, they're okay. Nancy is safe and sound back at home, and your mother is down the hall." Amanda's body tensed, and Professor Hoffman quickly added, "Don't worry, she doesn't know we're talking to you. She lied repeatedly to the police about who Anthony is and about the facts of the kidnapping. It was Nancy who told the detectives who he is and what really happened."

Then his voice became very gentle as he said, "Nancy told them that when she saw how dangerous Anthony was, she had to choose between the risk of Anthony hurting others and keeping her promise to you. She refused to tell the detectives the whole story, but she did tell them about

Anthony's childhood. Amanda, Anthony had a gun. He said he was going to kill them both."

Amanda slammed her hand down on the table and yelled, "God damn him! He promised me he wouldn't hurt anyone!"

Instantaneously she noticed Fearless' ears back and that he was ready to bolt. She immediately stroked him and apologized. "I'm so sorry, Fearless! Did I scare you? I shouldn't have done that. Sorry, sweet boy." The moment she began stroking Fearless her anger vaporized. It was replaced by a heavy sadness. Her shoulders sagged, her head dropped and her body slouched forward. "How did everything get so screwed up?'

In the softest, kindest voice possible, Professor Hoffman said, "I don't know, sweet girl, I don't know. But I do know that it doesn't have to stay screwed up."

Amanda kept her head down, sighing repeatedly. Now she, too, faced an extremely difficult choice. As she stroked us both, we sensed her deep sorrow. It felt like a big black hole.

Professor Hoffman persevered. "All these weeks, although you haven't told me what really happened to your father, we've talked quite a bit about your childhood and your life with him. I know you loved your Dad very much. You often said you always felt you were responsible for taking care of him because your mother had abandoned him, and how her leaving him made you sadder than the fact she also abandoned you. I've talked to you a lot about how, no matter how much we want the people we love to be happy, we're powerless over their emotions and what they do. No matter how hard we try, they and they alone are responsible for what they feel and the choices they make. Amanda, sweet, sweet girl, it's time for you to stop taking care of everyone else. It is time to take care of yourself. Whatever happened, and whatever they did, it has to be on them, not you."

Amanda started to cry, "But they promised, they promised!"

CHAPTER  77

Professor Hoffman, Fearless, and I stayed exactly where we were as Mom, Frank, and Mrs. Jackson entered the room. If Amanda was going to be brave enough to talk to them, the least we could do was make her feel a little safer.

Frank was kind. "Amanda, your friend Nancy obviously cares a great deal about you. We all should have such devoted friends. I want you to know that Nancy didn't betray you. She refused to tell us what happened to your father, although I think she knows the truth. Professor Hoffman has told you about the kidnapping and murder threats Anthony made. I've spoken to your mother, and she remains adamant that Anthony did not kidnap them and they went with him freely. She says she'll testify to that in court. Since her version of what happened is completely different from Nancy's, it will make it difficult to prove that they were actually kidnapped. We can charge Anthony with unlawful possession of a firearm. Nancy told us, and we believe her, that he threatened to kill them. However, once again, your mother's version is completely different. She says Anthony never threatened anyone at all. She claims that she never saw any gun until *after* we arrived, so we must have planted it, and that is also what she'll say in court. So we have two victims, one a teenager and one an adult, with two completely different accounts. We can charge him with assault with a deadly weapon, but proving it will not be so easy. In addition, Nancy told me she won't testify against your brother if you ask her not to. We can force her to testify but I don't think that will go well at all.

"So the bottom line is, if you stick to your story then in all probability you'll go to prison for a very long time, and Anthony could go free. Everyone in this room believes that's not the way it should be, but you're the only one who can change it."

Professor Hoffman placed his hand tenderly on Amanda's arm, and Fearless added his paw. The Professor leaned in to Amanda and gently said, "It's time, sweet girl, it's time."

Amanda sighed and then said, "I've had a lot of time to think about everything that's happened. In fact, I wish I could stop thinking about it. It's become a horror movie continually playing in my head. I can't shut it off. Parts of it I did myself, some parts I only saw, and other parts I was told about. The rest of it is still a blank. But I'll tell you everything I know."

Finally, Amanda was going to tell the truth.

CHAPTER 78

As Amanda began, she spoke in a quiet monotone with no emotion. She seemed detached from her words, as if she were talking about someone's else life.

"Anthony told me that when our mother kicked him out of her house in New York, she gave him a thousand dollars in cash and my cell phone number and address. He drove out here, found a cheap motel, and began watching our house. That was how he learned what time I usually got home from school and that Dad didn't get home until about two hours later. Then one afternoon, just after I got home, he called me. He said he had a big surprise for me and he hoped I would like it. Then out the blue, he told me he's my brother. Of course, I didn't believe him. I thought it was a scam. But as he kept talking, I realized he knew way too much about my parents and me. I was confused and suspicious, but he convinced me that until we had more time to talk, I should keep it a secret. So I did.

"After that we talked on the phone several times a day, and finally I agreed to meet him at the coffee shop. As soon as I saw him I saw his resemblance to my mother. The

326

pictures he had of them together and everything he knew about Mom's apartment and about my early life convinced me that he really was my mother's child. The good part was he didn't act like my mother. He was considerate, charming, sweet, and seemed sincerely delighted that he had finally found his sister. I began to really care about him. The more I heard the sad details of his life, the more I wanted to help him. I guess I was feeling horribly guilty that my life had been so good, while his had been so rotten. I thought his whole life could change if he lived with us and was finally part of a good family. I convinced myself that once Dad met Anthony, he would see what a good person he was. That was a stupid idea! I should have done it differently, but I didn't. I took Anthony home, but it didn't go the way I planned.

"Dad was shocked to have Mom's twenty-one-year-old son, who was not his son, standing in his living room. But he was gracious, and listened quietly as Anthony told the story of his life. Afterwards Dad politely explained that he and I needed time to ourselves to process all of it. After Anthony left Dad paced around the backyard by himself for about twenty minutes. Then he sat me down and said the reason he never told me about Mom having another child by another man was that she told him she'd given the child up for adoption. Dad said he hadn't even known whether the child was a boy or a girl, and he thought that if my mother wanted me to know, then she should be the one to tell me. He never dreamed that the child would actually show up on his doorstep! He knew I was happy that I might actually have a brother, but he thought I was blind to the fact that Anthony was high and that he'd been drinking.

He said all I had to do was look at Anthony's pupils and smell his breath.

"I don't know why, but I tried to defend Anthony. I started yelling at my father, telling him that he was wrong, and so what if Anthony was high? He had good reason to be, because he'd had such a crappy life, but once he was part of a good family I knew he'd be fine.

"Dad didn't buy it. He said Anthony was twenty-one years old, an adult, and needed to get his life in order on his own. He said he wasn't about to let a druggie ex-con we knew nothing about live under our roof. He said it wasn't safe, and it wasn't going to happen.

"Then I totally lost it. I started screaming that he wasn't even trying to give Anthony a chance. That he was really pissed at my mother and taking it out on Anthony. That it wasn't Anthony's fault Mom had slept with someone else. I went on and on about how Dad didn't know Anthony like I did, and how sweet and kind Anthony was, and how he wouldn't hurt anyone."

Amanda shivered as if a chill went through her. "I guess I got that one wrong too, didn't I?"

She didn't wait for an answer, but kept going. "Dad listened to me yell and then he walked over and put his hands on my shoulders. He was so calm it was spooky. He said I needed to remember addicts are chameleons and liars. To get what they want they'll become whoever you want them to be and say whatever you want to hear, but eventually, their addiction will demand to be fed. Then you'll see what they truly value. He said, 'How do I know? Because, I married one.' He told me he loved me and was sorry I was hurting, but his duty was to protect me. He said Anthony wasn't allowed back in our house. He told me he wasn't saying I could never see Anthony again, but that I should never be alone with him. It wasn't safe.

"Later that night, God help me, I was so angry, I called Nancy and screamed that I wished my father were dead.

"If only I could take back those words!"

CHAPTER 79

"Not a moment goes by that I don't wish I'd obeyed my father. But I didn't. I went ahead and saw Anthony the next day, and told him what my father had said. I thought he'd be furious, but he wasn't even angry. He actually comforted me, saying that my father just didn't know him like I did, and with time he knew he could win him over. I told him that would never happen. Once Dad made up his mind, it was a done deal.

"I was so angry at my father for refusing to help Anthony that I was oblivious to how Anthony was using my anger to his advantage. He was the one who suggested that I give my father a taste of his own medicine and see how he liked rejection. It was his idea that I tell one of my teachers that Dad was abusing me. I immediately thought Mr. Whitehead would be perfect. I knew he'd totally believe it, and he did. I told him I'd hurt myself if he told anyone, but I knew he wouldn't be able to keep it to himself. I truly believed he'd tell someone, and soon the gossip would knock my dad off his high horse. No way did I ever think wimpy old Mr. Whitehead would show up at my house!

"But he did. Early the next morning, there he was on our doorstep saying he wanted to talk before school. I was standing behind my father shaking my head and waving my hands, trying like hell to get him to shut up, but I swear, he acted like he was on a mission. He seemed determined to protect me. When Dad turned and looked at me, the look on his face broke my heart. I could see he was fuming, and when he stormed into the kitchen we followed. I guess Mr. Whitehead was angry that Dad had turned and walked away from him, because when he got to the kitchen he grabbed Dad and they started shoving each other. I started bawling and told them it was all a lie! Mr. Whitehead looked shocked, and the look on Dad's face was even worse. I kept saying over and over how sorry I was and begging them to forgive me. I guess neither Dad nor Mr. Whitehead could stand my crying, so eventually everyone calmed down and said they forgave me."

Amanda's voice trembled, and her bottom lip began quivering.

"After Mr. Whitehead left, I hugged Dad and told him again how sorry I was and how much I loved him. Dad said that he too was sorry, for not seeing how angry I was about him rejecting Anthony. He hugged me, kissed the top of head, and told me he loved me too."

Tears were flowing down Amanda's cheeks. She gulped air and said haltingly, "Those were the last words I ever heard my father say."

She took several deep breaths, forcing herself to calm down, and then she again forged ahead.

"After that Dad went into the kitchen to finish making breakfast. I already knew he was fixing one of my favorites,

331

watermelon. I went upstairs to get ready for school, but before I got into the shower I called Anthony and told him about Mr. Whitehead showing up, and I told him I'd been lying. He was not pleased. Then, like every other morning, I got into the shower, cranked up my music, and started singing.

"I never heard the doorbell. But when I got out of shower I heard voices downstairs. I thought maybe Mr. Whitehead had come back, so I pulled on my sweats and ran down the stairs."

Amanda buried her face in her hands. Her sobs grew louder and deeper. "Dad was dead. My God, all that blood... That horrible knife sticking in him..."

For weeks now, Amanda had only recited her mantra and refused to let her emotions show. She had built strong walls, but thankfully, they were not impenetrable. As those walls began to crack, the flood could no longer be contained.

Now Amanda's grief was mixed with rage. She yelled, sobbed, ranted and pounded the table with her fists. "I killed him! I didn't stab him, but I killed him. God help me, it was my fault! It was all my fault. I murdered my own father!"

Without a sound we all agreed it was time for a break. Mom, Frank, and Mrs. Jackson, silently got up and went out, leaving Joe, Fearless, and me alone with Amanda again. Mom returned with a box of Kleenex and two cans of Coke. Before she slipped out again, she gently draped her own sweater over Amanda's shoulders.

Professor Hoffman moved closer and put an arm lightly and tentatively around Amanda to see if she wanted that kind of comfort. Her answer was immediate. She collapsed into his chest as if it was the safest place in the world. Professor Hoffman knew that right now silence was better than words.

Amanda's sobbing escalated to wailing, and then shrieking. "It's my fault! I killed him! I killed my father!" She gripped Professor Hoffman's shirt and pounded her head into his chest over and over. He never pulled away. His arms stayed lightly about her, and he made soft, soothing sounds. Slowly her hysteria lessened to body-wrenching sobs and gulps, and then to blubbering and whimpering. Finally she was limp and sniveling. Professor Hoffman poked a wad of Kleenex toward his chest, and Amanda took it. Eventually she sat back and blew her nose. Professor Hoffman's shirt was covered in tears and snot but, bless his heart, he couldn't have cared less. He wore it like a badge of honor.

After rehydrating Amanda with a Coke and feeding her gentle words, Professor Hoffman asked if she wanted to quit for the day. She straightened her shoulders, raised her head, stared him square in the eye, and said, "No way in hell am I quitting now!"

Although our critter applause was silent, it was nonetheless heartfelt.

CHAPTER  80

After a few minutes everyone returned to the interview room. Amanda looked exhausted, but acted stronger than before. A good cry seems to have a profound effect on humans.

Frank began by saying as gently as he could, "So, when you came downstairs, your father was already dead, is that right?"

Amanda nodded.

"Who else was there?"

"Just Anthony. He was in the hall by the front door. He turned and told me something terrible had happened. When his eyes darted toward the kitchen I ran in there, and that's when I saw Dad on the floor. I began screaming, and I collapsed. I remember Anthony pulling me up and holding me and making shushing sounds, as if I were a baby. I then felt myself going down a dark hole. I knew I was screaming, but I couldn't hear my own screams. I don't know how long I was hysterical, but when I came back to my senses Anthony was yelling at me. He was gripping my arms so tight that it hurt. He shook me and ordered me to snap out of it. He said I had to help him or he'd go back to jail, and there was no way he was going to let that happen. Once I spoke to him, he immediately calmed down. That was when he told me what had happened.

"He said he'd come over to tell my father that he understood why he was being so cautious. He said he'd just wanted to talk, but that my father had gotten really angry and exploded like a crazy man and punched Anthony in the gut. Dad screamed that Anthony had better stay away from me, or he'd kill him. Anthony said Dad then picked up the watermelon knife and lunged at him. They fought over it, and Dad got stabbed. Anthony said there was nothing he could do. He was defending himself.

"Then Anthony started crying and said that, with his record, the cops would never believe him. He said he'd kill himself before he ever let anyone put him in a cell again. He told me I was the only person who'd ever believed in him, and now I was the only one who could save him. He pleaded with me to call Mr. Whitehead and tell him that I said I lied because I was afraid of my father, and to say that after Whitehead left my father started kissing and touching me. When he wouldn't stop, I picked up the knife but that I only wanted to threaten him so he'd stop; but he grabbed me, and the next thing I remembered was seeing him dead on the floor."

Amanda blew big puffs of air as if trying to blow the memory from her mind. Then she continued. "The whole time Anthony was talking, I think I was nodding my head. All I remember was feeling numb, and that everything sounded muffled. But when he took my hands

335

and tried to put them on the knife, I remember pulling back. He said my prints had to be in the right place, or the cops wouldn't believe me. He kept begging me to help him, so I let him press my fingers against the handle. He kept saying the cops would believe I was defending myself, because I'd already told Whitehead about the abuse. Besides, the cops would assume that something terrible must have happened for a teenage girl like me to stab her own father. Over and over he said that if I just stuck to the same story, I'd be fine. Then he'd be safe and we could finally be a family. He told me what to say, and I said it, over and over and over…"

Amanda paused, looked over at Professor Hoffman, and said, "All this time I never told Professor Hoffman what really happened, but he was very kind and talked a lot about the traumatic effect of seeing my Dad dead like that, and what that kind of shock can do to a person's mind. I was living a nightmare, but I now understand that I'd actually stepped outside of my own sanity. I had only one recurring thought: my dad was dead, my mother was a miserable drunk, and the only person I had left was Anthony. If he killed himself or ran away, I'd have no one. I'd be alone. He was my brother. I had to save him."

And so the lie was born.

Then Amanda stopped talking and there was silence. It was a silence of respect.

Frank finally broke the stillness by clearing his throat and saying, "Amanda, it took a lot of courage for you to tell us all that. I want you to know that I believe you, and I'm going to do everything I can to help you get out of here.

Right now, though, I need you to answer one question for me. Do you believe that Anthony stabbed your father in self-defense?"

Amanda looked Frank straight in the eye and said, "No."

CHAPTER 81

Amanda was finished and it was time for us to go, but Professor Hoffman said he would stay with her a while longer. Fearless rubbed against her face and I kissed the tip of her nose, and we followed Mom, Frank, and Mrs. Jackson out of the room.

Before anything else could happen, Mom said it had been a long morning and she wanted to take us outside. Being Mom, she first retrieved the cat harness and one of the extra leashes she always keeps in the car. Fearless wasn't thrilled about the harness, but he did have to pee, so he consented. Once we all were back inside, Mom set down a bowl of water and we drank heavily. Amanda wasn't the only one who needed hydration after the night's excitement.

Amanda's guardian had departed, and Frank was sitting at his desk with a tray of fresh coffee and bagels.

"Thank goodness," said Mom. "I'm starving!" She broke off a small piece of bagel and gave it to me. Fearless declined; after all, it wasn't an eggroll.

Frank took a sip of coffee, then said, "Now we have to fill in the blanks. I guess our best bet is for Tony and me to go talk to Anthony, and see if we get anywhere."

"I grant it's good for us, but it's weird that Anthony hasn't lawyered up." Mom said as she nibbled on her bagel.

Frank held up his hand in a defensive gesture. "Hey, not my fault. I personally Mirandized the man twice and he signed statements, both times, affirming that I did. I've gone above and beyond what I had to do to protect his rights but he says he doesn't need a lawyer."

Mom cocked her head. "Why would he think that?"

Frank smirked. "He told me he's been in the system so many times he knows what a lawyer would do. And he said he's done nothing wrong and we have no witnesses to say anything different. So what does he need a lawyer for?"

Mom sighed. "Arrogance may be his own worst enemy. Speaking of arrogance, what are you going to do with Ruth Pederson?"

"I guess they won't let me send her to Siberia, huh? Right now I have diddly-squat on her. It's her word against Nancy's, so I have to cut her loose."

All heads turned as Professor Hoffman came out of the interrogation room and walked over. He said nothing, but gave a tired grin when he spotted the coffee and bagels. The three of them relaxed as they replenished their bodies and talked about what Amanda had said. Mom complimented the Professor on what a great job he had done with Amanda.

"All this time I didn't think I was getting anywhere," he admitted, "but apparently trust was silently being built.

Maybe that connection helped her feel less alone, so she could finally tell the truth."

He then sighed and shook his head. "But that poor girl's going to need a whole lot of help to get past all this—if she ever can."

Mom put her arm around his shoulder and said, "Well, I happen to know two therapists who would be more than willing to help her."

"But first," said Frank, "we've got to get her out of here. Why don't you two go down to the diner and get some real breakfast while Tony and I try talking to Anthony? You want to leave the critters here?"

Mom shook her head, "Uh-uh. I'll drive, and they can sleep in the car while we're in the diner."

Great idea, Mom! If I'm right outside in the car she'll be far more apt to remember my share of the bacon.

CHAPTER  82

After the diner, Professor Hoffman headed home and we found Frank back at his desk rubbing his temples.

"I brought you and Tony some hamburgers and fries," said Mom. "I figured you could use more nourishment than coffee and bagels."

Frank smiled. "Indeed I could. Thanks. Tony's in the break room, if you want to give him his. Would you bring me back some napkins, please?'

Mom chuckled. "There are three napkins already in your bag, sir, along with your extra ketchup and mustard."

Frank's smile grew. "Ah, you're a good woman, Hannah."

Mom smiled. "How true. How true."

When Mom returned from bringing Tony his food she pulled up a chair next to Frank's desk. I claimed her lap, while Fearless stretched out on the corner of the desk. "Any luck with Anthony?" Mom asked.

Frank shook his head. "Nah. We told him Amanda's version of events, and said we didn't believe he killed Pederson in self-defense. His face showed his anger when he heard Amanda had changed her story, but the only words we got out of him were, 'She's lying to protect her own ass.'"

Frank took a big bite of hamburger and mumbled, "Ah! That's good." Then he his brow furrowed. "You know, there are some suspects I'd love to get alone in a room with no mirrors. Right now that feeling's really strong. I guess it's a good thing there are so many laws against using excessive force."

I barked.

Frank jumped. "Spunky, I'm glad you agree with me, but could you do it a little more quietly?"

I growled.

Frank looked at Mom and asked, "What's that about?"

Mom shrugged and hesitantly said, "I'm not sure. All I know to do is go back to the last thing you said before she barked. It was about laws against using excessive force."

I barked twice, stared Frank straight in the eye, cocked my head, and growled.

A grin spread across Frank's face. "Ah-ha! There may be laws against *police officers* using excessive force, but Spunky and Fearless aren't what a judge would call police officers."

Mom held up her hand, "Now wait a minute, Frank, Spunky isn't biting Anthony just to make your day!"

I turned and kissed Mom's nose. She didn't see the bigger picture, but Frank did.

"Spunky isn't going to bite anyone, Hannah. Let's say that, just to be nice, I take Anthony a cup of coffee and a bagel and I tell him I'll be back later to see if he's ready to talk. However, by happenstance, I don't see that Spunky and Fearless have followed me into the room. So when I leave, those poor babies end up locked in there with Anthony. Hmm, just the three of them locked in a room. But *I know* they won't hurt Anthony, right Spunk?"

I woofed softly.

"I'll follow procedure and leave the camera running so there's visual proof that Anthony wasn't harmed. Does that sound about right to you, Spunk?"

I woofed in the affirmative and off we went.

CHAPTER 83

When Frank went back into the interrogation room where Anthony was waiting he immediately began talking and shaking the bag of bagels. He also blocked Anthony's view of the door. While Anthony's eyes were on the bagels, Fearless and I silently crept in, crawled under the table, and waited.

"So, do you feel like talking yet? No? Okay. Well, if you bend forward slightly you've got just enough slack in your handcuff chain to get a bagel and a cup of mud to your mouth, so you'll be fine. I'll be back in a while to see if you've changed your mind."

Frank's voice held an obvious smile.

When the door shut behind Frank, the only sounds were Anthony's slurping and chewing. Then Fearless reached out and tapped Anthony's leg.

Anthony jumped. When he looked down all he saw was our two handsome faces staring up at him.

"What the hell? How did you two get in here? Nice doggie. Nice kitty. Here want some bagel?" He dropped a morsel. As hard as it was to ignore that tasty tidbit, I wouldn't give him the satisfaction. Our eyes stayed locked on his.

Then we slowly began to move. Fearless hissed as he crept under Anthony's chair. I followed right behind him with a very nasty growl. Anthony wiggled around like a fish on a hook. We turned and faced his plump butt protruding through the back of the folding chair. We knew full well where the camera was, in front of Anthony. No one could see us. Fearless rose and tapped Anthony's butt. I followed suit. We had a grand time playing patty-cake on Anthony's rump.

Anthony jumped up. But the short chain kept his hands tethered close to the table and prevented him from standing straight up. He could only move a few inches in any direction. He twisted his neck backwards but could not turn around. Multiple times he attempted to kick us but we knew which leg would lash out by how his weight shifted and we simply scampered out of harm's way. His frustration grew. He alternated between whimpering and yelling for someone to come help him. Guess what? No one came. As we crawled back under the table, once again I growled and Fearless hissed. In order to see us he spread his feet apart and bent sideways. That was when, just for fun, I raised a lip, growled and locked my eyes onto his groin. You should have seen how fast that man sat down and clenched his knees together!

Given the way Anthony squirmed in his chair, he must have been ready to wet himself. His cries for help now changed to "Okay, I'll talk! Just get them out of here!"

Amazingly, Frank came to his rescue at that very moment. "Did I hear you say you were ready to talk?"

"Yeah, yeah, but now I want a lawyer. Get me one and I'll sing like a bird. Just get these two out of here?"

Frank sounded very confused. "Two? Who are you talking about? You've been in here all by your lonesome. It's just you and me, pal. Just you and me."

Anthony's head spun like a top as he tried to find us. But Frank had left the door open a crack, so when Anthony was looking the other way Fearless and I made our break. Of course I made sure to grab that morsel of bagel first!

CHAPTER  84

Frank put in a call to the Public Defender's office and let Anthony rest in a cell while we all waited. About an hour later, a lawyer named Mr. Seagers arrived. Frank told him the charges against his client and allowed them time to meet alone. About thirty minutes later, Frank went in with a smirk on his face and me on a leash.

Anthony started sputtering and squawking when he saw me. But Frank just said, "My house, my rules. She's completely under control." He sat down, patted his lap, and up I jumped. "Besides, I'm much calmer when she's on my lap—and you do want me nice and calm, don't you?"

It made sense to nod, so they did. Anthony's lawyer tried to cut a deal by offering what Anthony knew in exchange for lessening the charges.

All Frank would give them was "I'll think about it. But I know one thing for sure: I'm going to charge him with first-degree murder right here and now if he doesn't start talking."

That's when Anthony began talking.

"Okay, okay." he said. "I'll tell you what happened."

Mr. Seagers advised Anthony to remain quiet. Anthony brushed him off. "I got this covered, man."

Mr. Seagers said, "Let the record show that my client's ignoring the advice of counsel."

Anthony rolled his eyes. "Now, if I may continue, here's what happened. I knew there was no way Pederson was going to let me live at his house, so I decided to have some fun. I called Ruth in New York, just to piss her off. I made up this awesome story about all the horrible names Pederson had called me, including Ruth's bastard boy. I especially liked the part I told her about how he ranted and raved that she was a bitch and a drunk-ass whore who never cared about anyone but herself. Man, it was a work of art! I knew there was no way she'd let him get away with talking that shit about her. She started yelling how she was going to call and give him a piece of her mind, but she got much quieter when I said that revenge was always sweeter up close and personal. Sure enough, the bitch got on a plane, and the next day we began plotting. It didn't take long at all to figure out how to settle the score. Ruth may be a bitch, but the broad really knows how to do payback.

"When Amanda called and said she caved in after that damn teacher showed up, we made our move. I knew I could get Amanda to agree with me, she's such a dummy, but we had to get to her before she left for school."

Mr. Seagers said, "Anthony, once again, I advise you to stop talking right now."

"Don't worry. It's cool." Anthony leaned back, puffed up his chest and a grin spread across his face. "Man, you should have seen Pederson's face when he opened the front door and saw us standing there."

I growled. My nose knew Anthony's scent had not been at the front door. Frank had no idea why I growled, but being a clever man he jumped right in. "That's a lie," he said.

Anthony furrowed his brow and cocked his head, mystified how Frank could know he was lying, but he did change his tune. "Okay, so Ruth said he wouldn't open the door if he saw me standing there. She told me to go around back and watch and listen for her cue."

He paused, waiting to see if Frank would say anything. Since I knew Anthony had indeed gone in through the back door I stayed quiet, and so did Frank.

"Okay, so as soon as Pederson let her in she started yelling at him about all the nasty names he had called her, like I told her. She never gave him a chance to get a word in edgewise. Ruth stormed into the kitchen. I was out back, peeking through the kitchen curtains so I could see and hear everything. Pederson followed her into the kitchen and she played her ace. She smugly threatened that if he didn't apologize and help me out with a job at the bank, she'd move back in with him. Yup, I told you the broad has a knack for payback! She told him she'd just move right back in, and of course her son would be moving in with her. Legally she knew she could do that, but to seal the deal she threatened that if he tried to get a restraining order against her she'd gladly tell the judge, his priest, and anyone else who would listen that she left him because he was smacking her around. Ruth said Pederson's reputation was important not only to him but also to the bank's board of directors. The plan was for me to wait outside until he apologized and agreed to her terms—but that never happened.

"Pederson refused to play along. In no uncertain terms he told her that she and I would never set foot in his house again. But she wasn't about to let him win. She grabbed his arms and started calling him every name in the book. He pulled her hands off him, spun her around, pushed her toward the front door, and told her to get out of his house. That was the gasoline on the fire. When that bitch spun back around, she grabbed that big freaking knife off the counter, and rammed it into his gut. Ol' Pederson went down bleeding like a stuck pig."

Mr. Seagers jumped to his feet. "This meeting is over, detective! I need to confer with my client."

Anthony raised his voice. "Sit back down, mister lawyer man. I didn't kill the old man. I told you it's all cool."

Mr. Seagers sat back down, leaned in and whispered into Anthony's ear. Anthony waved him off and said, "It's over when I say it's over. Man, don't be such a candy-ass."

Anthony was obviously enjoying himself. He was not ready to relinquish the spotlight. "Ruth let me in, and that's when I took over. When I heard the shower running I told Ruth to get the hell out of there, keep her mouth shut, and I'd handle everything. Her butt barely made it through the front door before Amanda came running down the stairs. From day one, I had that stupid girl eating out of the palm of my hand, so I knew I could get her to take the rap. I just didn't think the dummy would make it so freakin' easy."

Mr. Seagers leaned again and told Anthony he needed to stop talking. Anthony slammed the table. "Listen asshole.

I'm in charge here, not you. I'm gonna fire your ass if you keep interrupting me! Now, where was I? Oh, yeah. I knew Ruth had never taken off her driving gloves, so all I needed to do was get Amanda's prints on that knife and it would be a done deal. I told her what to do and what to say, and then I left the house."

Wrong! My nose knew Anthony had gone up the stairs and into the little office. I growled. Frank looked at me and then spoke his line. "That's a lie!"

I admit, it was fun seeing Anthony so baffled. "All right, already! I went upstairs, but I didn't touch anything."

That one got two growls. Frank smiled. "Do I have to say it again?"

Anthony huffed and puffed in frustration. "How the heck…? Okay, you win. I rummaged through the old man's desk. I took his gun and five hundred bucks. But I didn't stab him. His darling wife did that all on her on. I never touched the dude."

I growled. Frank was quick, although this time he did ad lib. "Another lie! Your prints were on the body."

Anthony took the bait, "No way! I put on those kitchen gloves…" His voice fell to a whisper, "… before I took the money from his wallet."

Now who's the dummy?

CHAPTER 85

Frank came out of the interrogation room all smiles.

Mom was sitting by his desk petting Fearless. "My, my!" she said when she saw his smile. "Something must have gone right in there."

Frank chuckled. "I took Spunky in there to intimidate that moron, but I got a bonus I never expected. This pooch is the best lie detector I've ever seen! You should have seen her nail him in one lie after another. How in heaven's name she knew he was lying is beyond me, but she did. She really did!"

Mom smiled proudly. "She can be quite amazing."

Perhaps Frank realized that he was having way too much fun, or maybe reality set in. He took in a deep breath, exhaled all his excitement, and got serious. "Have you seen Tony?" he asked.

"Yes, he left about ten minutes ago. He said to tell you he had to go talk to a witness for the Macklin case."

"Oh, yeah I forgot." Frank furrowed his brow and said, "I'm not really sure what the next step is. I know what I'd like to do, but legally I've hit a wall."

Mom leaned forward. "Care to elaborate, oh wise one?"

"Amanda says Anthony told her he killed Pederson. But Anthony says Ruth killed him, and if I question Ruth she'll probably tell me Amanda did it, and then we're right back to square one. The problem is, all I have is Anthony accusing Ruth, but not one shred of hard evidence. Ruth's prints weren't on the knife. No one except Anthony even knew she was in town until she showed up at Mrs. Swanson's house asking for a key. We've already searched the house thoroughly and didn't find a shred of evidence linking her to the murder. Add to all this mess, Ruth was released hours ago, and I'll bet she's already packing her bags and getting ready to fly the coop."

"Can't you now arrest her on suspicion of murder?"

"Based on what? The accusation of an ex-con druggie who is looking to make a deal? I don't have one piece of solid evidence to support a search warrant. And if I go talk to the woman, we both know she isn't going to give me squat. I wouldn't be any better off than I am right now. Dang it, I need evidence, hard proof of who the killer really is!"

Fearless and I had been gnawing on that exact same bone. We didn't need a search warrant; we just needed to get back into Ruth's house. But first we had to get out of the police station.

I whined. Mom looked down and said, "What is it, girl? You need to go out again?"

I gave a soft affirmative bark, and Mom attached my leash "Okay, off we go. Fearless, do you want to come with us?"

Fearless didn't budge. He appeared to be asleep on Frank's desk and didn't open an eye. "I guess that's a no. Frank, would you please keep an eye on him for me?"

"Sure thing."

Fearless didn't move a muscle, but I saw his eyes go from shut to slits. He watched our every move. As soon as Mom opened the outside door, he came off the desk like he'd been shot from a cannon. Frank yelled, Mom turned, and I pulled hard on the leash so I was now standing outside the door. Mom was now exactly where she needed to be, between a rock and a hard place. She couldn't shut the door because I was on the other side, but she needed two hands free to stop Fearless, which meant she would have to drop my leash. Fortunately for her we were considerate and made her predicament short-lived. Fearless streaked through the open door and was halfway down the street before Mom could say, "Fearless, don't you dare…"

After watering a nearby bush and listening to Mom's agitated babble, I headed for the car. As I expected, Mom put me in before going back inside to tell Frank she had to go home and make sure Fearless got there okay. Even though she knows we are accustomed to traveling about on our adventures, the fact that Fearless bolted had her concerned. By my calculation, if Fearless had already found Goliath at his campus abode, he'd probably be home before us.

Sure enough, when we got home we found Fearless grooming himself on the back porch. The worst punishment he had to endure was Mom swooping him up and hugging the stuffing out of him. After she fulfilled her parental obligation and scolded him, she went in for a cup of tea and we got down to business.

"Did you find Goliath?" I asked Fearless.

"I sure did. He's now on his way to fetch Tito. Einstein headed *(breath)* over to the Pederson house to make sure that window is still unlatched. *(Breath.)* They'll wait outside until we arrive to coordinate a plan. *(Breath.)* I sent Bobby and Sweetie out to find Ollie *(breath,)* in case we needed air support *(breath)*, and I asked him to alert the GPS squad. *(Breath.)* Anything else we need to do?"

"Nothing except get our butts over there. Come on, my friend, let's see if we find Frank something he can use. We need to clean up this mess and get Amanda out of that jail!"

CHAPTER  86

When we arrived at the Pederson house Goliath, Tito, and Einstein were already there. Goliath had recruited several dogs and a bunch of extra felines. But although I smelled them, I didn't see them, for Goliath had them well hidden in the shrubbery. This wasn't the time for a neighbor to call animal control.

Einstein confirmed that the window was still unlatched, and therefore a viable entry point. We mapped out an exit plan in case we got trapped inside, but the immediate problem was how I was going to get inside. There was a long drop on the other side of the window with nothing in between for me to land on. Tito could easily run down the wall, and Fearless could brace his front paws against the wall and make the leap, but as for me, at my age I avoid spine-wrenching risks. How would I get in without breaking my neck?

Einstein went in through the window to scope out the situation. A few minutes later he reappeared and out he came with the end of a clothesline in his mouth.

"And that helps us how?" I asked.

Goliath looked around and asked, "Einstein, is there enough rope to reach that oak tree?"

Einstein took the clothesline and ran to the tree, pulling the line behind him. He not only made it to the tree but all the way around it, with rope to spare.

I peered over the windowsill and assessed the situation. "Okay," I said, "if I'm seeing the same plan you're seeing, then keep on pulling. Okay, stop right there."

I pulled up the remaining length of rope, held it in my teeth and spun around in tiny circles until the rope was in a small coil at my feet. Then I went back to the window and looked again at the distance from the floor to the tree. It looked workable to me.

"Okay, that should do it. Goliath, how many critters do you think you'll need at the tree?"

"Hang on a minute." He explained the plan to his volunteers in the bushes, then returned and said, "When you're ready, two labs and a German shepherd will come out of the bushes and take hold of the line. Their muscle, plus resistance from wrapping the line around the tree, should be enough to hold you. Just say when."

"Tito, Fearless," I said, "you go in first, then get out of my way." In they went.

"Okay," I said. "Bring out the ballast." The dogs emerged and grabbed hold of the rope. I picked up the coil at my feet, locked my jaws on it, and nodded.

Goliath gave the commands. "Okay, tree-huggers, pull out the slack. Good! Now brace yourselves. Okay, Spunk, go!"

I stepped through the open window with my jaws clamped tight.

"Okay," said Goliath to the dogs, "ease her down. That's it, slow and steady. Keep that rope tight, no slack. Good!"

Down I went, to a perfect soft landing.

Fearless was there to greet me. "Have a good trip?"

I snorted, "Einstein actually lived up to his name this time! That doggie elevator was pure genius."

CHAPTER  87

Since Tito was the least likely to be seen, we sent him upstairs for recon.

"Any idea what we're *(breath)* looking for?" Fearless asked.

"Nope. Just start sniffing and see what your nose can find." While we waited for Tito we explored the basement area room we were in, but we found nothing useful.

A few minutes later Tito returned and said the first floor was clear. Mrs. Pederson was busy packing her suitcases in the upstairs bedroom. We headed up to the first floor.

Tito stood guard on the stairs, leading to the bedrooms, while Fearless and I sniffed our way around. We had just finished our initial scan when he squeaked, "Here she comes!"

We bolted. Fearless and I hid behind the recliner, while Tito dove under it. We heard Mrs. Pederson go down the stairs and into the kitchen, and open the refrigerator.

"Okay," Tito said, "I'll go see what she's up to. Be right back."

A few seconds later he returned. "Good news. She's making a sandwich."

"Okay," I said to Tito. "We're going upstairs. You stand guard at the top of stairs while we scope out the rooms up there."

Up we went.

Fearless headed for Amanda's room. I went into Mr. Pederson's bedroom and found Ruth's clothes and suitcases on the bed. A few seconds later I knew exactly what we were looking for—because I had found it.

Her driving gloves.

But there was a problem with where she had hidden them. They were crammed way back against the wall under a heavy dresser. The only part of me I could fit under the dresser was my nose.

Fearless walked into the room. "Didn't smell anything unusual in Amanda's room."

"That's because what we need is in here. Can you get your paw far enough back there to snag those gloves?"

Fearless hunkered down and stretched out one of his long, lanky leg as far as it would go. "Nope," he said. *(Breath.)* "I'm just a few inches short of it."

"Okay." I said. "You go stand guard, and send Tito in."

In a moment a small squeak said, "Whaddaya need, boss?"

I explained my idea, and with a quick nod of his head Tito scrambled under the dresser. Soon a tiny muffled voice said, "Okay, I'm in. Here I come."

I lay flat so I could watch. One of the gloves, with a tiny bump inside, began slowly walking itself across the floor in my direction.

The glove stopped part way. From inside came Tito's tiny, muffled voice. "I may be mighty but did you forget I'm a mouse? This leather glove is awful heavy!"

"You can stop right there, Tito, it's perfect. After you rest a moment, do you think you can move the other one forward that far, too? "

"Sure can."

I took over guard duty and sent Fearless back into the bedroom. In no time, he returned. "Worked like a charm *(breath)*. Tito moved both gloves up far enough *(breath)* for me to snag them *(breath)*. They're in there waiting for you."

I ran back into the bedroom. The gloves were on the floor in front of the dresser. Since they were black, it was hard to see anything peculiar about them. I lowered my nose.

Yep. We had the evidence Frank needed.

Henry Pederson's blood.

CHAPTER  88

Tito whispered, "Now what?"

"It'd be real simple if I could just take these gloves to Frank, but I can't. Humans have all these crazy rules about tampering with evidence. He needs to find them right here all by himself. We need to get him over here, but even then he can't come up here without a search warrant or Mrs. Pederson's consent. Until we figure that out, I'll push the gloves back under the dresser far enough that they stay hidden, but within reach. Okay, that's done. Now let's get out of here."

"I know how I'm getting out," said Tito, "and Einstein already proved that a cat can make the leap up to the window, so Fearless should be fine. But what about you, Spunky?"

"Just get us down there without us being seen, and I'll show you."

Tito went down the stairs to spy on Mrs. Pederson. He reported back that she was sitting at the kitchen table, eating her sandwich with a bottle of booze open on the table. Her back was to the stairs, so down we went. She never heard a thing.

Once we were down in the basement area, I explained my plan to Tito and Fearless. They both went out the window to tell Goliath. It was a thing of beauty watching Fearless leap straight up like that.

Within moments Tito's tiny head reappeared. "Okay, Spunk they're ready when you are."

I grabbed the coil of rope I'd left on the floor, nodded my head, and up I went.

Too bad my mouth was so full. I really wanted to do my Tarzan yell.

CHAPTER  89

Our team reconvened in the woods, and it didn't take us long to figure out how to get Frank into the house and implicate Mrs. Pederson. Then Fearless and I headed home, while Goliath and Einstein went on the tricky mission of recruiting the actors we needed for our sting operation. Ollie went along for their protection and to provide added inducement if needed.

Fearless and I waited at home for confirmation. There was no sense getting Mom and Frank involved until we knew if we could muster the necessary players. But a short time later a member of the GPS squad arrived.

"Ollie said you'd understand why he couldn't deliver the message himself. He said to tell you it's a go. Back window, twenty minutes. Is that enough time for you?"

"If Mom and Frank cooperate, yes. But would you please send a GPS messenger back to us, in case I need to alert them to a change?"

"Sure thing, Ms. Spunky. I'll send a pair over here pronto."

Off he flew, and in we went to fetch Frank's sock. That aromatic sock had proven its value and we had kept it well hidden. As far we were concerned, it was never to leave our house.

Fancy-Pants retrieved the sock, and I dangled it in front of Mom. She furrowed her brow, "Another sock! Where did you find—"

I shook the sock and looked her straight in the eye. Mom chuckled. "Okay, message received! Do you want me to call Frank now?"

Silence. I turned my head and looked at the back door.

"No phone call, huh? Do you want to see Frank?

A sock muffled woof confirmed she was correct.

"Do you want Frank to come here, or should I go get him?"

While I appreciated Mom's quick discernment, she should know better than to ask me two questions at the same time. I shook the sock again and growled softly.

Mom was on a roll. "Okay, I get it. You can't answer two questions at once. So, do you want Frank to come here?"

Silence. That would be a waste of time.

"Do you want me to go pick him up?"

I dropped the sock and barked in the affirmative. Mom got up her keys. As she walked to the car she phoned Frank and explained that I was asking for him and we were on our way to pick him up. Fearless and I jumped into the car. The boys knew Mom would never let all of them go with us, so they just ignored her and headed for the Pederson house on their own.

When we got to the police station, Frank and Tony were waiting by their car. Frank said, "Since we don't know where Spunky's taking us or what she's getting us into, I want my radio and my stuff with me, so we'll follow you."

Off we went. But as soon we pulled up at the Pederson house, Frank expressed his concern. "Hey, Spunk, I can't go barging in there. I don't have a warrant."

Patience, my friend, patience. As I walked to the door Mom said, "We just have to trust her, Frank. Come on."

They followed me. What they didn't see was Fancy-Pants staring out from under the bush next to the porch. He was the start of the cat phone line that I knew wrapped all the way around the house. I was sure our arrival had been announced. Now all that remained was my signal.

Frank rang the doorbell, but the poor guy didn't have a clue what to say when Mrs. Pederson answered. I didn't make him stand there very long.

I woofed, and within seconds a baby started wailing.

Mrs. Pederson abruptly turned back into the house and said, "What the—?"

Frank's went on alert. "What's that?" he demanded. "Sounds like a baby in terrible trouble."

Mrs. Pederson was dumbfounded and shook her head. "I don't have a baby in here!"

Frank might not have known what was going on, but he only had one option. He quickly turned to Tony and said, "Detective, do you hear a baby in distress?"

Tony was already moving forward. "I certainly do."

Frank gently pushed Ruth out of the way and said, "Ma'am please step aside. We have to help that child."

Bingo! Frank had his probable cause, and in he went.

Once inside Frank said, "Sounds like the kid's in the basement. Let's go."

Frank led the parade down the stairs. Obviously, we needed him upstairs, not downstairs, but he still needed Ruth's permission for that. When his feet reached the bottom step, the wailing suddenly ceased. Before anyone could investigate too closely, we kicked off act two.

Barney, the barn owl flew in though an open window and played his part perfectly. Goliath had specifically recruited him for his dramatic sound effects. In case you didn't know, a barn owl's call is a terrible blood-curdling screech, and Barney put the woman in *Psycho* to shame. Every human ducked for cover. Barney followed the script, flew over their heads, and went up the stairs.

Now Mrs. Pederson was the one screaming. "What *is* that thing? Do something! Get that creature out of my house!"

Yup, you heard it. She just gave Frank permission to go upstairs.

Barney flew around the living room until we were all present, and then flew up the stairs to the bedrooms. Everyone followed. As instructed, Barney perched on the curtain rod in the bedroom and waited for us to arrive. Mrs. Pederson was right behind me, and I was right behind Frank.

The humans came to an abrupt standstill and stared aghast at Barney. As instructed, he kept flapping his wings to assure all eyes stayed on him. This gave me ample time to slip my paw discreetly under the dresser.

I nodded, and Barney quit flapping. I barked. All eyes now turned in my direction. Astonishment registered on Mrs. Pederson's face as she said, "How the hell did my gloves—?"

The moment those words were out of her mouth she knew she had said too much, and she clamped her lips

367

shut. I watched as Frank's eyes went from confusion to recognition. As I hoped, he remembered what Anthony had said: "Ruth never took off her driving gloves." A smile pulled at the corners of his mouth.

"Tony," he said, "am I mistaken, or are those gloves laying there in plain sight?"

Tony answered, "They certainly are. Right there in front of God and everyone else."

"Tony, would you get our bag out of the trunk," Frank said. He reached into his pocket and pulled out a pair of blue gloves, and put them on. Mrs. Pederson turned and tried to head back down the stairs, but she didn't get far. There was a nasty-looking, hissing cat blocking her way. Just then Tony returned and led her back into the bedroom, and Fearless left his post and proudly sauntered in to join us.

Tony handed Frank the bag. "Here you go. This should help." He switched off the overhead light, and the room darkened.

Frank took a UV black light from the bag and held it over the gloves.

The resulting fluorescent glow brought a smile to Frank's face. He looked at me and gave me a clandestine wink. He now had exactly what he needed—hard evidence.

"Ruth Pederson, I'm arresting you for the murder of Henry Pederson. Anything you say can and will be used against you..."

CHAPTER 90

The DA charged Mrs. Pederson with second-degree murder, as well as obstruction of justice and criminal conspiracy. Anthony was charged with aiding and abetting in the murder of Henry Pederson, kidnapping, theft, assault with a deadly weapon, parole violations up the ying-yang, as well as criminal conspiracy, extortion, and blackmail.

Once Amanda knew they were both locked away, she felt safe enough to reveal her final secret. Anthony had threatened that if she didn't keep her mouth shut and take the rap, he would kill Mrs. Pederson. Although Amanda had a slew of conflicted feelings about her mother, she would never wish her dead. Initially, she had confessed in order to protect Anthony; later, she stuck to that confession in order to protect her mother. What she hadn't known was that Anthony was also blackmailing Mrs. Pederson: if she didn't pay up, he would tell the truth that she was the one who stabbed Henry. He also said he was more than willing to reveal that it was her idea to frame Amanda so that she would get all of Mr. Pederson's assets herself.

In the end, all she inherited was a jail cell.

The good news was Amanda was now free. Better still, she had not built new walls. She acknowledged that she needed help and accepted Mom's and Professor Hoffman's gifts of counseling. They knew it would take time for Amanda had lost so much in so many ways, going all the way back to when she was a child. The shock of losing her father was compounded by all the events that followed, up to and including the slamming of cell doors on her remaining family. Her mother had killed her father, her brother had kidnapped and threatened to kill her mother and her best friend, and both her mother and brother had been willing to let her stay in jail for the rest of her life.

Nevertheless, Amanda still carried far more than her share of guilt over what happened. She still believed it had all been her fault. In time, Mom and Professor Hoffman hoped to be able to ease that burden. For now, Amanda promised Professor Hoffman that she would first try to take care of herself. She agreed not to visit her mother and brother in jail. She said she would wait until she and Professor Hoffman decided she was ready.

But the best news of all was that Nancy's mother, Mrs. Evans, turned out to not be so weird after all. The day after the kidnapping, when Mom met with Nancy and her mother, she saw that Susan was a smart, warm, caring woman who also happened to be a germaphobe. A phobia doesn't define a person's character. This fine woman turned out to be the one who set in motion the plan for Amanda to live with her and Nancy, and to help her create a new family.

With Professor Hoffman's guidance, Amanda had the assets from her father's estate put into a trust. She was to receive an allowance to live on, but she also made a specific request. She asked that the trust pay Mrs. Evans for room and board as compensation for her moving in with them. Given this extra income, Nancy's mom no longer needed to work two jobs, and now she could be home at night. Everyone was pleased.

There was another unforeseen benefit. Nancy and Amanda reported they were having a grand time ignoring Pamela and her clique. Amanda said that in light of all that had happened, the kids at school were supportive of her and not about to believe Pamela's vile gossip. Mom and I were delighted that Pamela's social status had taken a significant hit.

Frank even pitched in his share of good will and agreed to help Mr. Whitehead try to locate his daughter.

Not long afterwards, Amanda approached Mom about her desire to reach out to the woman who had raised Anthony, Anna Reynolds. She wanted her to know where he was and what had happened. Mom suggested that Ms. Reynolds should also know the truth about Mrs. Pederson's alcohol abuse during her entire pregnancy with Anthony. Mom said that although Anthony might not have shown any signs of fetal alcohol syndrome at birth, in all likelihood he had been affected by it. Not knowing of his birth mother's addiction, no one, not even Anna Reynolds, could have guessed there might be a medical reason for his attention deficit and hyperactivity, which contributed to him being a problem child. Anthony was still responsible for his actions, but Mom and Amanda agreed Ms. Reynolds should know that there was far more to it than she could have ever known.

Without a doubt, however, Nancy was the happiest of all. That girl could not stop smiling. She not only had her best friend back, she had a sister.

CHAPTER 91

A bout two weeks later, after conferring with Amanda, Mom offered to host a backyard gathering as a memorial for Henry Pederson. People from all over Clearwater came to honor his memory and to celebrate Amanda's release. Everyone brought their own chairs or blankets and feasted on grilled chicken, hot dogs, and hamburgers, with loads of sides and all the fixings. When we got to the coffee and cupcakes, everyone sat down and shared stories about Mr. Pederson. Amanda had no idea that her father had been so admired and loved. Person after person told of how he had treated them with respect even if they didn't have a bank account, let alone a big one. He always made everyone feel welcome. It was amazing how many people he had helped to get loans when no other bank would even talk to them. Everyone said they worked hard to repay those loans, because they believed if they didn't honor their commitment then it would make it more difficult for him to help the next person.

Everyone had a grand time, including our crew. Mom welcomed Lion King, Goliath, and Einstein as part of the family. Frank even tossed chunks of chicken up to Ollie, who was perched majestically in the oak tree. Mom knew from our previous encounters that many of the feral felines would remain hidden, so she followed her tradition and dumped an ice chest full of fish at the far corner of the field—downwind, of course. She also placed bowls of dry cat food around the perimeter so everyone could partake. One might never see the ferals, but they could make a bowl of food disappear in no time. We made sure our canine friends as well as Bandito, Roxie, and the other raccoons knew about the bowls of food in advance, so they could get their fair share.

Mom guessed there might be others I would want to thank, so she brought out a small plastic basket and filled it as often as necessary with an assortment of goodies. I was the meals-on-wheels transporter, delivering delectable snacks to my friends hidden here and there around the yard and in the woods.

Tito and Belvidere had their own charming dining area tucked away in the barn, because we all knew humans wouldn't be thrilled to see mice at their picnic. Belvidere honored us by bringing a guest, his new friend Sophia. She told us Nancy's mother was not only afraid of germs, but also determined to be prepared for any emergency. Belvidere said it went way beyond a pantry. It was a room with shelves stacked to the ceiling, loaded with food. There was so much stuff that Sophia had been living a grand life in there for months and was still undetected. There were boxes of cereal, crackers, dried fruit, and even bags of nuts. The shelves were packed so deep that she and Belvidere could live off the back row alone for years to come. A mouse's proverbial Garden of Eden.

After watching Sophia and Belvidere nuzzle each other, I nudged Sweetie and said, "Mark my words: Soon we'll be getting teeny-tiny invitations to a very English mouse wedding."

Sweetie purred, "Ah, good! I'm a sucker for weddings, no matter how small they are."

When I headed off to the edge of the woods carrying two hot dogs for one of my friends, I didn't know I was being watched. But when I returned, Frank came over to me, knelt down, and gave me a good head-scratching. To anyone watching, it looked like he was just saying hello, but he had an ulterior motive. This good ol' country boy had figured out our secret weapon.

He leaned in close and said, "I admit it, girl, you had me stumped. I couldn't figure out how on earth you managed that tormented baby sound at the Pederson house, and then— *poof*—silence. But I just figured it out. It was that beautiful red fox you just graced with those hot dogs. One night when I was a kid I heard a horrifying screaming howl and ran to my dad yelling that there was a baby outside in horrible trouble. He went out, listened, and told me that it was actually a female fox calling for her mate. I forgot all about it until just now, when I saw that vixen peeking out from under the bush over there. How you got a fox, a barn owl, and all those cats to work together without killing each other is beyond me, but my hat's off to you girl. It was an amazing act."

Frank leaned in closer. "Don't worry, Spunk. Your secret's safe with me. You might need to use her again someday, and if you do, I want everyone to think we're rescuing a real baby. Besides, I'm having way too much fun watching Hannah and Tony try to figure it out. I am right, aren't I? It was the fox, wasn't it?"

I remained silent. I wasn't about to confirm or deny this one. If we had to deploy Foxy's yowl again, it would be far better if Frank also had a little room for doubt.

As I sauntered away, Frank laughed and said, "Oh, so you're gonna keep that one to yourself, huh?"

Rule number four: Keep your ace in the hole until game time.

Once all the thank-you treats had been delivered, I sat down to enjoy my own. Lest you think I forgot anyone, earlier in the day I had carried two hot dogs to Nosey. Then I came back and snatched a paper bowl of Mom's diced fruit salad for Ms. Massey. Boy, that gal really loves bananas!

As things began to wind down, I lay down to enjoy the music. The humans couldn't comprehend or appreciate the sounds coming from over the hill, but we critters did. Back and forth, echoes rang of Nosey howling and Ms. Massey braying. It might sound like noise to humans, but to me it was a symphony of two new friends having a wonderful chat. I turned and saw Frank walk up to Mom, sweetly put his arm though hers and whisper in her ear. Mom's spontaneous laugh and relaxed body said it all. It was good to see these two old friends again at ease with each other.

When the crowd had headed home and everything was cleaned up, Amanda came to say goodbye. She gave Frank, Mom, and Professor Hoffman each a hug and a sincere thank-you.

As she and Nancy walked away arm in arm toward Nancy's mother's car, Amanda stopped, turned back, and asked Nancy to wait right there. Amanda ran back, knelt down and gave Sweetie and me the best of hugs. She reached for Fearless too, but he sauntered away.

Amanda laughed. "That's okay, Fearless, you can't escape the fact I love you too." She stroked me and Sweetie. "Thank you. You guys saved my life. I'm not sure how, but I know you did. I'll love you forever and ever. Come see us real soon, okay?"

My woof sealed the deal.

As Amanda walked away, I sensed that she missed her father more than ever. But she also carried a new level of pride that she was his daughter.

CHAPTER  92

Humans have their traditions, and Fearless and I have ours. When it got dark and all was quiet, we took our stroll toward the barn.

Fearless said, "Seems like everyone ended up *(breath)* right where they were supposed to be."

I nodded. "Yup, the winners won, and the losers lost."

Fearless nudge me. "I'll bet you got a rule for that one too *(breath)*, right?"

I snorted. "Sure do. Rule number thirty: You will know the truth, and the truth will set you free.

Fearless said, "That's not exactly a Spunky original, you know."

"I know. But it works for me."

We sat surrounded by the night and indulged in the rich silence of two good friends who didn't have to talk.

Then, out of the night, a soft, sweet voice behind us said, "Spunk, don't forget about tomorrow."

I turned and said, "Thanks for the reminder, Sweetie. Do you want to join us?"

Sweetie ducked his head bashfully and said, "No thanks. I'm off to see Miss Gidget over at Tidwell's. She and I have a date."

I swung my head around, "You've got a date?"

Sweetie stood straighter and said, "I may be neutered, but I ain't dead!"

I chuckled, "Well, you must be brave. I thought she was Lion King's gal."

Sweetie snorted. "Miss Gidget ain't no tom's property. She's a true free spirit!"

"Good for her! Hope you have a good time, but please get some rest tonight. You know I'm going to need your help tomorrow."

"I'll be ready and able. Good night, guys."

Fearless brought up his paw, scratched his ear, and asked, "Did I forget something? *(Breath.)* What's tomorrow?"

I said, "You know Mom's been talking a blue streak to that wonderful dog rescue lady in Alabama, the Fairy Dogmother. Well, tomorrow around noon the transport arrives to deliver the newest addition to our family."

Fearless said, "And?"

"All I know is that he's a young pup, his name is MacDuff, and—"

Fearless finished my thought, "—and—he's gonna have to learn the rules!"

POST SCRIPT

A joyous woof to our very special friend, Glenda Wilhite. She is certainly not a make believe character. She is a real-life Fairy Dogmother.

All profits from the sale of this book will go to support the Fairy Dogmother Rescue & Rehab in Baileyton, Alabama: a 501(c)(3) organization dedicated to making good things happen for dogs in need.

Check her out for yourself at: www.facebook.com/fairydogmotherrescue

You can also see our wonderful canine friends who are still waiting for their forever home at: fairydogmother1.petfinder.com

Spunky's rule number seven: support duly licensed animal rescues, not puppy mills.

In real life, our four-legged family have all been rescues. Spunky hopes yours are the same.

ADDENDUM

Spunky and her cohorts hope you enjoyed their latest adventure. As you have seen, Spunky's rules help guide her decisions, her relationships, and her life. She thought you might like to have your own copy. She plans to share more rules as they appear in each new book.

The Nose Knows humans need rules too. Please feel free to live by any of hers. She'd love it!

SPUNKY'S RULES

Number Two	Your word is your bond and must be honored.
Number Three	You may not see the solution to a problem, but never stop believing you'll figure it out. Keep the faith and keep moving forward.
Number Four	Keep your ace in the hole until game time.

Number Five	Trust requires time to build but only seconds to shatter.
Number Six	Tenacity and creativity will always serve you well.
Number Seven	Support duly licensed animal rescues, not puppy mills.
Number Eight	You can't put marrow back into a bone.
Number Ten	Never deploy all your weapons at once. Maintain a reserve.
Number Fifteen	Never let vanity interfere with the mission.
Number Eighteen	Every problem has a solution if you are willing to see it.
Number Thirty	You will know the truth and the truth will set you free. (John 8:32)

Spunky would love if you would visit her and her pals on her website at spunkymysterybooks.com.

You could really make their tails wag if you'd take the time to write your review of their story on Amazon.com or on your own favorite book site.

Reviews are like treats—we love them! Woof-Woof (Thanks!)

www.ingramcontent.com/pod-product-compliance
Lightning Source LLC
Chambersburg PA
CBHW020913110726
47900CB00001B/121